# HEX THE HALLS

*A Hexed Christmas Romance*

*B Wills*

Golden Light Publishing House

ISBN: 978-1-970692-00-6

This book is dedicated to the bold, the curious, and the "I can fix him—well maybe not, but I'll let him ruin me anyway" crowd. Enjoy my beloved feral gremlin, *enjoy*.

# Trigger Warnings

Explicit sexual content, BDSM dynamics, possessive romance, supernatural violence, demonic themes, emotional abandonment, relationship-related distress, family dysfunction, curses, and occult imagery.

If you're sensitive to any of the topics above, please take care of yourself before diving in. This book contains demons with opinions, witches with boundaries, magic that doesn't ask permission, and relationships that get intense in ways both emotional and physical.

If any of that isn't your cup of tea, it's okay to set this one down.

But if you're here for chaos, consent, devotion, a morally gray demon who worships his woman, and a fluffy black cat who absolutely runs the household—welcome. You're exactly where you belong.

# PLAYLIST

1. A Nonsense Christmas – Sabrina Carpenter

2. Believe It – Jared Benjamin

3. When Did You Get Hot? – Sabrina Carpenter

4. Nonsense – Sabrina Carpenter

5. Is It New Years Yet? – Sabrina Carpenter

6. Fuck Being a Princess – Esme Rose

7. STFUATTDLAGG – Ruby Darkrose

# CONTENTS

# CHAPTER 1

*Piper*

If Snowglobe Hollow had a town motto, it would be... *We Wish You a Merry Christmas, Whether You Like It or Not.*

The evidence?

Mariah Carey is already screaming through my bedroom window, and it's barely sunrise.

I groan and shove the blankets off my body, peeling myself from the warm nest I'd built overnight. My curls—thick, dark, and forever plotting my downfall—spill around me as I sit up. They're frizzed into a halo of chaotic energy, sparking faintly at the ends in a way that says the curse is awake before I am.

*Great.* Just what I needed.

The floor is freezing when my feet hit it, and I bite out a curse under my breath. My entire apartment smells like cold air and a hint of cinnamon from the candle I forgot to snuff out. I tug my tank top straight over my chest—big boobs and gravity have been in a long-term feud—then pad into the kitchen, thighs brushing pleasantly with every step.

The coffee pot gurgles like it's chewing gravel.

"Don't even think about it," I warn.

It explodes anyway.

Not destructively—just a violent puff of steam that blasts peppermint grounds across my counter and coats my cheeks in warm, sticky grit. I glare at the machine through lashes dusted in coffee shrapnel.

The Bellamy Holiday Curse strikes again.

Every December, the curse wakes like some ancient, bored creature stretching its limbs. Our magic—usually stable, manageable—turns feral. Overly emotional. Overreactive. Spells slip their leashes. Charms misbehave. Enchantments twist into something darker, louder, messier.

Magic reacts to mood, and mine?

Decidedly stabby before caffeine.

My grandmother used to call us the Winter Witches. My mother used to call us walking hazards. I just call it another Tuesday.

I wipe the mess from my porcelain-pale skin, the pink of my lips going redder from the friction. My striking blue eyes—which my aunt always said were "Bellamy blue, storm-bound and stubborn"—catch my reflection in the toaster. I look like a sleep-paralyzed Victorian ghost who happens to be wearing *Target* pajamas.

*Perfect.*

I yank on jeans that hug my hips and a sweater thick enough to count as armor, then shrug into my coat. When I step outside, a blade of cold air slices across my face, waking me up instantly. The street is buried under twinkling lights and fake snow, wreaths hanging from poles, garlands draped across every doorway.

Snowglobe Hollow doesn't decorate.

It *blazes* Christmas spirit.

The whole damn town smells like pine sap and gingerbread. My breath clouds as I walk, boots crunching in perfect rhythm with a distant choir warming up in the town square. My curls snag on my scarf, static biting at my ears.

The curse *always* heightens my senses.

The world feels too loud—too bright. More...

*alive.*

I feel magic, even mundane magic, like temperature—an ambient pressure curling against my skin, prickling along my ribs. Today it hums beneath everything, restless and metallic like a storm wanting out.

I make it to my shop—Bellamy's Hearth & Home—just as the bells above the entrance tinkle on their own. Not the simple chime they're supposed to give. No. It's a freaking melody—a jaunty little tune, like they're auditioning for a fantasy musical.

"I swear to the spirits," I mutter, "if you're about to sing—"

They chime again. Innocently... Mockingly.

Inside, the shop reeks of lavender, dried rosemary, and faint smoke. My senses stretch, cataloguing the changes immediately. My potions are stacked in a rainbow gradient I never arranged. A spell jar labeled Noise Reduction throbs with bass like it wants to DJ my morning. And every bundle of mistletoe I prepped for tomorrow's craft fair?

They're all dragged into a pile in the center of the floor.

Staring at me like a predator. Sentient even. "Back up," I tell them.

They rustle like they're offended.

I sigh and lock the door behind me. This is what happens when the curse builds—magic starts... thinking for itself. Bending things. Nudging things. Rearranging my life like an overbearing mother-in-law I don't have.

I drop behind the counter, letting my weight settle into the stool. My thighs spill warmly against the seat, grounding me. The curse claws at my spine again, a tremor of static whispering beneath my skin.

This is getting worse. Earlier. Sharper.

I pull the grimoire from the drawer—heavy, leather, older than every building in Snowglobe Hollow combined. The worn cover feels warm, familiar, comforting in a nostalgic, mildly terrifying way.

The pages flutter open without permission... directly on a warding ritual. Simple. Elegant. Meant to stabilize magic.

My pulse races, sending me into a tizzy. "This is fine," I whisper. "A *ward* is fine."

My curls crackle. The lights flicker, shimmering back and forth with a faint buzz. The mistletoe pile scoots an inch to the left like it's settling in for a show.

I gather ingredients with hands that won't stop trembling. Salt. Chalk. Rosemary. Belladonna. A pinch of sugar because I'm exhausted and improvisation isn't a crime yet. I draw the circle slowly. Carefully. The chalk line glows faint silver when I complete it—never a great sign.

My magic surges in my chest and it feels like swallowing a sparkler—bright, hot, frayed at the edges.

The curse responds, tightening like cold fingers around my ribs. I take a breath. My lips part around the incantation.

"Just a ward," I remind myself. "Not a summon. Not a binding. Just—"

My magic leaps, sparks flying. Candles roar to life. The grimoire slams shut. The air explodes outward in a wind that isn't wind—cold and hot at the same time, rippling down my spine like a voice whispering finally. The chalk ignites. Flame spirals up in a ring, consuming the circle in a flash of blue-white light.

And I feel it. Something ancient... *powerful*. Something answering.

"Oh... *no*."

Magic snaps through the room like a whip. Every candle dies. The mistletoe pile flees behind the register. And the floor hums with the unmistakable resonance of a summons.

Not a ward.... Nor a charm. And absofucking-lutely *not* harmless.

It's a summoning.

"*Shit*." I scramble to the floor, sitting on shaky knees. The floor hums harder—deep, resonant, vibrating through the soles of my boots. Air thickens like syrup. The smell hits next. It's smoke, cedar, winter wind, and something darker—something sinful. "Oh, come on," I whisper. "I said *ward*. *WARD*. Like, the magical equivalent of putting a baby gate on my powers. I did not order a—"

The circle detonates. Blue-white fire shoots upward, then collapses inward, like the air is folding itself into a form. A person-shaped structure.

My heartbeat goes rabid. My hair floats like static-bloomed smoke around my head. Even the mistletoe peeks out from behind the counter like it's watching a horror movie through its fingers.

The flames twist, pull, compress—splitting open. A figure steps through, rising from the dying fire like a man built out of shadows and bad decisions.

*Oh. Oh no. Oh hell no.*

My eyes rake over him. He's tall, stupidly broad, muscles for days, carved like he was sculpted by someone who had clearly been in their feelings about "vengeful hotness."

Boots hit the wooden floor with a heavy thud. Black hair falls in slightly messy waves around his jaw, glossy as spilled ink. His eyes—*Gods* help me—are green. A bright, unnatural, dancing green that flicks over me like he's assessing both my soul and my credit score.

His presence fills the room like gravity decided to pick a favorite.

He looks at me. And *smirks*. I'm going to die, I think. And he's going to be smug about it.

His voice drops like velvet dipped in smoke. "Well," he drawls, "you're not what I expected."

I blink. "Excuse me?"

He glances around my shop with bored disdain, like he's rating it one star on Yelp. "This is... quaint." His gaze lands on the mistletoe pile. "And deeply pathetic."

"Those are sentient," I snap.

He lifts a brow. "Then they should be ashamed."

My jaw drops. "Okay, listen—whoever you are—this was an accident, and you need to—"

"How do you *accidentally* summon a demon?" he interrupts, stepping fully out of the circle as it fizzles into glittering ash. "You either have catastrophic impulse control or you're stupid."

My blood pressure skyrockets, and I'm suddenly seeing red. "I'm *not* stupid," I hiss, "and that *wasn't* a summoning. It was a simple ward. Emphasis on simple. It's not my fault the universe hates me."

His mouth curves in a slow, dark smile. "I don't think the universe hates you, Piper Bellamy."

My entire body freezes. He *knows* my name. "How the fuck—"

"I knew the moment your magic touched me."

He says it like it's obvious. Like this is normal. Like he isn't standing there looking like temptation incarnate.

His eyes sweep over me—my thick thighs still braced in a defensive stance, my sweater stretched across my chest, my wild curls floating with residual static, my lips parted in shock. Something flickers in his expression. A spark? Interest, maybe. *Heat.*

He masks it with annoyance. "You're... very *noisy*," he mutters.

"I'm noisy?" I choke out. "You literally just crawled out of a magical inferno like you're auditioning for a metal album cover."

He steps closer, then another. He is VERY big. And very shirtless. And very... *everything*. "Who are you?" I demand, trying not to look directly at the abs that are practically sculpted invitations to sin. "And why did you come through my circle?"

He tilts his head, eyes gleaming with wicked amusement. "I'm Slade Athalar." He lets the name hang in the air like thunder. "Demon," he adds, unhelpfully.

"No shit."

"And I didn't come through your circle." His smile sharpens. "You *pulled* me."

"I did not—"

"Oh, you did." He steps even closer, his heat rolling off him despite the cold draft swirling around us. "You reached for power—and found me."

"That is NOT what happened!"

He grins. "I felt your magic all over me."

"Can you *not* say it like that?"

His gaze drops to my lips, and I watch, stuck frozen in place as he bites his bottom lip. "I can say it any way I like."

My stomach swoops. *No.* Absolutely not. *Bad Piper. Bad hormones.*

He extends a hand, like he expects me to take it. I don't. "Put your hand away," I say flatly.

Slade looks offended. No—shocked. Like no one has ever said no to him in the history of time.

"You summoned me," he says slowly, "and now you're *refusing* me?"

I cross my arms. "My bad. I didn't realize demons came with customer service expectations."

His nostrils flare. The lights flicker. Somewhere behind me, the mistletoe lets out a weak squeak.

He's *too* close, an array of scents assault my nostrils—smoke. Pine and sandalwood. Cold winter air mixed with scorch. The scent hits me like a memory I've never had. He leans down, voice a low warning rumble. "You shouldn't have called me, Piper Bellamy."

"I didn't call—"

"Because now," he murmurs, "I'm bound to you."

Bound... wait. *Bound*?! My heartbeat stops. Then races. Then vaults out of my ribcage entirely. "No," I whisper. "No, no, no—absolutely not. You are not bound to me. I do not have a demon. I barely have time for a cat."

He smirks. "You did this."

"I DID NOT—"

"You summoned me with emotion instead of ritual. That's a bond invocation." His grin is devastating. "You didn't just summon any demon, witch."

He leans in, close enough that his breath ghosts across my lips. "You summoned *me*."

# Chapter 2

*Slade*

Most summons feel like hooks. Violent. Abrupt. A yank through realms that tears the soul sideways. This one?

It felt like fingers sinking into my chest. Warm. Emotional. *Too* intimate.

I should've ignored it. And I usually do. But something in it—something sharp and bright and stubborn—sank deep.

Then the circle opened, the flames parted, and I stepped into a cramped little witch shop lit by twinkle lights and scented with dried herbs and panic. And *her—Piper Bellamy*. Sitting there in jeans hugging thick thighs, curls wild around her head, chest rising in quick, furious breaths. A pendant glows at her neck—Amethyst, maybe?—and crescent-shaped moon earrings dangle from her ears. Blue eyes like frost and fire all at once. A body soft in ways I shouldn't immediately notice.

Yet I do... *Unfortunately.*

She looks at me like I'm a home invasion. *Fuck.* I don't get bound, or summoned by accident. And I certainly don't get dragged through realms by witches who look like sin wrapped in sarcasm. But here we are.

She's ranting now—hands flying, curls bouncing, chest heaving—and the more she spirals, the more I feel the bond tightening around my ribs. Annoying... Intriguing... *Dangerous*. "What are you staring at?" she snaps.

"*You*."

Her breath stutters. "Stop that."

"Stop what?"

I step closer. Deliberately. Slowly.  Her back hits the counter with a satisfying little gasp. "Stop looming," she demands, shoving weakly at my chest.

I let her shove me. She might as well punch a wall made of iron. A heated, amused spark crawls through me. "I'm not looming," I say. "This is just how tall I am."

"You're doing it on purpose."

I smirk. "Maybe."

She crosses her arms, trying to look intimidating. It only draws my eyes to her breasts. I drag my gaze back to her face before she notices. Barely. "Why are you here?" she demands.

"I could ask you the same question."

"I LIVE here."

"And I don't," I counter. "Yet you dragged me into your realm anyway."

Her jaw drops. "I didn't drag anyone!"

I step closer. Close enough to feel her breath. Close enough to see panic spark in those blue eyes. I lift my hand slowly. Her lips part—and I wrap my hand around her throat.

Not to restrain. Or hurt. Just to claim the space between us.

Her pulse leaps against my palm like a struck match. Her thighs press subconsciously together. Her voice goes faint. "What... what are you doing?"

"Confirming something."

Her lashes flutter. "C-confirming what?"

"That you *feel* it."

"Feel what?" she whispers.

"The pull."

The bond. The tether. The magic that should never have touched me—let alone chosen me.

She shoves at my chest again. "Get away from me."

I lean in, thumb stroking her pulse. "I don't think you want that, sweetheart."

Her breath catches. Her magic flares, brushing against my aura like a curious animal. "This is insane," she mutters. "I don't even know who you are."

Good. That's better. *Safer.*

But the bond squeezes hard, demanding the introduction. Demanding the connection. I give in. Just barely. "Like I said, I'm just Slade."

The name rolls through the air like thunder. Her eyes widen, pupils dilating. She feels it. The click. The lock. The ancient recognition.

*Fuck.*

I pull back before I do something reckless—like push her onto the counter and taste that pink mouth.

She bolts toward the shop door. "I—I need to close. Now. I need air. I need..." She grabs her phone, throws up a post on her social media about a "family emergency," and flips the sign to CLOSED.

Then she turns and points a shaking finger at me. "You're not following me."

I follow her anyway. Down the street. Through the cold. Up the stairs to her apartment. She keeps looking back like she expects me to vanish. Or... combust. Or explode into bat wings.

*Cute.*

She unlocks her door and steps inside. I cross the threshold—and something launches at me. A cat. Black. Round. Feral. It attaches itself to my boot like a tiny demon attempting murder. I stare down at it, bewildered confusion mixed with annoyance.

Seriously?

"Newt!" she shrieks. "Let go! He's—he's not a chew toy!"

"He attacked me," I say flatly.

"You walked through the door!"

"That's hardly justification."

She runs to pry him off.

I lift the creature by the scruff, eye to eye. "You're lucky she's cute," I inform him.

"HEY." She snatches the cat away.

I step deeper into her apartment—warm, cozy, cluttered with books, plants, and blankets. Soft lighting, colors, and apparently a soft witch. It smells like vanilla, cinnamon, magic, and her. The bond twists in my chest—hard.

Too hard.

I drag a hand through my hair, grounding myself before I do something catastrophically stupid—like press her against the wall and introduce her body to mine. She rounds on me, cheeks pink, curls wild. "You're staying, aren't you?"

I lean against her wall, arms crossed, holding her gaze like it's a leash. "Sweetheart," I murmur, "I'm not going *anywhere*."

# CHAPTER 3

*Piper*

There should be rules about demons following you home. Like... *Don't*. Or at the very least... call *first*. But Slade stands in my living room like he owns oxygen, arms folded over his stupidly muscular chest, green eyes glowing faintly as they track every inch of me. It's unsettling. Infuriating. It's... *annoyingly* attractive.

"Make yourself at home," I mutter. "By all means. I just *love* unexpected supernatural intrusions during the holidays."

He doesn't move. Hasn't blinked. Just watches me like a predator. Like he's waiting for me to bolt so he can chase. The heating kicks on with a soft rumble. My curtains sway from the draft, brushing against the faint hum of magic still clinging to Slade like a second skin. I tap my fingers against my thigh. "So. Ground rules."

His lips twitch. "Rules. For me?"

"Yes."

"Bold." His green eyes flash mischievously.

"Shut up."

He smirks, stepping closer. My breath catches — damn him — because he moves like a threat and a promise wrapped into one. "What are your rules?" he asks, voice low and ruinous.

"Rule one: You're sleeping on the couch."

"If I wanted a bed," he says, leaning in, "I'd take yours."

Heat crawls up my neck. "No. You will not be taking anything." Another step. I retreat instinctively, bumping into my bookshelf. His eyes dip — briefly, hungrily — to my throat. "Rule two," I whisper, "you can't just... touch me. Whenever you want."

His gaze darkens. "I'm already restraining myself, little witch."

I hate how that affects me.

Newt leaps onto the bookshelf beside my head, hissing at Slade with theatrical disgust. I stroke between his ears to soothe him. Slade glares back, unimpressed with my furry bodyguard. "That creature has a death wish," he mutters.

"His name is Newt," I correct. "And he's family."

Slade scoffs. "I've slain warlords with less ego."

I roll my eyes. "Rule three... Stop making everything sound like a threat."

His expression turns wicked. "Sweetheart, everything I say is a threat."

And I believe him.

I exhale, pushing past him toward the kitchen. My apartment smells like cinnamon, vanilla, and my favorite winter candle — *Frostbound Hearth* — something I usually find comforting. Tonight it feels... intrusive.

Slade shadows me like a large, ominous storm cloud. Every motion radiates heat. Every breath vibrates with something dark and ancient.

"Stop looming," I snap again.

"I'm observing," he says.

"You're hovering."

"I'm ensuring you don't pass out," he says with an eye roll.

"I am NOT going to pass out!"

"You're flushed," he says, eyes dragging over my face. "Your breathing is uneven. Your magic is—"

"Stop analyzing me like I'm a blood pressure reading!"

He steps closer again, stealing the distance between us. "*You* summoned *me*, Piper."

"FOR THE LAST TIME... I *ACCIDENTALLY*... summoned you."

He laughs, soft and deadly. "There's no such thing as accidental magic when it comes to a bond."

My stomach drops. "Stop saying *bond* like it means something."

"It does," he murmurs.

I cross my arms, trying to hide the tremble in my hands. "Look. I'm going to get water. You are going to sit on the couch. Quietly. Like a... demonic houseplant."

"I don't sit."

"Well, you're going to tonight."

"I don't take orders."

"You do now," I shoot back, trying on confidence I absolutely don't feel. "Because you're in my apartment, demon man."

He steps forward until his chest brushes my shoulder. "So brave," he murmurs. My heart slams painfully.

As I reach the kitchen counter, the pendant lights flicker. My magic swells unexpectedly, reacting to something in the air — something from him. "Why is the entire apartment suddenly acting like we're in a haunted Hallmark special?" I mutter.

Slade breathes in — slow and deep, like he's tasting the energy. "The curse," he says. "It's responding to me."

"Responding how?"

He leans close enough that his breath grazes my ear. "It recognizes the bond."

I whip around. "Stop. STOP saying bond. There is *no* bond. There is *no* tether. There is *no* cosmic matchmaking conspiracy."

He laughs again. Dark. Knowing. "I can feel your magic," he says softly. "And you feel mine. You're trembling from it."

"I'm trembling because you're terrifying!"

His gaze drops to my lips, a sinful smile slowly spreading across his face. "You're trembling because you want me."

My jaw drops. Heat floods my cheeks. "You—! Arrogant—! Lantern-jawed—! *Hell... REJECT!*"

His grin widens. "Adorableeee."

"Get out of my space," I whisper.

He doesn't. Slade catches my wrist — gently, maddeningly gentle — and guides my hand to rest on his chest. His heartbeat thunders against my palm, strong and wrong and intimate. "Feel that?" He whispers.

I swallow hard. "What... what is that?"

"A demon recognizing what's his."

My breath leaves me in a rush. Before I can form a coherent response, Newt leaps between us onto the counter, screeching like a tiny warlord defending his queen.

Slade snarls. "I swear to every infernal god, I'm going to banish him."

"You TOUCH that cat," I warn, "and I will hex your dick."

His eyebrow lifts. "You assume yours is the only magic affecting it."

The air between us crackles — magic, heat, fury, tension — thick enough to choke on. I break first. "Fine," I mutter. "One night. ONE. And you sleep on the couch."

He leans in, brushing a curl from my cheek with a touch too soft for my sanity. "Sweetheart," he murmurs, "I don't sleep." Then he steps past me and throws himself onto my couch like he owns it.

I stand there speechless. Newt jumps onto my shoulder like an angry fur scarf. And I realize... I have a demon in my living room, a curse reacting to him, and a bond I *refuse* to acknowledge.

And exactly... *zero* plan.

# CHAPTER 4

*Piper*

I wake up to the smell of cedar, smoke, and pure demonic arrogance. *Fantastic.*

My curls are a disaster, my face is flushed, and my magic is prickling under my skin like static begging to misbehave. I sit up slowly, scanning the living room. Slade is standing by the window. Just... standing there.

Back turned, shoulders broad enough to block out half the damn morning light, arms crossed as he stares outside at Snowglobe Hollow like the town owes him money. His black hair is messy, his muscles unfair, and his entire presence is screaming... *I hate joy.*

He glances over his shoulder. "You slept," he says flatly.

"Yeah," I mutter, pushing my curls back. "That's what humans do."

"In case you forgot... demons *don't.*"

"I don't care."

He turns fully toward me—slow, predatory, gorgeous. "I wasn't asking for permission for you to care."

My stomach dips. I ignore it. "Okay, demon boy." I grab my robe and tie it tight. "We need to set some *actual* fucking boundaries."

"Boundaries," he repeats dryly, crossing his arms, somehow making a plain black shirt and fitted jeans look sinful. "Between bonded souls? How cute."

"I *will* throw you out the window."

He smirks. "I'd survive."

"Don't test me."

Newt hops onto the back of the couch, fixing Slade with a homicidal glare. "Your familiar is deranged," Slade mutters.

"He's not my familiar," I snap. "He's my cat."

"He attacked me," Slade mutters in disdain.

"You existed!"

Slade's lip twitches. I have to get out of this apartment before I combust. I grab my phone, scrolling through my Bellamy contacts until I reach the only person insane enough to understand this.

Rhea Bellamy—resident chaos witch, egotistical and successful CEO of House of Rheadora, a fashion empire that she's built from the ground up. It's inspiring, *and* slightly intimidating if I'm being honest. It helps she's my older cousin by three years, Elle's older sister—the lesser of the two evils—but *she* happens to be away in Milan. But... on the other hand. Elle *would* set the moon on fire if it looked at her wrong.

I hit the call button anyway.

She picks up on the first ring. "PIPER LEIGH FUCKING BELLAMY," she screeches before I say a word. "I felt that magical spike from THREE TOWNS OVER. What the hell did you do?"

I wince. "Good morning to you too."

"Oh no," she says, voice going gleefully feral. "No, no, no. Don't you dare try to downplay this. The entire Bellamy line just hiccuped. Spill."

I swallow. Slade is staring at me like he can hear every word. He probably can. "I—uh—may have attempted a ward."

"A ward?" Rhea cackles so loud I pull the phone away. "A WARD? In DECEMBER? You absolute

MORON. Piper, *honey*, sweet baby witch, the curse is at its PEAK."

"I KNOW!" I screech back.

Slade snickers. I flip him off.

"What exactly happened?" Rhea demands, equally delighted.

"There was a circle," I mumble. "And... candles. And basically... well... my magic was being rude."

"And then?" She prompts.

"And then something came through."

Silence. Then—"OH MY GOD YOU SUM- MONED A DEMON."

She is shrieking with joy. Actual fucking *hysterical* joy.

"It was an accident!"

"There is NO SUCH THING as accidental de- mon summoning," she cackles. "Piper, what the FUCK were you thinking?"

"I WASN'T—"

"You never do," she interrupts. "Which demon is it? I swear to god if it's the Imp King I'm going to piss myself laughing—"

"A higher demon," Slade calls from across the room, bored.

Rhea gasps so loud it whistles through the phone. "Oh. My. GOD. A HIGHER DEMON? Piper, you're DONE. You're DEAD!" She squeals dramatically, then pauses like something just clicked in her head. "OR... You're MATED."

"I AM NOT—!!!"

I almost throw my phone. Slade smiles, slow and wicked, all while Rhea continues screaming in my ear. "Send me a photo RIGHT NOW. If he looks like a decaying corpse I'm breaking the curse myself. No cousin of mine is mating with a demon that isn't hot."

I squeak. Slade leans against the wall like a magazine centerfold. "Is he hot?" Rhea demands.

"No," I lie.

Slade raises an eyebrow.

"You're lying," Rhea says practically cackling all over again. "You only sound like that when you're lying or orgasming. You remember that time when I walked in on you and—"

"*RHEA*," I bark.

Slade visibly perks up at the word orgasm. Andddd... I contemplate walking into traffic. "I've got to go," I say, mortified. "Work. Life. Panic. Goodbye."

"NO—SEND PICTURES—"

I hang up. Slade's smirk is catastrophic. "No," I warn him.

"You have an *interesting* family," he says, clearly amused.

"No." *Is that seriously the only word I know?*

"She's not wrong about the bond."

"NO." *Yep, it's definitely the only word I'm capable of saying right now.*

He steps toward me—slow, deliberate, heat radiating off him like a storm. "Piper."

"Nope." *Oh! One for the win. Gods, I need help.*

"You're trembling."

"That's fear," I lie.

"That's arousal."

"No the fuck it's—WHY ARE YOU LIKE THIS?" I screech, eyes widening a fraction as he stops directly in front of me. He's close enough that my breath hits his chest.

"Because you summoned me," he murmurs. "And now I'm in your world. Your home. Your orbit. And whether you accept it or not..."

He lifts my chin with two fingers. "...you are *mine*."

My heart flatlines. Newt hisses like a disapproving chaperone. Slade doesn't blink. I break first, stumbling back. "I'm going to work," I croak. "You are going to stay here and not talk... Or... breathe loud. Or touch *anything*."

Slade leans against my doorway like sin incarnate. "I go where you go."

"You go NOWHERE."

He only grins, and my heart plummets to my ass all over again. I'm in over my fucking head. And he knows it. Fucking bastard. A very big, very sexy, very *smug* bastard who is currently leaning in my doorway like he's posing for a demon-themed advent calendar.

"Stay," I tell him.

Slade lifts a brow. "I'm not a dog."

"Then stop acting like you're going to follow me everywhere."

He steps closer. Too close. His voice drops into that deep, I'm-your-problem-now rumble. "I go where the bond leads."

"No," I hiss, poking his chest. "You go WHERE I SAY."

His grin is slow and devastating. "Say *please*."

I shove past him before I lose my last functioning brain cell, turning around to yell, "STAY. HERE." It comes out like I'm yelling commands at a toddler or malfunctioning Roomba.

Slade leans against my kitchen counter, arms crossed, smirk sinful. "For a little witch who summoned a higher demon, you give terrible orders."

"Stay," I repeat, jabbing a finger at him.

"Make me."

I nearly scream. Newt does scream—hissing from atop the fridge like my feral hype man.

Slade snorts. "I'll consider staying." His eyes drag over me, slow and molten. "If you say it nicely."

"I hope your horns grow crooked."

He... *laughs*. Actually laughs.

Great. Add "demon delighting in my misery" to the morning checklist.

Finally, *finally*, I storm out and slam the door.

# CHAPTER 5

## *Piper*

I'm living a lie. A beautiful, *peaceful* lie... But, a lie nonetheless.

Bellamy's Hearth & Home is in full chaotic swing. The curse has settled to a dull buzz, my customers are blissfully unaware, and everything smells like peppermint candles and pastry spells.

Frost sparkles harmlessly across the windowpanes. The register sings its little tune. My morning line stretches out the door.

People are already asking questions...

"Why were you closed yesterday?"

"Are you okay?"

"Did the curse flare early?"

"Did a spell backfire?"

"Did the mistletoe attack again?"

"Was it a BOY?"

I choke every time.

"No emergency," I lie. "Just... family things."

Rhea texted me twelve laughing emojis and a GIF of a dumpster fire two minutes ago. I'm ringing up a bundle of snow-protection charms when Mrs. Alderberry leans over the counter conspiratorially. "You look flushed this morning, dear."

"I'm fine," I answer quietly.

"Did you meet someone?"

"I'm going to die." I spit out, then smack myself in the head for saying it out loud.

"Oh! So it WAS a man!"

Before I can throttle myself with my own apron—bells over the shop door chime. Not normal chimes. A low, resonant sound like the opening note to a very dangerous symphony. My stomach drops. No.

*No no no*—he *wouldn't*. Fucks sake! He *did*.

Slade steps into my shop like he owns dimension and fucking air itself. And the women of Snowglobe Hollow collectively lose consciousness. I swear half the town swoons on the spot.

He's wearing dark jeans and a black Henley I did NOT give him, stretched over muscles that should not be legally visible in public. His black hair is tousled like he just stepped off a romance cover model set. His eyes—those impossible, dancing green eyes—sweep the shop and land on me.

Heat flares under my skin. He feels it. I know he feels it. The room fills with feminine sighs.

"Who is THAT?" ... "Oh my GOD." ... "He's gorgeous!" ... "Is he... with Piper?" ... "They look like a couple." ... "She deserves it. Look at those shoulders."

Slade eats it up. EATS. IT. UP.

His smirk is obscene. He stalks toward the counter with slow, confident steps, like every human here should be thanking him for breathing.

I hiss under my breath, "I told you to stay home."

He leans against the counter, entirely too close, voice a low purr only I can hear. "You told me many things, little witch." His eyes glint. "I listened to none of them."

I want to strangle him with a garland. Mrs. Alderberry clasps her hands, starstruck. "Oh Piper, dear—is this your... *boyfriend*?"

I nearly swallow my tongue. "No—NO—he's not my—this isn't—"

Slade places a warm, heavy hand on my lower back. I freeze. He says—loud enough for the entire shop to hear—"I'm hers."

A chorus of gasps detonates. I make a noise only bats can hear. Slade's grin widens, wicked and triumphant. I elbow him sharply. "Stop it!"

"I thought I was making things easier," he murmurs with faux innocence.

"You're making things worse!"

Mrs. Alderberry fans herself. "Oh my."

Slade leans down, voice brushing my ear. "You're welcome."

I glare at him with the force of a thousand collapsing stars. He just smiles. The fucking *bastard*.

I don't think. I grab Slade's wrist—hot, solid, arrogant—and yank him behind the counter. "Back room. NOW."

A few customers gasp. Someone whispers, "Oh my..."

Slade, of course, looks positively delighted. I march him through the beaded curtain, slam the door behind us, and whirl on him, ready to unleash holy hell—He's already leaning against a shelf. Arms crossed. Smirk sinful enough to get us both arrested. "You wanted privacy?" he asks.

"I wanted to yell at you."

"You can do that in private too."

Gods. Give me strength. I poke him in the chest. Hard. "What. The fuck. Was that?"

He cocks his head. "The truth."

"You told them you were mine."

"Should I clarify?" He leans forward. "Should I specify in what ways?"

My face bursts into flames. "STOP. Talking."

His voice drops. "Make me."

Oh no. NO *sir*.

Slade steps off the shelf, closing the distance in a single predatory stride. Then he cages me against the door. Again. "But I told you—" he murmurs, "I go where you go."

I shove his chest. He doesn't budge. He moves like a mountain—like he's letting me push him for his amusement. "Slade," I warn, "your behavior is—unwelcomed."

"Liar."

My mouth falls open. "You can't just say liar whenever you want!"

"I can when it's accurate."

I growl.—actually growl. He laughs. His hand slides to my waist—slow, warm, claiming. My brain automatically short-circuits. "Don't touch me," I whisper.

He leans in, breath warm against my jaw. "I think you like when I do."

"I don't." It's a lie, we both know it.

"You tremble when I do," he counters.

"That's the curse!"

"Is it?" he asks softly. "Or is it me?"

My pulse stutters. Something crackles overhead. The lights flicker. The shelves rattle faintly. A jar of moon-bloom salt hops an inch like it's trying to escape the tension.

Slade's smile sharpens. "The curse is reacting to us."

"Then STOP being so—so—"

"Devastatingly attractive?"

"ANNOYING."

He chuckles low. "Sweetheart, I was *born* annoying."

"Born annoying," I mutter. "And built like a temptation trap."

His eyes gleam. "You think I'm built well?"

"I am NOT answering that."

"You just did."

This can't be happening. A soft rattle comes from the shop floor outside the back-room door. Just one. Someone murmurs, "Did you feel that?" Someone else gives an uneasy laugh.

Slade's damn smile goes nuclear, sending a wave of nervous energy bouncing around in my stomach. The lights flicker again. A stack of spell tags flutters off a shelf. A dried herb garland sways like there's a breeze—though there isn't. Magic ripples through the room, sharp and electric. Slade steps back slightly, listening. His expression shifts from amused... to intent. "The curse is mirroring you," he says.

"Mirroring what?"

"Your emotions," he clarifies. "They're unstable. So the curse is unstable."

"That's not—I'm *not*—unstable—!!"

He lifts a brow slowly.

I sag. "Okay, FINE, I'm unstable! *You're* destabilizing!"

Slade actually looks pleased. "If I affect you that much, maybe you should reconsider fighting the bond."

"The bond can eat my ass."

A pause. A *very* heavy pause. Slade tilts his head. Dead serious. "...Is that an invitation?"

"NO—Slade STOP—WHY ARE YOU LIKE THIS—"

From the shop floor, a patron calls gently through the curtain, "Everything okay back there?"

I slam my palm over my face. Slade leans in, mouth inches from mine, eyes burning green fire. "This town is very supportive."

"Get. Away," I groan.

"Say it nicely."

"I will STILL hex your dick."

He laughs. "Still *not* a deterrent."

I shove him again. This time he lets me. He steps back with a little bow. "Your wish, little witch."

I crack the door open—just barely. The shop looks mostly normal. Just... jittery. A few customers shifting awkwardly. A candle flame fluttering against nonexistent wind. Magic humming faintly under the floorboards. Mrs. Alderberry glances my way, eyes narrowing. "Oh dear," she murmurs. "You've got a glow about you. What happened?"

I slam the door shut. Slade crosses his arms, smug. "You're welcome."

"SLAAADE."

"This is fun," he says.

"THIS IS A NIGHTMARE."

He smirks. "Not for me."

"Get out."

He saunters to the door like a lazy predator. Instead of leaving, he leans against the frame, smoldering. "You told me to stay put," he says. "And I did."

"This is NOT what I meant!"

"It's what the *bond* meant."

I scream into my hands. The shelves tremble again. And Slade? Slade wears a smile that is pure, unadulterated sin incarnate. And I still want to strangle the living daylights out of him.

I've got to find a way to break this curse... this *bon*d... whatever the fuck it is.

Before I lose my god's damned mind.

# CHAPTER 6

*Slade*

The day drags. Humans talk too much, touch too much, breathe too loudly, and yet Piper moves among them like she belongs—like someone born to warmth and soft lights and glittering shelves of charm-laced nonsense.

I watch her... All day. I've tried to stop... But, I can't help it.

She doesn't notice me most of the time, too busy ringing customers up or laughing at something someone says, curls bouncing around her shoulders in ways that make my hands itch.

But I notice everything.

The way her magic flickers gold around her fingers when she's focused. Or the way she tries, and fails, to hide each spike of irritation when I hover nearby. And the way she keeps glancing at me like I'm a ticking bomb she can't defuse.

She's wrong. I'm the one trying to defuse her.

I find myself wandering the shop—casually, like a predator pretending to be a house pet—trailing fingertips over jars of herbs and glass ornaments, feeling the faint hum of old Bellamy magic stitched into the walls.

She watches every time I touch something. Suspicious. Tense. So adorably cute.

*Gods*, since when do I use the words cute and adorable?

At one point she mutters under her breath, "If you break anything, I'm billing Hell directly."

I hum. "Send the invoice to the Ninth Circle. Mark it attention to Slade."

She glares, and I enjoy it way more than I should.

I keep circling her, observing her from different angles. Her movements. Her scent. Her mood shifts. I'm looking for clues. Because she insists—loudly, repeatedly, and with increasing fury—that she didn't summon me.

She did. Like I told her... Emotion is a stronger conduit than ritual.

Whatever she felt last night was strong enough to punch a hole between realms and drag me through. But what emotion? Fear? Longing? Desperation? Anger? Or something else—something she refuses to name.

Every time I get close enough to her magic, it pulses toward mine like a hand reaching in the dark—hungry, curious, even familiar.

*Bound.*

She's fighting it so hard she's exhausting herself. Near closing, she's rounding up stray candles while muttering to herself. "...doesn't make sense... I didn't summon anything... I was warding, not conjuring—"

I lean against a shelf beside her. "Still denying the obvious?"

She jumps, and I grin.

"Slade," Piper warns. "You're giving me wrinkles."

"You should thank me. Fated mate wrinkles are flattering."

She smacks a box of tea charms against the counter harder than necessary. "I'm not your fated *anything*."

"You keep saying that," I murmur, "and your magic keeps disagreeing."

She narrows her eyes. "Stop analyzing me."

"Stop being interesting."

Her lips part—offended and flustered. What a *lovely* combination.

She flips the sign to CLOSED, turns off the main lights, and begins locking the door. Her movements are brisk, practiced, a little shaky.

I can tell she's pretending she's in control. I let her pretend. For now... I follow her outside, taking in the small and sleepy town.

Snowglobe Hollow glitters under early evening light, frost collecting along the cobblestones. Piper pulls her coat tight, curls spilling from her hood in a dark, stormy halo. She keeps walking fast enough that she thinks she's outpacing me. I stroll lazily beside her, matching her every step without effort.

"Stop hovering," she mutters.

"I'm walking," I reply, arching a brow.

"You're hovering while standing."

"That's called existing *near* you."

She groans dramatically. "I need a vacation."

"You need answers," I retort.

"I need wine."

"You want to know about the curse."

She stops walking. Looks at me. Really looks. Her breath clouds the cold air, cheeks pink from wind and frustration. "I don't want your help," she says softly.

"But you want the truth."

Her jaw flexes. She says nothing, which is as good as a yes. I step closer—not touching her, not yet—but close enough that the magic between us shivers in recognition. "You didn't summon me by accident," I say quietly. "Something inside you called for something stronger."

Piper swallows hard. "I don't want to talk about this outside."

That's fine. I like her walls. They're fun to break.

And I do intend to break them down...

***

The moment she opens the door, the cat waits for me. Newt sits proudly in the entryway like a tiny gargoyle, tail wrapped around his paws.

Piper sighs. "Newt, *don't* start. Mommy's had a day."

I step inside. Newt stands, approaches... and rubs against my leg. *Purring*. I stare down at him. The creature looks smug.

Piper blinks. "...what are you doing?"

Newt headbutts my shin. She squints at him like he's betrayed the entire Bellamy bloodline. "Newt. Sweetie. Wh—why are you—why are you being NICE?"

I crouch, scratch the cat behind the ear. Newt melts like butter under my hand.

Piper's eyes widen. "WHAT DID YOU DO TO HIM?"

"Nothing," I say truthfully.

"You bribed him with demon treats."

"Demon treats don't exist."

"Well they SHOULD," she snaps, pacing and pointing accusingly. "Because my cat does not trust easily, and he is not cuddly with strangers, and he definitely doesn't like you—"

Newt hops into my lap. Stretches. Purrs even louder.

Piper stares at us like she's witnessing the fall of civilization. "Oh my god," she whispers. "He *likes* you."

I give her a slow, satisfied smile. "I told you," I say quietly. "Your familiar recognizes the bond."

"HE IS NOT MY FAMILIAR."

"Sure," I say, stroking the cat. "Keep telling yourself that."

Her glare could melt stone. But underneath it, her magic flickers, curious and unsettled. I lean back against the couch, cat sprawled across me like a traitor, and watch her unravel in slow motion. And I know... she's already mine.

She doesn't realize it—not deep down, not consciously—but her magic does. It keeps reaching for me. Testing the edges. Pulling like a subtle gravitational force.

Piper crosses her arms hard over her chest, as if that alone could keep me out. "Okay, demon," she snaps, "since you're already turning my life into a train wreck, let's cut the shit. What do you know about my curse?"

I stroke the cat absently, watching her. "Not enough to give you the answers you want."

"Not enough," she repeats, incredulous. "Are you kidding me? You're a higher demon. You should know *something*."

"I know pieces."

"Start connecting them."

I tilt my head. "You didn't say please."

"Slade," she hisses, "I am two seconds away from snapping and you haven't even seen me cranky yet."

Gods, she's exquisite when she's angry. "I know the curse is ancient," I say slowly, "Old-magic. Tied to emotion. And reactive. Very reactive." My gaze drags over her deliberately. "Especially for you."

She rolls her eyes. "Wow. *So helpful*. I could've googled that."

"And I know," I continue, letting my voice drop, "that there are places—*old* places—where your family kept records. Histories. Spellwork diaries. The kind you witches love. One of them might still exist."

Her expression cracks, just a little. "Where?"

I shrug. "I have an idea."

"Slade. I swear, if you don't pony up the information, I will—"

"You're getting impatient," I murmur. "Interesting."

"Of COURSE I'm impatient! I summoned a demon, accidentally bonded with said demon—"

"You *did* summon me," I agree.

"—and my CAT likes you now—"

"I'm very likable."

"—and the town thinks I'm attracted to you—" she groans.

"They're not entirely wrong."

She sputters. "EXCUSE ME?"

I stand slowly, letting Newt slide off my lap. Her eyes widen as I tower over her. "You feel it," I say softly.

"That is NOT what I feel!"

"Your magic thinks otherwise."

She shakes her head so hard her curls bounce. "Absolutely not. I am NOT—under ANY cir-cumstances—attracted to some arrogant, broody, musclebound—"

"Keep going," I murmur.

"—horny HELL-spawn—"

"Mm."

"—with an ego the size of the moon and no concept of personal space—"

"I do enjoy your space," I retort.

"—and a face that's—" She clamps her mouth shut. Hard.

I step closer. Predator close. Heat rolling off me in waves. "A face that's what?" I coax.

She shoves my shoulder. "PUNCHABLE."

I laugh—low, delighted, hungry. She has no idea what she just did to me. My demon surges, slow and thick and possessive. "I could help you," I say quietly. "With all of this. With the curse. With the pull you're feeling."

"I AM NOT FEEL—"

"There's a very simple way to ease the bond's pressure."

Her mouth opens—and snaps shut. Piper's voice drops to a horrified whisper. "If you say sex..."

I smile.

Her eyes go huge. Horrified. Flustered. Pink creeping up her throat. "You are UNBELIEV-ABLE," she sputters. "I cannot—are you out of your infernal MIND—sex does NOT solve CURSES—"

"It would solve this one."

"No it wouldn't!"

"*Yes* it would."

"No—NO." She points at me wildly. "We are not doing ANYTHING. EVER."

I step in. Close enough that she bumps into the wall behind her. Her breath stutters.

"You insult me," I murmur. "And it excites me."

Her breath catches in her throat. "Don't—don't say things like that—"

"Why?" I ask. My hand comes up. She freezes. I slide my fingers along her jaw, down her neck, curling softly, possessively around her throat. Not squeezing—just holding. Just claiming territory I know belongs to me.

Her eyes flutter. Her lips part. Magic crackles between us like static in a storm.

"Slade..." she whispers, voice breaking.

"You want answers," I say.

My thumb brushes her pulse. "Fine. We'll find them."

She shivers. "But right now," I murmur, leaning in, "you need to sleep. Before the curse gets another foothold."

I press my lips to her temple—slow, warm, intentional. A kiss that is not a kiss. A claim disguised as comfort.

Her knees soften. A soft, helpless sound escapes her throat—barely audible. Heat floods off her in waves. Sweet. Wild. Unmistakable. Piper's scent shifts—warm, sultry, blooming with magic she can't hide.

*Desire.*

I inhale once—slowly—and it hits me like a blow to the chest. She's *wet...* for *me.*

She stiffens immediately, sensing the change in my breathing, the way I go still. Her eyes dart up to mine, wide and defensive, like she knows I've just discovered a secret she didn't mean to reveal.

I lean in, my lips brushing her temple. "Go to bed, Piper."

She tries to scowl at me, but the edges of it tremble. Her pupils are blown, pulse fluttering against my fingers. Her magic skitters over her skin like sparks desperate to leap. I tilt my head, inhale again—purposefully this time. And she goes bright red. "Slade," she hisses through clenched teeth, "don't."

"You're soaked for me," I murmur.

She lets out a shocked, furious noise—somewhere between a gasp and a squeak. "That is—NO—it's—SHUT. UP."

I smile against her cheek. Dark. Slow. Knowing. "Liar."

She shoves me again—weak, embarrassed, and absolutely melting under my hand. "I hate you," she snaps.

"No." I step back just enough to let her breathe. "You *wish* you did."

She whirls around and storms down the hallway, curls bouncing violently, indignation in every step. I stay where I am. Listening.

Her heartbeat—fast, uneven, desperate. Piper's magic—humming, needy, reaching even as she tries to push it down.

The moment she throws herself into bed, I hear it. A soft, helpless exhale of frustration and want. A woman trying very, very hard *not* to think about me.

*Exactly* as intended.

# CHAPTER 7

*Piper*

Morning filters through my curtains in a soft wash of winter light, warm enough to tease but too faint to soothe. I wake with a start—not dramatically, just a sharp inhale that hits the back of my throat and reminds me of everything I'm trying very hard not to remember.

Slade's hand on my throat. His breath against my skin. His mouth brushing my temple. The way my body answered him—quick and helpless—as if it had been waiting for that moment longer than I've been alive.

*Absolutely not.*

I shove off the blankets and roll out of bed, willing my legs not to wobble. They do anyway. I pretend they don't. What can I say? A girl deserves her delusions.

The scent reaches me before I turn the corner—something warm and savory, threaded with the faintest curl of smoke.

He's in my *kitchen*. Of course he is.

I pause at the threshold, silently pleading for a moment of grace, but the universe refuses. Slade stands at the stove, bare from the waist up, cooking like it's the most natural thing in the world. Strong shoulders taper into a broad back, smooth and powerful, every line of muscle shifting with infuriating ease.

He glances back, sensing me. "Good morning," he says, as if we didn't practically melt into each other's magic last night. "You slept well."

My voice catches. "I'm fine."

"That's not what I asked."

"It's what you're getting."

He returns to the pan, unfazed. There is a confidence in him so complete it almost feels like serenity—if serenity were carved into muscle and smirked like a sinner.

Before I can formulate a coherent thought, my phone rings on the counter. Rhea's name flashes across the screen like a warning label. I grab it before Slade can decide he has opinions about my family. My phone rings again before I'm even halfway across the kitchen.

Of course it's Rhea. I answer out of reflex, bracing myself. She doesn't even greet me.

"Piper Leigh Bellamy," she snaps, "I checked your house wards this morning and they're humming like they've been having a night of their own.

What the *hell* happened last night, and why am I the LAST to know?"

I drag a hand over my face. "Rhea, it's too early—"

"Oh gods, your voice." She gasps dramatically. "You sound wrecked. Did you—did he—Piper, if you got ravished by something infernal and didn't FaceTime me to give me the—"

"RHEA."

Slade turns, amused, stirring the pan like he's been waiting for this exact circus to occur.

Rhea continues, completely relentless. "Is he still there? Wait—don't answer. I can feel trouble through the phone. I KNOW you're not alone. Are you clothed? Is he? Are you clothed... but *barely*? Do I need to stage an intervention or a celebration—because I can go either way—"

"I'm going to hang up," I warn.

"You will NOT—PIPER—DO NOT—"

I hang up.

Slade chuckles low, plating breakfast. "Your cousin is... *passionate*."

"That's one thing she is, yes."

"She's also observant."

I stiffen. "About what?"

He looks at me over his shoulder, voice smooth. "Your attraction. You're trying so hard not to show it."

Heat prickles across my skin. "You're delusional."

"No," he says simply. "Just paying attention."

I fold my arms, grounding myself in irritation because anything else feels too dangerous. "Just give me food. Maybe chewing will stop me from hexing you."

Slade sets a plate in front of me with slow, deliberate care. "Unfortunately, breakfast won't solve your problem."

"You are unbearable."

"And you," he says softly, "are blushing."

"I am NOT—"

"You've been flushed since you woke up."

I stab my fork into my eggs with unnecessary force and shove a bite into my mouth to avoid acknowledging him. Then it happens. A faint creak above the refrigerator. I look up, stomach sinking.

A sprig of mistletoe dangles precariously above me, shifting as if caught on a breeze that... doesn't exist. "Oh, for the love of—no. No, we are NOT doing this."

It wiggles. Slade doesn't turn around. "Mm."

"Slade," I warn, backing away as the mistletoe dips closer.

He finally glances over his shoulder, obviously amused. "It's reacting to your magic again..."

"It's *hunting* me."

"It's *enchanted* to encourage intimacy," he counters, clearly amused at my panic.

"I didn't enchant it!" I screech at him.

"And I didn't either."

"Then WHY is it—oh gods—"

The mistletoe swoops. I yelp and duck as it dives dangerously close to my face. Slade catches it in one smooth, effortless motion, holding it up between us. He studies it like it's mildly amusing instead of a predatory plant with romance-based murder in its heart. "Harmless," he says, mouth curling up in amusement.

"It's *plotting*," I argue. "Put it outside."

"It will return."

"It can find... NEW FRIENDS."

He tosses it into the sink. It hops out again, cheery and malevolent. Slade smiles. "Persistent. Just like the bond."

"Stop. Saying. Bond," I grit out, grabbing a wooden spoon like I'm about to declare war.

He watches me with a slow, warm amusement that makes my blood hum. "If you hex me every time I'm right, you'll wear yourself out." His tone changes—low, dangerous, enticing. "Careful, Piper."

My pulse jumps. I hate that he sees it. I straighten, dragging air into my lungs. "Rhea said something about old spellwork. You said the Bellamy line kept records. If you know something, you're going to start talking."

"I will."

"When?" I ask, obviously wanting a clear answer so he can't back out of it later.

"After breakfast."

"Slade."

He steps close—too close—and slips a finger beneath my chin, tilting my face up with disarming gentleness. "We'll look today," he says. "I'll take you to what remains of your family's archives. Some were lost. Some were hidden. Some only demons know the location of."

A cold shiver crawls down my spine. "And you know this how?"

"I've lived long enough to see where witches hide their secrets. Your bloodline is predictable in that way."

"That's not an answer," I argue.

"It's the one you have."

Heat slides up my neck. "You're impossible."

"And you," he murmurs, letting his thumb brush the edge of my jaw, "are learning to lean into what you pretend you don't feel."

I forget how to breathe. He leans in—not kissing me, but letting the warmth of him settle over my skin in a way that dissolves thought.

"Good girl," he whispers.

The curse responds instantly. Lights flicker. Warm air ripples through the kitchen. The mistletoe shivers like it's preparing a second assault. I step back, cheeks burning, trying to hold myself together. "We need to go," I say, voice strained. "Before this gets worse."

Slade watches me like a man enjoying a secret only he knows. "It will," he murmurs. "Just not in the way you fear."

I don't say anything to that, turning away instead, still pretending he doesn't affect me at all.

But I know... he doesn't believe me in the slightest. And I'm starting to wonder... do I even really believe myself?

***

Slade doesn't push me the moment I step back from him, though the look in his eyes suggests he wants to. The curse hums in the air like static before a storm, subtle but restless, and the mistletoe in the sink gives one last irritated tremor.

I decide I need shoes, coffee, twelve layers of emotional camouflage, and—to my misfortune—Slade.

He watches me while I throw myself together in the living room, coat half-zipped, curls barely tamed, to-go mug clutched like a lifeline. His expression is unreadable in a way that makes my skin tingle. "You ready?" I ask, trying to sound neutral and definitely not flushed from that earlier good girl comment.

His smile is a slow, dangerous thing. "I've been ready since you woke up."

"Congratulations," I mutter. "Let's go."

Slade steps outside like the cold doesn't exist. I, on the other hand, immediately regret being human. Snowglobe Hollow's winter air cuts through me, crisp and clean and laced with the faint scent of pine.

We walk in silence for a few blocks, my boots crunching in the snow, Slade's footsteps soundless as shadows. "You never answered my question," I say finally, adjusting my scarf. "Where exactly are we going?"

"A place that specializes in information."

"That is incredibly vague," I say with a frown.

"Intentionally."

"And you thought taking me was smart?"

"I didn't say it was smart," he replies. "But it's necessary."

"How reassuring."

The next city over isn't far—just fifteen minutes by car—but every one of those minutes feels heavy. Slade's presence fills the vehicle, warm and consuming, like the cabin itself is too small to contain him. He watches the passing trees with mild disinterest, but occasionally, when he thinks I'm not watching, his gaze flickers to me.

By the time we reach the outskirts of Frostharrow, dusk has already crept across the sky. The neon sign flickering outside the dive bar reads *THE HOLLOW TANKARD*, though half the bulbs are dead and the rest are trying their best. It looks like a place where hope comes to die. "Charming," I mutter.

"It's a front," Slade says simply. "Humans see a rundown bar. Magic sees doors."

I eye him warily. "Have you... been here before?"

"Yes."

I blink. "Do you come here often?"

His smile sharpens. "Sweetheart," he says, leaning close enough that his breath warms the air near my cheek, "my reputation keeps me from needing to 'come often' to any establishment. When I walk in, people talk."

I hate that my stomach flips.

Inside, the Hollow Tankard smells like old whiskey, pine sap, and something metallic that makes the back of my throat prickle. The lights are low, more shadow than illumination, and the patrons are a collection of misfits—witches, fae, shifters, things I can't immediately categorize.

Every head turns when Slade enters. Not in fear. Not exactly... But in acknowledgment. He moves like a storm given legs—dangerous, hungry, familiar to every dark corner of this place.

I stay close to him. Not because I need protection. No. Absolutely not. But because my magic stirs uncomfortably when people brush too close.

"Don't wander," he murmurs, eyeing the patrons with obvious distrust.

"I wasn't planning to."

He leads me to the bar, where a woman with iridescent eyes and pale silver braids stops wiping a glass mid-motion. "Slade," she says, voice low, almost melodic. "Didn't expect you for another decade."

"I work irregular hours." He gestures toward me. "We're looking for Bellamy records."

Her gaze slides to me. A spark of recognition flares. "You're one of them," she says with certainty.

"One of who?" I ask.

But she ignores me, leaning in further. "What kind of Bellamy are you seeking, demon?"

"Old ones," Slade replies. "Origins. Curse work."

The woman stills. No—she *freezes*. Her fingers curl around the bar, knuckles whitening. When she speaks again, her voice has dropped to a hush. "That's dangerous history."

Slade tilts his head. "Not that dangerous."

She gives a dry laugh. "Everything connected to that lineage is dangerous. But you already knew that." She studies me for a long, suffocating moment—eyes flicking over my face, my aura, the faint shimmer of magic that's probably still reacting to Slade's earlier proximity.

Finally, she exhales.

"There's not much left," she says quietly. "Most of the older Bellamy records were either hidden too *well*... or destroyed before anyone could get to them."

My stomach twists. "Destroyed by who?"

She lifts one shoulder in a grim half-shrug. "Witches. Hunters. Time. No one really knows anymore. People are good at erasing the things that scare them." Her gaze drifts to Slade. "Or the things they can't control."

Slade's jaw tightens, just enough for me to notice.

"But," she continues, leaning closer, "one fragment survived. Just one. Old enough that it predates most living bloodlines." Those iridescent eyes lock on mine. "Rare enough that even speaking of it tends to attract attention."

I swallow. "What fragment?"

Something flickers behind her expression—hesitation... or fear. "The first name," she whispers. "The first Bellamy touched by the curse. Five centuries ago."

My pulse stutters. Slade goes very still beside me. "Who?" I ask, breath catching before the word even forms.

"*Veda Bellamy*," the woman answers. "The origin point. Or the closest thing anyone's been able to confirm."

A shiver rolls down my spine. "What happened to her?" I ask, even though I'm terrified of the answer.

"No one knows." She shakes her head slowly. "Some say she disappeared. Others say she broke under whatever the curse demanded. Some say she survived it."

Her eyes grow distant—haunted. "But all that's left now is a name—a whisper, really—and a warning."

Before I can ask anything else, the front door of the bar swings open with a sharp crack. A wave of energy ripples through the room—subtle but unmistakable. My skin prickles. The air thickens. Conversation dies instantly.

The bartender's eyes widen. "She shouldn't be here," she murmurs, gaze flicking toward me. "Not with the curse waking. Not now."

Slade moves before I can breathe. One step, then another—smooth, controlled, predatory—until he's a wall of heat at my back, eclipsing the room behind him. His voice is soft but final. "We're leaving."

I nod, throat tight.

Outside, the cold hits like a warning. Snowflakes tumble under the glow of the neon sign, the wind whispering through the narrow alley beside the bar. Slade guides me to a waiting car with a hand at the small of my back—light, steady, grounding.

When we reach the passenger side, I finally manage words. "So... Veda Bellamy. Five hundred years ago." I swallow hard. "First recorded curse-bearer."

Slade meets my gaze, eyes burning with something unreadable—dark, thoughtful, almost protective—but there's something else beneath it. Something older, more wary. "And we're going to find out what happened to her," he says.

"Why?" My voice comes out smaller than I intend, trembling at the edges.

He takes one slow step closer, boots sinking slightly into the snow. The wind curls around us, cold biting at my cheeks, but his presence is warm—too warm—like he's radiating heat from somewhere beneath his skin.

"Because whatever touched her bloodline," he murmurs, "is touching *you* now."

It's not enough. Not anymore. I cross my arms tightly. "That's not an answer."

His gaze flicks away—just for a heartbeat—but it's the first time I've seen him look... unsure.

"Slade." I take a step toward him. "You dragged me out here. You inserted yourself into my life. You keep talking about bonds and curses and fate. If you know more than you're admitting—start talking."

He huffs a quiet laugh, not amused. "Careful, little witch."

"No," I snap. "No more warnings. No more riddles. Tell me the truth. Why do you care what happens to my family? Why does any of this matter to a demon who wasn't supposed to answer my summoning in the first place?"

He goes very still. The snowflakes drifting between us pause in the air like they're waiting. "I didn't say it *didn't* concern me," he murmurs.

"That's not an explanation."

He exhales slowly, fog curling from his lips. "Because your bloodline didn't just create a curse, Piper." His eyes lift to mine, piercing, ancient. "It broke something first."

A cold knot forms low in my stomach. "Broke... what?"

He takes another step closer, the distance between us shrinking until the air feels electric. "Five centuries ago," he says softly, "Veda Bellamy wasn't just the first to carry the curse. She was bound. Promised. Marked to another."

My breath catches. "A mate?"

"An intended," Slade corrects. "Magic chose for them. Fate sealed it."

"And she refused?" I whisper.

His jaw tightens. "...Yes."

"So the curse wasn't just born from a Bellamy," I say slowly, pieces clicking into place. "It was born from betrayal."

His silence is confirmation. I swallow hard, forcing the words out. "And the person she betrayed—who were they?"

Slade's eyes darken, the green deepening until it's nearly black. The wind gusts around us, stirring his coat, ruffling my curls. He leans in, lowering his voice to a gravel-soft whisper that seems to echo with something older than language. "My ancestor."

The world tilts. For a heartbeat, all I hear is the rush of my own pulse. "*You...*" I breathe. "Your line was her original match."

"Yes," he answers.

"And when she rejected that bond—"

"The curse manifested," Slade finishes. "On her. On her descendants. And—by extension—on mine."

The revelation sinks into my bones like ice water. "So you're not helping me," I say, voice thin. "You're helping yourself."

A muscle jumps in his jaw. "It's both."

"No. You're using me."

He steps closer, heat rolling off him. "If I intended to use you, Piper, you'd already be mine."

The words shouldn't make my stomach flip—but they do.

My breath trembles out in a cloud of frost. "So you're bound to this because of some ancient Bellamy witch and a choice she made five hundred years ago?"

"Not just bound," he murmurs. "Entangled."

I shake my head, trying to make sense of it. "You keep saying the curse responds to me. But if your bloodline was part of the original break—why isn't it destroying your life every Christmas, too?"

A slow, dangerous smile curves his mouth. "Because demons don't break the way humans do."

My heart stutters.

"And because," he adds, voice dipping lower, "the curse wants something from us. Something it didn't get last time."

I swallow. "What?"

His gaze burns hotter. Older. Hungry. "The completion of the bond."

The snow seems to hush around us. My pulse thunders. "No," I whisper. "You can't just—no. I didn't sign up for that."

"You summoned me," he reminds gently. "Magic answered. Fate followed."

"I didn't summon fate," I protest.

He steps close enough that the cold can't reach me. Close enough that his breath warms my cheek. "That may be true... But it still summoned me."

The night closes in—quiet, heavy, alive. And with his bloodline tied to mine, with Veda Bellamy's shadow looming behind us and the curse beginning to stir...

For the first time since Slade walked into my life, I'm not confused. Not overwhelmed, or annoyed.

I'm *afraid*.

# CHAPTER 8

*Piper*

The next morning begins with exactly three goals... Run my shop. Pretend everything is normal. Keep Slade at least ten feet away from me at all times.

Goal one is questionable. Goal two dies before breakfast. Goal three was always delusional.

I fling the front lightswitch with a little more aggression than intended. The shop hums awake—twinkling fairy bulbs, lingering incense, soft chimes near the window. Comforting, familiar, safe.

Unlike the demon currently leaning in my doorway.

Slade's silhouette fills the frame, arms crossed, posture loose and predatory, green eyes bright with amusement like he's already won some argument I haven't started yet. "You're scowling," he says.

"I'm TRYING," I mutter, pinching the bridge of my nose.

"To scowl?"

"To *pretend* you *don't* exist."

He steps inside. "I can help."

"No." I point at the floor. "Stay there."

He raises a brow. "You're giving a demon boundaries?"

"*Yes*," I snap. "Healthy ones."

"Mmh." His gaze travels slowly—too slowly—down my body and back up. "You look delicious when you're flustered."

I nearly throw a candle at him.

Customers begin trickling in as the morning settles. Locals, tourists, magic-aware folks, gossip-mongers. The usual mix of curious and nosy. I force a smile, answer questions, ring up purchases. All while Slade prowls the shelves like he's casing the joint—or, worse, like he's guarding it. And me.

Every time I glance over, he's there. Like smoke, or fucking gravity. Like he's incapable of not orbiting me.

And the customers notice.

Two older witches by the incense rack whisper loudly. "He's still here," one mutters.

"He's following her like a storm cloud," the other notes.

"A handsome storm cloud," the first says.

"I heard he carried her home," a third newcomer says, eyeing me with curiosity. I pretend not to notice that, too.

"I heard he claimed her," the second says in a near whisper.

Slade smirks, and I want to scream. I force my focus onto a cauldron-shaped wax warmer someone is purchasing. "Did you need this gift-wrapped?"

"Yes, please," the woman says sweetly—but her eyes keep darting to Slade. "Is that your... um... *boyfriend*?"

"No," I say firmly.

"Not yet," Slade offers.

The woman's eyebrows shoot up. "Oh my."

I slam the register shut with unnecessary force. Slade finally drifts closer—close enough that his body heat radiates against mine, close enough that my pulse reacts before my brain catches up. "You're tense," he murmurs. Like that thought offends him.

"Gee," I whisper back, "I WONDER WHY."

"I could relieve it."

"Slade," I hiss, "I am WORKING."

"That doesn't change my offer," he says with a feral grin.

I swear my soul tries to exit my body. I storm away to restock crystals, hoping distance will fix something—anything. Instead he trails me, a silent shadow with too much presence. "Stop following me," I mutter under my breath.

"I'm not," he argues.

"You are literally breathing down my neck."

"I like the way you smell."

I choke, sputtering as I try to regain my composure. A jar of rose quartz rattles. That damn curse is listening again. "Go *away*," I plead.

"No."

"Why?"

He steps in front of me, cutting off my escape route. "Because the moment you walked out of that bar last night, you decided you hate me more than you actually do."

My breath catches. "I don't hate you."

"Correct," he says softly.

"That doesn't mean I LIKE you."

His head tilts. "Your magic does."

"That is irrelevant," I argue, dismissing him with a wave of my hand.

He leans closer, voice dropping. "You're my mate, Piper."

I freeze. "And you didn't know it would be me," I whisper.

"No." His expression softens—not much, but enough that it cracks something inside me. "I expected someone ruthless. Power-hungry. Vicious. Someone who would destroy me before I could destroy them."

My throat tightens.

"But I got you instead." His voice roughens almost imperceptibly. "And you are... *infuriating-*

*ly* human. Stubborn, bright. Braver than some demons I know. Soft in ways I don't deserve."

That catches my breath. But I shove the moment aside because I can't—can't—accept this. "You only want my help because of the curse."

"No." He moves closer, crowding into my space, heat rolling off him. "I want *you*. The curse is incidental."

"That's a lie."

"Demons don't lie," he says quietly. "Not about this."

Something beats hard against my ribs. I step back. "I don't want any of this."

He doesn't chase me this time. He just watches. Patient... Hungry. Certain. "Liar," he murmurs.

Before I can react, the front door bursts open and Rhea barrels in like a chaotic missile wrapped in a peacoat. She stops dead, sees Slade, then me, and how close we are. "Oh," she says slowly. "Well. This looks... *charged*."

I bury my face in my hands. Slade grins like he's been handed a holiday gift soaked in gasoline.

Rhea drops her purse. "Okay. Someone start talking. Preferably Piper. Slade looks like he's seconds from doing something... irreversible."

Slade's gaze flicks to me—low, dark, promising. "I won't do anything irreversible," he says lazily. "*Yet.*"

Rhea fans herself. "Yup. I'm staying."

I groan. "Please leave."

"No," both of them say at once.

I glare up at the ceiling, searching for divine intervention. Instead, a strand of tinsel on the nearest tree twitches and floats toward Slade like it wants to perch on his horns. I smack it down.

He smirks. Rhea squeals. The curse hums, and I realize—with bone-deep dread—that keeping him away from me?

Is becoming impossible.

***

"Okay," Rhea says, planting her hands on her curvy hips, brown hair spilling in glossy waves past her shoulders. Her amber eyes glitter with mischief and concern—*heavy* on the mischief. "Someone explain the tension in here before I spontaneously combust."

"You won't combust," Slade says with a lazy smirk. "You would sizzle."

Rhea blinks. "Oh my gods, he finally speaks."

"He talks too much," I snap.

Slade tilts his head, amused. "You enjoy it."

"No, I don't."

Rhea's lips curl into a wicked grin. "Oh, she enjoys something, alright."

"Rhea," I warn.

But she's already circling me like a shark drawn to drama. "Pipes, babe, I love you, but you look like you slept three minutes and have been refusing to process something emotionally significant. Spill.”

I grit my teeth. “Not here.”

“Why not? Because of him?” She jerks her chin toward Slade, eyes gleaming.

“Yes!” I hiss. “Because of him.”

Slade smiles like I handed him a compliment wrapped in velvet. “She means she’s distracted by me.”

I whirl on him. “I mean I cannot think straight with you *breathing* near me!”

His brows lift. “My breathing affects you?”

“Everything about you affects me!” The words fly out before I can choke them back. Rhea makes a noise suspiciously close to a celebratory shriek. I slam a hand over her mouth, and she licks my palm. “Rhea!”

She shrugs. “Don’t put your hand near my face if you don’t want consequences.”

Slade’s shoulders shake with quiet, entertained laughter.

I snap toward him. "Stop enjoying this!"

"Impossible," he says simply.

I might explode. Explode... and then haunt everyone out of spite.

Rhea loops an arm through mine. "Okay, come here. Girl talk. Private. Away from Captain Demon Thirst Trap."

"No," Slade says immediately.

Rhea freezes. "I wasn't talking to you, shadow boy."

"It wasn't a request." He steps closer, voice a low rumble. "She doesn't leave my sight."

I jab a finger into his chest. "I am not *yours* to monitor!"

"You summoned me," he says for the thousandth time like a broken record.

"By *accident*! We are NOT rehashing this."

"You still did it," he argues smugly.

"That doesn't make me your property!"

His jaw ticks—just slightly. "I never said you were property."

"Then stop acting like I have a tracking collar!"

"I'm ensuring your safety," he practically whines.

"From WHAT?" I demand. "*You*? The mistletoe? The universe's poor life choices?"

Rhea watches the argument with visible delight. "Oh, this is *juicy*."

"RHEA," I bark.

"Sorry, sorry," she says, waving her hands. "I'll tone it down. But seriously—do you know what's going on with the curse?"

I stiffen. She notices immediately—because of course she does. "Piper." Her voice softens. "You've been avoiding my calls. Avoiding asking for help. What do you know?"

I swallow hard, glancing at the customers still browsing. "Not here."

"Then let's step into the back," Rhea says, tugging me gently.

Slade blocks the doorway like a six-foot-four stone wall with muscles and bad ideas. "She's not going anywhere alone."

Rhea stares up at him—unimpressed. "Big guy, please. I'm a *Bellamy*. I'm more likely to hex her into telling me the truth than hurt her."

"That," Slade says without blinking, "is exactly the issue."

I throw my hands up. "Both of you... *Stop*."

They look at me at the same time. Like I'm a rope in the middle of a very territorial tug-of-war. I inhale deeply. "*First*... Rhea, I have no idea what's happening with the curse."

Slade's eyes narrow.

"*Second*... Slade—back up. I can talk to my cousin without you hovering over my shoulder like a sexy gargoyle."

His lips twitch. "You think I'm sexy?"

"THAT IS NOT THE POINT."

"It's relevant."

Rhea gives a dreamy sigh. "It kind of is."

"Rhea!"

She winces, then motions me closer. "Okay, seriously. I came because the wardline in your house flickered. And the shift wasn't random. It was... resonant."

My stomach drops. "Resonant with what?"

"With someone," she says, glancing meaningfully at Slade.

He looks... smug. I glare murderously at him.

Rhea continues, lowering her voice. "We need to figure out what's triggering the curse. And what exactly you learned last night. Because the more information we have, the better chance we have of stopping this before it spirals."

Slade steps forward. "I can help."

"You already AREN'T," I snap.

His eyes flash. "You're pushing me away because you're afraid of what this means."

"I am pushing you away because you are overwhelming and territorial and—" I wave both hands at him, unable to articulate the rest. "And you know something and WON'T SAY IT."

Rhea's gaze darts between us. "Okay, wait—what does he know?"

Slade's expression shifts. He meets my eyes, slow and deliberate, voice dropping low enough that my magic thrums in response.

"I know what the curse wants," he says.

The room stills. Rhea's amber eyes widen, horror creeping across her face.

"Slade. No," I whisper.

He steps toward me—just one step—but it's enough to steal the breath from my lungs.

"The curse wants what it lost five centuries ago," he murmurs.

"And what was that?" Rhea asks, and I dread hearing the answer.

Slade's gaze burns through me. "You," he says softly. "Or rather—the Bellamy meant for my ancestor."

My heart lurches painfully. Rhea gasps. And for
a moment, the whole shop holds its breath.

# CHAPTER 9

*Slade*

Rhea spins around so fast her brown curls whip across her shoulders. Her amber eyes flare—bright, sharp, witch-lit—and she points a finger right at my chest.

"Oh, absolutely NOT," she snaps. "You do not get to stand here and tell us that our ancestor doomed our entire bloodline because she rejected your ancestor. That isn't how the curse works."

Around us, the shop hums with dormant magic. Piper stands between us, curls bristling, blue eyes flicking back and forth like she's watching a tennis match she did not consent to participate in.

I fold my arms—not because I need the stance, but because it seems to irritate both of them. "You don't know how the curse works, little Bellamy."

Rhea sputters. "Oh, you smug—overgrown—*hellspawn*—"

"Accurate," I cut in smoothly.

Piper shoots me a glare that could have cracked obsidian. "Slade, don't antagonize her."

I look at Piper. Really look. Her cheeks flushed from anger. Her chest rising too fast. Her power tugging at the air like an unstable heartbeat. She's perfect—*mine*. And she's walking blind toward a truth that should have been hers from birth. I exhale once, slow, a demon's version of restraint.

"Your curse is not about punishment," I say quietly.

Rhea stops mid-rant. Piper goes still.

"It's not?" Piper asks hesitantly.

"No," I answer. "And it never was."

Rhea folds her arms. "Then what exactly do you think it was about?"

I meet her gaze without blinking. "A lie."

The air in the shop tightens—like invisible fingers pulling everything taut.

Piper's brows knit. "A... lie?"

"Yes." I look between them. "Veda Bellamy lied about the curse's origin. Lied to your coven. Lied to mine. Lied to the entire magical world."

Rhea swallows hard. "That's impossible. Bellamys don't lie about bloodline magic."

I huff out a humorless laugh. "They do when they must."

Piper steps closer, fingers trembling against her skirt. "What did she lie about?"

Everything in me goes still—ancient memory rising like smoke from a dying fire. "Veda wasn't the victim," I say. "She was the architect."

Rhea stares. Piper's breath catches, and the magic in the store ripples like a chord being plucked.

I continue, voice low, edged with truth older than their entire bloodline. "Your ancestor didn't reject my ancestor because she feared him... or because fate forced her hand."

My gaze settles on Piper—my intended—because she deserves this truth more than anyone. "She abandoned the bond because she wanted more power."

Piper sucks in a sharp breath. "What?"

"She didn't run from destiny," I murmur. "She ran from accountability. From balance. From the one thing the bond would have demanded of her."

Rhea finds her voice first. "Which was?"

"A sharing of power," I say simply. "A merging of it."

The cousins stare at me as though I've ripped open centuries of silence—and I have.

"Demon bonds," I explain, "don't take from witches. They equalize and unify. They demand honesty and sacrifice."

Piper whispers, "And Veda didn't want that."

"No," I say. "She wanted supremacy."

Rhea's mouth falls open. "You're telling me our sweet, ancient, slightly spooky ancestor—"

"Was a power-hungry liar," I finish. "Yes."

Piper looks like she's been struck. I soften my tone. Only for her. Never for anyone else. "When she broke the bond, the magic snapped. It twisted. And because she lied about her reasons, the curse became a corrupted echo of the original bond's purpose."

Rhea takes a step forward, voice trembling with a mixture of anger and awe. "And what was the original purpose?"

I look at Piper—her curls. That stubborn chin. Those blue eyes shining with fear and defiance

and something fragile she won't name. "You,"
I say quietly. "You were meant to be the *cure*,
Piper—not the sacrifice."

Her breath shatters in the air.

Rhea's eyes go wide. "Holy shit."

Piper shakes her head. "Slade... stop."

"I can't," I whisper. "Not anymore."

I step toward her—and she doesn't move. "You
think I came here to take advantage of your bloodline?" I say. "You think I want you for your curse?
For some ancestral debt?" I lean forward, letting
her feel the heat of every truth I've held back. "I
didn't know fate was offering me the one thing my
line has waited five hundred years for."

Her lips part.

"And it isn't power," I murmur. "It's you."

The curse stirs—lights flickering overhead, a
low hum vibrating through the shelves.

Rhea inhales sharply. "Oh no. Nope. Nope. The
air is doing that *thing* again."

Piper closes her eyes—just once. Then opens them again. Blue fire... Fear... Want... Anger... All braided together. "Slade," she whispers, voice trembling, "why didn't Veda tell the truth?"

My answer is a blade. "Because she didn't want anyone to know she gave up the one person she was ever meant to love."

Piper flinches. Then, Rhea curses under her breath. And the curse pulses so hard the ornaments on the nearest tree tremble.

They're not gonna like it, but... This is only the beginning.

***

Silence.

Thick. Unmoving. Crushing.

Piper stares at me like I've just rewritten five centuries of Bellamy history with a single sentence. Rhea's amber eyes are blown wide, hands trembling at her sides. Magic hums in the walls, in the floorboards, in the lights overhead—an unstable, jittering pulse echoing Piper's heartbeat.

The shop itself seems to flinch under the pressure.

Rhea finally whispers, "So we're cursed because Great-Great-Grandmother Veda wanted more power and ghosted a demon?"

I blink. "That's... not an inaccurate summary."

Piper looks like she might pass out... or hex me... or *both*. "I need air," she murmurs.

"You're inside," I point out.

"SLAADE," she warns.

The shelves rattle again, louder this time. Glittering tinsel wriggles like startled snakes. An entire rack of spell candles flickers in synchronized panic.

Rhea glances around, wide-eyed. "Oh gods."

Piper drags both hands through her curls, muttering Bellamy curse words I haven't heard in two centuries. The magic crackles, then—BANG.

Something slams against the shop window so hard the glass shivers.

Rhea jumps. "What was THAT?"

Piper and I both turn. Outside, framed in a blizzard of twinkling snow and streetlamps, stand a group of grinning townspeople—carolers.

Except... Not normal ones. These have glowing red cheeks, too-bright smiles, and matching holiday cardigans knitted with unsettling precision. All of them holding sheet music like weapons.

Rhea whispers, "*Piper*... why do they look like cult members on Christmas break?"

Piper presses a trembling hand to her temple. "Because my life is hell."

"Correction," I say softly, moving toward her, "your life is cursed."

The lights flicker as the carolers begin tapping on the glass. In unison. A synchronized, eerie rhythm.

Tap. Tap. Tap-tap-tap. Oh, that is absolutely a summoning cadence.

Rhea pales. "Oh no. Oh HELL no."

Piper whispers, "They're going to sing, aren't they?"

The carolers inhale. And then— "DING DONG MERRILY ON HIGH"—but it's too loud, too sharp. Too magically charged.

The windows vibrate. The ornaments tremble. A row of enchanted bells begins chiming aggressively, the sounds clashing in disharmony.

I step in front of Piper automatically. "They're enchanted."

"No shit," Rhea mutters. "Those are MENACING altos."

Another bang rattles the door. One caroler—an elderly man with a disturbingly jolly grin—presses his face to the glass and sings with possessed fervor, "AND THE BELLS ARE RINGING—FOR SLAAADE AND PIPERRRR—"

Piper chokes. "OH MY GOD—THEY KNOW YOUR NAME—"

I roll my shoulders. "They *shouldn't*."

"Slade," Rhea snaps, "fix it!"

I gesture to the window. "They're affected by the bond. And the curse. And your family's questionable magical filtration system."

"Just—JUST—GO TALK TO THEM!" Rhea squeaks.

"They're hostile," I smirk. "I like hostile. It's festive."

Piper grabs my sleeve. "Slade. Please."

Something in my chest tightens. Then I turn, and open the door. The carolers pivot as one creature, their smiles stretching too wide to be natural.

"HELL-O SLAAAAADE," the old man bellows.

Behind me, Piper squeaks. Rhea swears.

I step fully outside, letting the cold bite across my skin. The carolers swarm closer—too close. One woman leans in, eyes glassy. "Do you WOR-SHIP the season—?"

"No," I say. "Back up."

They don't. They sing louder. "GLORI-AAAAAA—IN EXCELSIS DEOOOOOO—"

My eye twitches. I could immolate them. I could snap my fingers and disperse the enchantment with the efficiency of a scalpel. Instead... I growl, voice layered with demon command. "Silence."

The carolers choke off mid-note, expressions drooping. Their shoulders slump. One drops a tambourine.

Behind me, Piper whispers, "Holy shit."

Rhea whispers, "Can he do that again?"

The carolers blink in a dazed rhythm before slowly shuffling away, muttering confused fragments of lyrics like traumatized mall Santas. When the last one disappears down the snowy street, I shut the door.

Piper exhales a long, shaking breath. Rhea flops dramatically onto a counter. "Pipes. Babe. You NEED to break this curse. I don't care if you have to kiss him, bind with him, or marry him on Christmas Eve—but I am NOT living through demon-adjacent carolers again."

Piper's jaw drops. "Rhea!"

Rhea shrugs. "I'm just saying. That was *horrify-ing*."

Piper turns to me. She's angry, and equally terrified. Confused. Too beautiful for her own good. And she whispers, "Slade... what's happening to me?"

I step closer—slow, careful, gentle in a way demons aren't taught to be. "The curse is waking," I murmur. "And it recognizes you."

Her breath trembles. "As what?"

I meet her eyes. "The one who must finish what Veda never did."

Her pulse stutters, but she doesn't balk. I take that as a good sign.

Rhea's amber eyes widen again. "Oh... shit."

The ornaments tremble. Then, the lights flicker. And magic tightens around Piper like she's the spark at the center of a long-buried fuse.

# CHAPTER 10

*Piper*

My apartment smells like pine, cinnamon, and exhaustion. Mostly exhaustion. Because it's been days—maybe a week?  Time has lost meaning—since Slade wedged himself into every waking moment of my life—and I'm hanging on by a thread thinner than tinsel.

I'm so tired I could cry over a candy cane.

Slade, of course, is thriving. He doesn't sleep, doesn't tire. Slade doesn't even pretend to understand personal space. He just... exists. Constantly. Loudly. Hotly. And the worst part?

I'm not hating it as much as I should.

My resolve—the thing I held so tightly it practically left marks—is slipping. Little by little. Hour by hour. Touch by accidental, infuriating, devastating touch. I hate him. I want him.

Both statements *can* coexist, unfortunately.

It's the second week of December, and the whole town is drowning in garland and fake snow. The festive season is swelling like a tidal wave, threatening to pull me down with it, curse and all. So naturally, I decide that the best way to distract myself is... *decorating*.

Or pretending to.

I haul open my apartment closet—more like battle it—because the door sticks, the hinges squeak, and the top shelf is exactly where things go to die.

"Looking for something?" Slade asks from the kitchen, voice warm and amused like he knows I'm losing my grip.

"No." Yes. "I'm looking for my Christmas wreath."

A pause. He leans around the corner. "Your what?"

"My wreath."

He stares at me like I just said I collect the fingernails of ex-boyfriends. "Is this... important?"

"Yes," I snap, staring at him incredulously while reaching for the top shelf. "It goes on the front door."

Slade folds his arms, leaning against the doorframe like a sin carved into oak. "And this helps you... *how*?"

For the love of all things divine... "It's December," I say through gritted teeth. "I want normal.

I want something festive. I want a life that isn't being taken over by a demon who—"

"Who what?" he cuts in, voice low. "Who cares what happens to you?"

I freeze. The worst part is that he's right. And that it hurts to admit it. "Go bother someone else," I mutter, turning back to the shelf.

He doesn't move.

I grab the box labeled XMAS STORAGE—a disaster waiting to topple—and yank it down. It slides too fast, knocking loose a few things that were shoved beside it.

One smaller box tumbles out and hits the floor with a soft thud, and I frown. It's unfamiliar. Wrapped in old linen, tied with a fraying red ribbon. No label. *Definitely* not mine.

"What's that?" Slade asks immediately, all humor gone.

"I... don't know."

I lift it slowly, turning it over in my hands. It's heavier than it looks. Warm, almost. When I pull the ribbon, the fabric unfurls like it hasn't been touched in centuries. Inside is—a small brass bell. Plain. Tarnished. Worn smooth with age. Nothing special. Nothing obviously magical. Something I've never seen before.

But the moment I touch it—the air shifts. Not violently. Not like the curse's usual theatrical displays. Just a soft tightening. A pull—as if the room inhales around me.

Slade takes a step nearer, face sharpening with recognition. "Piper," he says quietly. "Don't ring it."

"I wasn't planning on it," I snap, then softer. "What is it?"

Rhea would kill to be here. She'd dig through ancestral records and pull out fifteen theories before Slade even finished one sentence. He doesn't answer right away. That alone terrifies me. "What?" I demand.

"It's not the bell itself," he says slowly. "It's... who it belonged to."

I look down at the small, innocuous thing in my palm.

"Slade." My voice trembles. "Whose was it?"

He meets my eyes—green burning, jaw tight. "Veda Bellamy's."

The world seems to tilt. "No," I whisper.

"Yes," he murmurs. "I didn't think any of her objects survived. She destroyed everything that could incriminate her. This... shouldn't exist."

My fingers tighten around the bell. A faint warmth pulses under my skin. Not a spark. Not a glow. Just a soft, steady heartbeat.

Like something sleeping—*wailing*.

For fucks sake it's like I'm Piper Bellamy, sleeping cursebreaker extraordinaire—*great*. Just. Fucking. Great.

Exactly what I needed.

I swallow hard. "So what does this mean?"

Slade steps closer, brushing his fingers beneath mine as if assessing the object's magic without touching it himself.

"It means," he says softly, "Veda left something behind. And it went to you for a reason."

My heart races, palms sweating as I grip the bell.

"Piper," he adds, voice dropping, "this is the first clue she ever left."

And maybe—just maybe—the truth hidden for five hundred years finally wants to be found.

***

Slade watches me for a long moment—too long—while I clutch the tiny brass bell like it's a live grenade with excellent manners.

I carry it to the kitchen table, setting it down gently. The metal catches the soft glow of the Christmas lights, shining dully like it hasn't seen daylight since before indoor plumbing.

I inhale. Exhale. Ignore Slade hovering over my shoulder like an overly attractive gargoyle. "Rhea is better at this," I murmur.

Slade hums—dark, displeased. "She's impulsive."

"She's also a *Bellamy*, and so am I."

He snorts. "She doesn't have what you have."

"And what is that exactly?"

Slade's gaze lowers to my mouth, slowly. Too intentionally. "Me," he says.

"Oh my god, Slade—*stop*."

He smirks. I pick up my phone and send Rhea one of our code messages: **REINDEER EMERGENCY. COFFEE? NO DEMONS.**

Her reply is immediate: **BE THERE IN TEN. IF SLED—SLADE—TRIES TO FOLLOW, I'LL HEX HIS HORNS OFF.**

I hide a smile and turn to the demon in question. "I need an hour," I tell him.

Slade tilts his head. "For what?"

"To meet my cousin. Alone."

Slade looks... *offended*. "I don't want to leave you alone when the curse is stirring."

"Well, you are today," I snap, completely flabbergasted.

His jaw clenches. "No."

"Yes," I argue.

The air crackles like it's considering becoming a lightning storm. Slade steps closer, shadows curling at his ankles. "Piper, if something happens—"

"Nothing will happen at the coffee shop."

He rolls his eyes. My jaw hits the floor. This man—*demon*—just *rolled* his eyes at me. "That's what every horror story begins with."

"It has gingerbread lattes and elderly couples doing crossword puzzles."

"Exactly."

I blink. "Are you... *scared* of crossword puzzles?"

"No," he growls, narrowing his eyes at me. "I'm scared of you being out of my sight when you're unraveling a five-hundred-year curse connected to my bloodline."

My stomach flips—but I stand firm. "Slade. I need this. I need space. And I need your word you'll stay with Newt."

Slade glances toward Newt—who is sitting on the counter, tail neatly tucked, staring at him like he's evaluating his worthiness to exist.

Slade scowls, Newt blinks. "I'm not staying with a house cat," Slade mutters.

Newt meows back, fully aware he's won.

I fold my arms. "Slade. Promise."

He watches me—hungry, frustrated, possessive—but not refusing.  And that's how I know his walls are crumbling too. "What will you give me in return?" he asks, stepping forward. "You never take without offering something back."

My body warms unpleasantly. "What do you want?"

Slade lowers his voice until it slides over my skin. "A deal."

"No," I say, shaking my head.

"You haven't even heard what I'm asking for."

"It's a deal with a demon."

"It's a deal with *your* demon," he corrects.

I almost choke on my own tongue. "Slade—"

"One condition," he says. "If Rhea can't give you the answers you're looking for, you agree to follow me to the Ninth Realm."

My stomach drops. "Ninth—no. Absolutely not. Hell is off the table."

"It's not hell," Slade says. "It's the Ninth Realm."

"That is *literally* hell."

His lips twitch. "Not the way you imagine it."

"I don't care what brand of hell it is, I'm not going."

"It's not torture," he says calmly. "It's a holiday ball."

I blink, utterly confused. "I'm sorry?"

"Yes," he says. "Lucifer celebrates."

I stare at him. Slade stares back. "Lucifer. As in the Lucifer," I say slowly.

"Yes."

"Has a holiday ball?" I ask.

"Yes."

"With what? Infernal garland and brimstone eggnog?"

A beat of silence. Then—"...Actually, yes."

I grip the back of the chair. "Slade. Why would I ever go to that?"

"Because the Ninth Realm has the oldest untouched archives in existence," he says. "Some predating witchcraft. Some predating humanity."

My breath catches.

"And those records," he continues, "may hold the truth Veda erased."

A shiver curls down my spine. I hate that he's right. I hate that he *knows* he's right. And I *especially* hate that part of me wants to say yes.

"So?" he asks softly. "Deal?"

I look at the bell. Then at him. Then at Newt, who is licking his paw like this is all beneath him. I blow out a breath, conceding defeat. "Fine."

Slade goes perfectly still.

"So long as Rhea fails to give me the answers," I say, lifting a finger, "only then do I agree. And only if you stay here with Newt for the next hour."

Slade's jaw flexes. He hates this. Truly hates it. But he nods. "Deal."

A demon's deal is binding. I feel it settle over my skin like a warm ribbon tightening around my ribs. Slade steps back, eyes burning. "Be careful."

"I'm going to get coffee."

"Exactly."

I grab my coat, the bell wrapped in linen, and my keys. Slade's voice follows me out the door—low, dark, entirely too intimate. "Don't make me come find you, Piper."

I slam the door shut before he can see the way that line turns my bones into molten sugar.

Newt hisses at him from the counter. Slade stares at the cat.

"Well," he mutters, "this will be hell."

I snicker all the way down the hall, not bothering to hide my choked laughter. It'll be a miracle if my apartment survives this. I grin, decidedly choosing to let the catastrophe unfold. Slade is Newt's problem now...

# CHAPTER 11

*Piper*

S now swirls lazily outside Bean & Bell, our tiny local coffee shop strung with warm lights and evergreen garland. The windows are fogged from the heat inside, giving the place a cozy, snow-globe quality.

Inside, everything smells like cinnamon, espresso, and comfort. Perfectly normal, and *exactly* what I need.

Rhea is already at a corner table, coat tossed over her chair, curls wild around her face. She's stirring her latte like she's trying to divine a prophecy in the foam. The moment she sees me, her amber eyes widen. "You look like you haven't slept in a week."

"That's because I haven't."

She pats the seat beside her. "Come. Tell me everything."

I slide into the booth, lowering the linen-wrapped bell onto the table between us.

Rhea leans forward, eyes narrowing. "Oh…That's a… *vibe*."

"It shouldn't be," I mutter. "It's just a bell."

"That's a Veda bell. It's NEVER 'just' anything."

I rub my temples. "I was hoping you'd say it's fake. Or decorative. Or an antique someone misplaced."

"Piper," she whispers, voice softening. "It's humming."

I go still. "You can feel it too?"

She nods, expression sobering. "It feels... old. And stubborn." She hesitates. "Kind of like you."

I glare. "Not helpful."

"Okay, okay." She folds her hands. "Let's take this one step at a time."

I meet her gaze. "What do you know about Veda?"

Rhea sighs. "Not much. She's practically a myth in our family. A name in a ledger. A sketch in an old book, if you will. The one who 'broke the balance'—whatever that means."

"Slade says she lied," I mutter, staring down at the tarnished little bell.

Rhea lifts both eyebrows. "Oh, I remember."

She waves a hand dramatically. "Veda wasn't the victim, she was the architect," she says, voice deepening into an overly dramatic imitation of Slade. "She ran from the bond. She wanted supremacy."

I pinch the bridge of my nose. "Rhea—"

She softens, leaning forward. "Look, Pipes... I didn't want to hear it either. But some of what he said lines up with the old coven rumors. Not the official stuff, but the things our great-aunts whispered when they'd had too much peppermint liquor."

I blink. "What rumors?"

"That the curse wasn't born out of punishment."

She lowers her voice. "But out of a choice. A... break. A severing."

My stomach tightens. "A severing of what?"

Rhea shakes her head helplessly. "I don't know. A bargain? A sacrifice? A bond she didn't want? But something this old—" She gestures toward the bell. "It would hide itself until the right Bellamy came along."

"And you think that's me."

"I *know* it's you," she whispers.

The words land heavy. Ancient. Inescapable. I swallow. "So what do we do?"

Rhea stares at the bell again, shoulders tense. "We investigate. Carefully."

She unwraps the linen, exposing the tarnished brass. Nothing glows. It doesn't rattle. Nothing hums. It looks like a trinket. Except when Rhea brushes her fingertips across the metal—a soft pulse of air ripples through my magic.

Rhea recoils instantly. "Okay. NOPE. That is definitely holding a memory. Or a message. Or trauma." She shudders. "Probably trauma."

"Fantastic," I mutter. "Super reassuring."

Rhea points at it. "Ring it."

"ABSOLUTELY NOT."

"Just lightly!"

"That doesn't lower the danger level!"

"Piper, it might be the only way to activate it."

I force a breathe in, releasing it in a whoosh. "You felt Slade's warning. He nearly growled when I picked it up."

Rhea scoffs. "Please. Demons say 'don't' like it's punctuation." She deepens her voice. "'Don't touch that.' 'Don't go alone.' 'Don't summon ancient powers by accident.'" She flicks her wrist. "And yet here we are—summoning demons and unraveling curses like it's Tuesday."

"I hate everything you're saying right now," I growl.

"You love it."

"I absolutely *do not*."

She takes a smug sip of her latte. "Your demon babysitting Newt right now says otherwise."

I groan into my hands. "Rhea. Slade made me promise that if YOU couldn't help, I'd go to the Ninth Realm."

Rhea spits her drink across the table. "THE WHAT?"

"The Ninth Realm."

She coughs violently. "As in Lucifer's Christmas Ball?!"

"Yes."

"PIPER LEIGH!"

"I KNOW."

"PIPER. LEIGH. BELLAMY," she screeches, drawing nearly every eye in the coffee shop. Then slaps the table, scandalized. "Why would you agree to that?!"

"Because the Ninth Realm has the oldest archives in existence!" I hiss, waving frantically trying to get her to hush. "Slade said they might have what Veda erased!"

Rhea freezes. Then leans in very, very slowly. "You want the truth?"

I nod, throat tight.

"Then we're way out of our depth."

My blood goes cold. "Meaning?"

"Meaning," she whispers, eyes on the bell, "this is older than anything I've ever studied. Definitely older than our coven. Maybe older than Bellamy magic entirely."

A quiet dread creeps under my skin.

Rhea inhales shakily. "Or, ya know. Maybe it's harmless," she says, sighing dramatically like she doesn't even believe herself. "Pipes... I can't help you. Not fully. Not with this." The words hit like a stone. I tighten my grip on the linen-wrapped bell.

Rhea reaches for my hands, squeezing gently. "But I can prepare you. And I can be at your back. No matter what you find."

My vision blurs for a second—emotion, fear, the weight of five centuries pressing down on me.

"You have to go," she whispers.

My throat tightens. "Slade will be *impossible* after this."

She snorts. "He was impossible *before* this."

I close my eyes. The truth cracks out of me in one whispered breath, "I think he wants *more* than the bond."

Rhea squeezes my hand tighter. "Oh sweetie. He does. We *both* saw it."

"But I don't know if I can handle that."

Rhea's voice drops, soft but sharp with honesty. "Then decide what scares you more. The curse... or letting someone actually see you."

The bell pulses. Once. Soft. Like the heartbeat of someone finally waking. And just like that—I know.

The Ninth Realm isn't optional anymore...

It's *inevitable*.

# CHAPTER 12

*Slade*

Newt is sprawled across my lap like he owns me. Which, frankly, is embarrassing.

I never intended to befriend the creature—yet here we are. He purrs like a tiny engine, kneading the muscle of my thigh with sharp little claws he absolutely uses on purpose. "You're manipulative," I inform him.

Newt purrs louder. I stroke behind his ears—apparently his favorite spot—and he melts like butter under my hand, tail twitching with smug satisfaction.

This cat has chosen me. And for reasons I cannot begin to articulate, that pleases me more than it should.

My phone vibrates on the table. Newt stretches, planting one paw on the screen as if claiming it. As if saying... *No work. Only cat.* "I have to answer that," I mutter.

Newt refuses to move. I sigh and slide the phone out from under his paw, which earns me a slow blink of reprimand.

Draven. *Of course.*

I answer. "What."

"Slade." His voice is pure fury wrapped in suspicion. "*Why* are you topside?"

I rub my temple. "Hello to you too."

"No. No greetings. You vanish for days. I can't reach you. You break protocol. And then—THEN—I hear rumor that you're walking around the mortal realm like some trench-coat-wearing menace. What the *hell* is going on?"

Newt headbutts my hand, demanding more pets. "I'm fine," I say.

"You're NEVER '*fine*.'" Draven snaps. "You're controlled. You're predictable. You follow rules like a self-righteous martyr. So if you're up there, something happened."

A long beat of silence stretches between us. I breathe once. Calm. Measured. Knowing I'm lying through my teeth.

"I found my mate."

Draven goes silent. Dead. Fucking. Silent. Then— "...the *fuck* you did."

I smile faintly. "Yes."

"A mortal?" he demands.

"A witch." A tiny pause as I gather my strength. "A *cursed* witch."

"Oh gods." Draven sounds personally attacked. "A WITCH?! A fucking *cursed* witch?! Are you *insane*?!!! "

Newt chirps as if agreeing.

Draven barrels on, voice rising, "Okay—okay—hang on—tell me you didn't CLAIM her. Tell me you didn't—"

"I haven't claimed her."

A long, heavy pause fills the line. Then Draven exhales—slow, sharp, like he's bracing himself. "Good," he says quietly. "That would've been... premature."

Newt flicks his ear, unimpressed. Draven continues, voice cooling into something more controlled. "Slade... you don't claim someone when you know nothing about the curse wrapped around her blood. You wait. You assess."

I roll my eyes. "I *am* assessing."

"You're terrible at assessing when you're emotionally compromised."

"I'm not emotionally—"

"Yes, you are," he cuts in. "Which is why I'm asking this next part very carefully." A beat passes before he speaks again. "Is there another reason *why* you're waiting?"

I rub the back of my neck. "Because claiming her binds us permanently. She's terrified. And barely tolerating me."

Draven mutters, "So she's sensible."

"Shut up."

He snorts softly. "I'm not judging you. I just needed to know you weren't hesitating because you're injured or poisoned... or controlled."

"I'm *fine*."

"You say that like it means anything."

"Do you at least know what *kind* of curse it is?" He asks with another long suffering sigh.

"I don't know all of it yet. It's old. Older than her coven records. Older than her bloodline, maybe."

Draven curses under his breath. "So you walked into a mate bond and an unidentified hereditary curse? Do you even LIKE surviving?"

I flex my jaw. "I didn't choose the timing."

"No one does," he mutters. "But a curse tied to a witch's bloodline? That's messy. Dangerous. Probably comes with expectations. And enemies."

He hisses a breath. "Slade. You need backup."

"No."

"You need information," he says, trying a different angle.

"I'm getting it."

"How?" He asks.

I glance at Newt. He stares back, entirely unimpressed. "...carefully," I say.

Draven groans. "Which means recklessly."

"I didn't ask for advice," I say flatly.

"You never do," Draven fires back. "You just brood until someone calls you and forces you to talk."

I grit my teeth. He's not wrong.

"I called because you disappeared," Draven continues. "Because something changed and I knew it was something delicious. You always did keep secrets better than me. You sound—different." Newt headbutts my hand again like a tiny traitor. I pet him anyway. Draven lowers his voice. "It's because of *her*, isn't it."

I don't answer. Which is answer enough.

A long exhale drags through the line. "Slade... *gods.* You actually care for her."

The truth lands like a blade between ribs—precise, undeniable.

More than I should. More than she knows. More than either realm would forgive.

Silence speaks for me.

Draven's voice shifts—less furious, more grim. "Then listen carefully. If she's cursed, she's your mate, *and* you're helping her? Whatever coils through her bloodline is now wrapped around yours."

I already know. Still... It doesn't make it easier to hear.

"And if she goes to the Ninth Realm—"

"She hasn't decided," I say, though even I can hear the doubt. Though, I'm sure she won't learn anything new with Rhea.

"She will." Draven sounds certain in a way only older brothers and prophets ever are. "Mortals always come to us when they want answers. Especially answers they shouldn't have."

Newt rolls onto his back, exposing his belly. I scratch lightly, and he purrs like a damn engine.

Draven continues, tone tightening. "And you need to remember something. The Ninth Realm may look like heaven. Peace. Warmth. Gardens and golden air. It fools mortals—makes them feel safe." A long pause that makes the hair on the back of my neck stand up. "But it's still hell, Slade.

And your mate will be surrounded by beings who would take her power, her curse, or her life if it gave them an inch of advantage."

My magic coils, dark and lethal. Protective. Possessive. "No one touches her."

Draven makes a tired, resigned noise. "Yeah. I knew you'd say that." Another pause. "I'll prepare for your arrival. *Quietly.*"

The line crackles—soft static, then nothing. I lower the phone. Newt shifts, crawls higher into my lap, and presses his warm little face against my chest with surprising trust.

I stroke his fur and stare toward the front door—toward where Piper walked into the world, still cursed, still stubborn, still so heartbreakingly mortal.

"She has no idea what she's walking into," I murmur. Newt purrs, a low, steady sound. "But... She won't walk into it alone."

Not ever again.

# CHAPTER 13

## *Piper*

I wake to an unsettling quiet. Not bad, or even, cursed quiet. Just... different. Like the air is holding its breath.

I push myself upright, blurry-eyed, curls falling into my face. My room hums faintly with leftover magic—warm, simmering, restless. The kind that usually spikes when Slade is far too close for comfort.

Except—that feeling isn't heat.

It's weight. Calm, heavy, dangerous weight.

*Something* in him changed last night.

I hurriedly pull on black leggings, a cream-colored oversized sweater, and pull my wild curls back into a clip, adjusting the pendant at my neck. When I'm done, I grab my socks and head out the bedroom door. I almost trip, yanking on my thick Christmas themed socks, as I creep down the hallway.

"Newt?" I call softly.

A thump. The sound of paws hitting the floor. He appears—stretching, tail flicking, but... unusually alert. Eyes wide, and ears perked. Like he felt whatever shift Slade did. I scoop him up. "Okay, buddy. What happened?"

Newt headbutts my chin, which is reassuring... until he twists in my arms and stares toward the kitchen with an almost warning flick of his tail.

"Great," I mutter. "Love that. What a vibe."

Slade is standing at the counter. And I freeze. He's... radiant. Not glowing, or sparkly. Just... *more*.

More presence—*power*. More demon prince energy he tries—and *fails*—to pretend he doesn't have.

He turns his head slightly. "Good morning."

My knees try to buckle and I silently curse them. "Hi," I manage.

His eyes sweep over me once—slow, assessing, not predatory but not not predatory. "You look like you slept decently," he notes.

"I tried."

His mouth lifts slightly. "You succeeded."

I roll my eyes to hide the treacherous warmth blooming in my chest. "Is Newt okay?"

"He's fine." Slade inclines his head toward the cat now weaving smugly between his ankles. "He is... comfortable."

Newt rubs against him like they've been best friends for a decade. *Traitor.* But there's another layer beneath it—something uneasy.

Rhea's voice echoes in my head. *"Let me take him if you go anywhere dangerous."*

I clear my throat. "Rhea said she'll take him for a few days."

Slade's expression softens just a fraction. "Good."

The tone beneath that one word chills me. "So," I say cautiously, "you're... different today."

He doesn't deny it. Instead, he turns fully toward me, arms crossing over his broad chest. And suddenly I understand exactly what changed. He's in full demon-boss mode.

No teasing, smugness, or lazy flirtation. Just full on power.

"Piper," he says quietly, "we need to discuss tonight."

My stomach flips. "Lucifer's Ball?"

His jaw flexes once. "Yes."

I swallow. "Okay. Discuss."

He watches me for a long moment, as if deciding how much truth I can handle. "There will be rules."

Great. Rules from a demon. So reassuring. "Such as?" I ask.

Slade steps closer. Just one step. But it feels like a declaration. "One," he says, voice low, "you do not wander. Not even a single corridor."

"Noted."

"Two. You do not drink anything that is offered to you, unless I personally hand it to you."

"I sense a story there."

"Several," he says dryly.

Okay then.

"Three," he continues, "the covens will be watching you. Some out of curiosity. Some, I suspect out of envy. Some because they'll suspect you *might* hold something ancient."

My heart thumps painfully.

"And four…" His eyes lock onto mine, burning green flame. "You do not take your eyes off me while we are in that realm."

I laugh before I can stop myself.

"Slade, I don't take my eyes off you here."

"Yes," he murmurs, stepping even closer, "but tonight, it won't be because you want to. It will be because you must."

My laughter dies. "Why?" I whisper. It comes out smaller than I'd meant it to.

He hesitates. His voice lowers—dark silk, quiet and potent. "Because tonight," he says, "all demon houses will attend. Every noble bloodline. Every heir. Every lord." He pauses, green eyes blazing with something I'd rather not put a name to. "And they will all know what you are to me."

A shiver runs through me. "And… *what* exactly am I to you?"

His throat works. "My *mate*." The room goes still. Even Newt stops purring. "And that," he adds softly, "will make you a target."

My breath stutters. "But you're just—you know. *Slade*."

His mouth twitches. Then he steps forward, so close my heartbeat stumbles. "Piper," he says quietly, "I have not been *just* Slade in a very long time."

The power rolling off him finally clicks into place. I inhale sharply. "You're a *noble*."

"A lord," he corrects softly. "By blood. By power. By birthright."

My pulse kicks hard. Slade's next words nearly melt my spine. "And when I walk into that ballroom with you at my side... they will all understand exactly what that means."

I grip the counter for balance. "Which is...?"

He leans in. Not touching. Not quite kissing. Just close enough to steal air from my lungs. "That you are under my protection," he whispers. "And mine to *claim*—whether I have formally made it or not."

My pulse roars in my ears. "Slade..."

He steps back slowly, letting the distance clear the heat between us—but not the tension.

"We leave at dusk," he murmurs. "Prepare yourself."

"How?" I choke.

"Dress," he says. "Arm yourself. Trust nothing. Stay close." His eyes roam my face with a softness so fierce it hurts. "And Piper?" he adds, voice dipping low.

"Yes?"

"When we enter the Ninth Realm..." His gaze burns through me, "...do not let anyone convince you that I am anything less than the most dangerous thing in the room."

I swallow hard.

"Because I assure you," he finishes, "I *am*."

# CHAPTER 14

## *Piper*

Rhea arrives like a holiday hurricane—coat flapping, curls bouncing, arms overflowing with shopping bags that probably cost more than my rent.

Newt bolts to the door, chirping excitedly.

"Okay," Rhea huffs, kicking the door shut with her heel. "I brought the beast's overnight bag, three days' worth of food, and—" She drops a glossy stack of shopping bags and garment bags onto my couch with a dramatic thump.

"—your wardrobe for Hell's fanciest Christmas ball."

I blink. "How did you even—"

"I called in a favor," she says sweetly. Then she winks. "And my plus-size section is divine, babe. You know that."

Slade appears from the hallway like he's been summoned by the words wardrobe and plus-size section. His eyes flick to the bags. Then to me. Then back to the bags. All while never blinking.

Rhea notices and smirks like the devil's favorite cousin. "Well hello, tall dark and demon-y. Do you approve?"

Slade's gaze never leaves me. "I'll approve once she tries them on."

My entire face goes nuclear. "Absolutely not!"

"Yes," Rhea says, earning a glare from me. "You *have* to. You need etiquette guidance so you don't accidentally curtsy to a lesser demon and start a blood feud."

I glare at her. "Why would that be a thing?!"

"Because demon nobility is petty," Slade answers dryly.

I throw my hands up. "*Great.* I'll go to Hell, insult someone accidentally, and die in a glittering explosion."

Rhea slaps a dress bag into my chest. "Try it. Now. Before you panic yourself into hives."

Slade leans against the doorway, arms crossed, looking maddeningly pleased.

I snatch the bag. "Fine! But not because either of you asked. I'm doing this because—because—"

"I have superior fashion instincts?" Rhea offers.

"Because you don't want to embarrass yourself in front of demon royalty," Slade adds, voice low and amused.

I whirl on him. "You didn't tell me they'd be *royalty*... royalty."

He lifts a brow. "I assumed that was implied."

"It was not!!!"

Rhea cackles. "Go. Change. I'll wrangle Newt."

Newt meows like, *good luck, mother*.

***

Tucked away in my bedroom, I pull out the first gown. It's crimson, velvet, and hugs every curve like it was custom-made for me. I look in the mirror and nearly pass out.

Oh... Oh NO.

I step out slowly. Slade straightens like someone hit him with divine lightning. His gaze drags over me—slow, reverent, hungry—and he very visibly forgets how to breathe.

Rhea fan-gasps. "Okay, bitch, you are a PROB-LEM."

Slade says nothing. But his hands curl at his sides like he's physically restraining himself.

"Say something," I whisper, heat crawling up my throat.

Slade's voice is rough velvet. "Turn."

My knees wobble, but I obey. The curse stirs instantly—lights flickering, warmth sliding across my skin like invisible fingertips.

Slade watches every inch of my spin with dark intensity. "That," he says quietly, "would start a war."

I freeze. "What?! Why?!"

He steps closer, but not too close—just enough to invade oxygen. "Because," Slade murmurs, "you look like temptation incarnate. Wearing that beside me would suggest you're already claimed."

My pulse thunders.

"And since you are not... every noble house would assume I'm making a statement."

Rhea points. "Okay, that's *hot* but also terrifying. Next dress."

Flabbergasted, I peel my jaw off the floor, practically running for the safety of my bedroom. I shut the door behind me, slip out of the gown, pull out the next... And promptly—*gasp.*

It's emerald green. Off-the-shoulder. Soft satin that pools at my hips.

I slip it on, inhale, and walk out.

Slade goes still again. More still than before. His pupils blow wide, and his jaw looks like it's clenched hard enough to crack teeth. "Slade?" I say.

He inhales sharply, jaw tightening. "Piper."

"What?" I whisper.

"You need to stop."

My stomach flips. "Why?"

"Because the curse is... *responding.*"

I frown, glancing around, only to realize he's right. The Christmas tree lights begin strobing like a rave. The tinsel shivers, like a snow has been summoned from the arctic. My garland slowly raises itself off the bookshelf like it's performing an exorcism.

*Oh God.*

"Slade..."

He steps toward me—slow, controlled, predatory—but he stops a breath away, hands flexing like he wants to touch and is forcing himself not to.

"I think if I come any closer," he says softly, "Your whole apartment might combust." He smirks, eyes shifting from me to the room.

The sink turns on. A snow globe shakes itself off the shelf. The mistletoe over my doorway wiggles ominously.

Rhea snorts. "Okay, okay, end this runway show before we summon Santa's horny ghost."

I whirl toward her. "RHEA."

She holds up her hands. "I'm just saying! The magic CLEARLY wants you two together."

Slade's eyes lock onto mine. I feel it instantly. Heat. The pull. *Gravity*.

"It does," he murmurs.

My breath goes shallow. He steps back—barely. But enough to let the tree lights settle into a slow pulsing glow. "Try the third one," he says, voice low, controlled, dangerous.

I swallow. "There's a *third*?"

"There are *six*," Rhea chirps.

I groan.

Slade's mouth curves into a sinful smile. "Let's see them all."

I tuck tail so fast I almost trip over the gown, darting into my bedroom door like he personally set my ass on fire.

Crossing the room, I aggressively yank the emerald green gown off, fingers deftly working on the final bag. I freeze halfway through, unexpected tears welling in my eyes.

I already know it's the one. It's black. Shimmering like starlight scattered across midnight.

A plunging neckline, but elegant. Fitted bodice. Flowing skirt. It fits like a glove, and I feel like royalty.

When I step out... even Rhea stops breathing.

Slade looks—*devastated*. Ruined. Worshipful, even. He steps forward—close, so close—then stops like something invisible yanked him back. "That one," he says, voice barely human. "That is the one."

Rhea claps. "YES. That one screams sexy-powerful-goddess-with-a-curse. Perfect."

The decorations begin rotating slowly in a lazy orbit above our heads. The tree lights glow gold. The sink shuts off. Even the mistletoe stays still, like it's bowing.

Slade exhales, slow and reverent. "That one. I want you to wear that into my realm."

Something in my chest twists. Something soft... and equally *terrifying*. "Okay," I whisper.

He nods once—sharp, controlled. But his eyes... His eyes burn like he's imagining peeling that dress off me in a thousand different ways.

Rhea fans herself. "Alright. Newt and I are leaving before the room catches fire."

Newt trots toward the door proudly, tail high. Slade and I remain locked in a stare neither of us knows how to break. The curse hums under my skin, warm and wanting.

"Piper." My name leaves him like a sin he's savoring.

The door clicks shut behind Rhea, her giggles fading down the hall, Newt's soft meow trailing after her like a warning I'm too distracted to interpret. And then it's just us. The apartment settles into a low hum. A pulse. A heartbeat that doesn't belong to me.

Slade's gaze drags over me once more—slow, reverent, starving—and something inside him fractures. Not a lot. Just enough to expose the raw edge beneath. He steps toward me. One step.

Then another. Like gravity tightened its fist and decided we belong in the same orbit.

I inhale sharply. "Slade..."

"You shouldn't say my name like that," he murmurs.

"Like what?"

"Like I'm allowed to touch you," he says, low, husky, filled with a longing I don't want to face.

My pulse stutters. "You are—not."

His mouth tips in a dark smile. "No?"

"No," I whisper, though my body betrays me, leaning in.

His eyes flick down to my lips. The curse surges instantly—my Christmas tree lights flash a brilliant gold, ornaments tremble, and a strand of tinsel slithers down the wall like it's trying to wrap around us both. Slade's breath catches. "The curse reacts to desire," he says quietly, like he's challenging me to say differently.

"It reacts to *you*," I shoot back.

He closes the final inch. His hand lifts—not grabbing, not demanding—just... brushing the back of his knuckles along my cheek, slow and reverent.

I shiver, and of course he notices. "Piper," he murmurs, fingers sliding into the curls at the base of my skull, guiding my head back the barest inch. "You have no idea how much restraint I'm using."

"I..."

My voice fades. Because his other hand settles on my waist. Hot. Strong. Possessive in a way that melts my bones. "Oh," is all I manage.

His forehead dips to mine. "Tell me to stop," he whispers.

I open my mouth. No sound comes out. Because every cell in my body is singing one truth... *Don't* stop.

He watches the realization hit me. His breath trembles. Then he kisses me.

It's not rough. Not forced, or dominating. It's a single, *sinfully* slow press of lips that steals thought, breath, and all my resistance. A low sound escapes me—pitiful and hungry.

Slade growls softly against my mouth, the sound vibrating straight through me. His hand tightens at my waist, pulling me into the solid, burning wall of his chest. I fist his shirt. Pulling him closer—*needing* him closer.

The curse erupts. The Christmas tree erupts into sparkling light. Ornaments tremble in joy. A wreath spins halfway off its hook. And my sink turns on full blast in the kitchen like it's cheering us on.

Slade breaks the kiss with a ragged groan, forehead pressed to mine as we both gasp for breath. I wobble, knees quaking like jello. He catches me instantly. "Easy."

"I—I don't understand—" I whisper.

"You're my *mate*," he says softly. "Your body knows it. Even if your mind is still catching up."

My knees threaten treason again. He steadies me with both hands now, fingers digging into the small of my back like he's holding onto sanity.

"Slade..."

He shuts his eyes like he's in pain. "If you stay right here, dressed like that, looking at me like this..." He inhales sharply. "I will forget Lucifer's Ball entirely."

My throat dries, but I play with fire anyway, letting the question slip between my teeth. "W-What would you do instead?"

His eyes open—green flame, hunger, devotion, all tangled into one devastating look. "I would put you against that wall," he says quietly, "and kiss you again. I would touch you, rip that dress off you, claim you fully and *ravish* you until you forgot your own name."

Heat floods every inch of me. "*Slade—*"

He steps back quickly, like the distance is the only barrier between sanity and catastrophe. "You need to finish getting ready," he says, voice rough. "We leave in two hours."

I try to breathe, but my body is humming like I swallowed electricity.

"You should go," he adds, nodding toward my bedroom. "*Now.* Before I change my mind and pull you back into my arms."

I take a shaky step backward. His gaze follows me like he's memorizing every movement. At the doorway to my room, I pause.

His voice drops, sinful and certain, "*Unless...* you *want* me to forget the Ninth Realm *entirely*?"

"Oh my god," I squeak.

He smiles—slow, dark, devastating. "Go, Piper."

I flee. Barely. It's more like a disgraced flailing of limbs and fabric.

Behind me, Slade exhales a breath that sounds like he's holding back a storm. And... truthfully?

I'm honestly not sure I want him to.

# CHAPTER 15

*Piper*

The air thickens around us before Slade even opens the portal—warm, shimmering, charged like before a storm. He stands beside me in his formal demon attire.

Black coat that clings to his shoulders. High collar embroidered with shifting sigils. A blade sheathed at his hip. His hair darker, his aura sharper, his presence... *enormous.*

He's not Slade-from-my-kitchen anymore. He's *him.* Lord Slade Athalar of the Ninth.

He lifts one hand. Reality parts. The portal blooms open like a tear in velvet—gold, crimson, black—revealing a realm that shouldn't exist.

A sky of shimmering aurora, streaked with silver and pale gold. Pathways of obsidian shot through with molten gold veins. Gardens made of crystalline trees that glow with warm light. Fountains of starlit water that float upward instead of down. Towers carved from midnight marble, spiraling elegantly toward the sky. Air that tastes like sweet smoke and winter spice.

It's... *breathtaking.* Wait... *This* is Hell? I'm so busy admiring the view that when I turn, I notice Slade's gaze isn't on the scenery. It's on *me.*

"Ready?" he asks, voice low and threaded with something protective.

"No," I whisper.

He offers his arm to me anyway. The moment my hand touches him, the curse stirs—warm, insistent, almost relieved. I give him one last lingering look, and then...

We step through.

***

The realm folds around us like warm silk, the portal sealing behind with a soft rush of air. For a moment, I forget to breathe.

Snow—soft as ash and faintly luminous—drifts from a sky swept in swirling ribbons of gold and amethyst. Lanterns float above the pathways like drifting constellations, casting long amber shadows across gardens carved from crystal and volcanic glass. Everything hums with a gentle, resonant magic... a heartbeat that doesn't belong to this world or mine.

Demons—elegant, dangerous, impossibly poised—move along the obsidian path toward the palace in their formal finery. Not monstrous. Not twisted. Just... breathtaking. Otherworldly. A blur of shimmering fabrics, dark eyes, and ancient power.

Every head turns as we step forward. Not with hostility. More... curiosity, mixed with something deeper. Like the air shifted the moment I arrived and they all felt it.

Slade's arm tightens beneath my grip, the slightest tension rippling through him.

"Is something wrong?" I whisper.

"They sense the curse," he murmurs. "And they... *smell* you."

OH. GREAT.

"And what exactly do I smell like?" I ask, voice tight.

He bends just enough that his lips brush the shell of my ear. The breath that accompanies his words sends heat spiraling straight down my spine.

"Something forbidden," he says softly. "*Rare.* Precious. And waiting to be claimed. I thought my scent would hide yours. Obviously... I was wrong."

My pulse jumps. I swear the lanterns brighten, as if agreeing. Slade straightens, jaw locked, posture turning sharp and regal as he guides me toward the palace.

And though the crowd doesn't speak aloud, the atmosphere shifts around us—an awareness, electric and unmistakable, following every step we take.

The weight of a hundred eyes settles over me. Some assessing, while some are startled. Other's are intrigued. Nothing overtly hostile... yet everything too focused for comfort.

"Do not let go of my arm," Slade says quietly.

I tighten my grip. He covers my hand with his, heat seeping through fabric and skin like a silent vow.

We walk on and let the realm watch.

The palace gates rise before us like carved constellations, sigils flowing across the obsidian surface in liquid gold. They recognize Slade first — bowing open in a slow, sweeping arc, as though the realm itself is greeting him.

Beyond them, the ballroom unfolds like a myth brought to life. A cathedral of midnight glass stretches upward into a sky that doesn't exist in this world. Chandeliers made from living constellations drift lazily above the crowd, dripping starfire. Music winds through the air — low, ancient, vibrating through my bones like a ritual drum.

Demons of every noble house swirl through the room in gowns and coats that shimmer like molten metal or shadow-woven silk. Some glance our way briefly. Others pause entirely, their attention drawn not with malice but with interest... something rising, shifting in the current of magic around us.

And then the room stills. Not loudly, or theatrically. Just subtly — like a ripple passing through a lake.

I follow the shift upward, and almost fall on my face as Lucifer descends the grand staircase.

He is impossible in the way of old things — ageless, calm, beautiful in a way that has nothing to do with vanity. His hair is silver, tied back with a black ribbon. His eyes glow faint gold, brightening as he approaches. His suit changes with every movement — shadow, starlight, shadow again.

But what strikes me most is not his appearance. It's the way every demon in the room subtly inclines their head as he passes. A king without a crown. His gaze reaches Slade's and warms, amusement curling through it.

"Lord Athalar." His voice is velvet and fire. "You return to us at last."

Slade's posture changes — straightening, shoulders settling into the quiet authority of someone who was born to command. He inclines his head, the faintest acknowledgment. "Your Grace."

Lucifer's attention shifts to me. And the air seems to inhale. Not a curse spike — not fear — just an awareness, electric and sharp, threading through the space between us.

"So, *this* is the witch." A faint smile plays at the edges of his mouth. "The Bellamy *spark*. I wondered when she'd appear."

Slade moves instantly, stepping half a pace in front of me — not blocking my view, but placing himself firmly between us. His hand finds the small of my back with a possessiveness so quiet it's almost tender.

"She stands with me," Slade says.

Lucifer's smile deepens. "That much is obvious. The realm noticed the moment you arrived."

A murmur moves through the gathered nobles — soft, restrained, dangerous. The sound of minds recalculating. Of old families adjusting their expectations.

No shrieking whispers, but a court registering a shift in power. The curse reacts to the attention — a low heat blooming beneath my skin, magic bending subtly toward Slade like a compass finding north.

Lanterns flicker in a soft ripple. Shadows lengthen and draw inward. A crystalline pillar near the wall cracks with a delicate chiming sound.

Lucifer's eyes glow brighter. "Ah. There it is."

Slade's jaw tenses. "Stay back."

"I'm not touching her," Lucifer replies, unoffended. "But your realm reacts to balance — or imbalance. And she carries both."

Another figure steps forward from the crowd — tall, elegant, wearing deep cerulean robes threaded with silver. His gaze lingers too long on me. Slade doesn't even look at him. "That's close enough."

The noble ignores him, moving closer. Lucifer's hand flashes out with the ease of centuries of rule, fingers closing around the man's wrist before he can take another step. "*Careful,*" Lucifer murmurs. "Lord Athalar is in a generous mood tonight. Do not test the limits of his restraint."

The noble pales and withdraws immediately. Slade's aura flares — not a scream of violence, but a quiet, lethal promise. I lean closer to him, my voice soft. "Is this... normal?"

"No." His hand tightens at my waist. "This is what happens when a curse, a mate bond, and a noble house collide under one roof."

My stomach flips. "So... Special then?"

His eyes burn into mine. "*Cataclysmic.*"

Lucifer observes us both with a thoughtful expression, then says lightly, "Do try to enjoy yourselves. Dinner will begin shortly. And, Lady Bellamy..." His gaze warms with something almost fond. "...do stay close to him. There are those here who would value you far more than they should."

Slade growls, low and lethal. Lucifer just laughs, elegant and unbothered, turning back toward the staircase as the music swells again. But the room doesn't resume its easy flow.

Every head tracks us. Every aura shifts as if reacting to our presence. The air feels poised on a knife's edge.

Slade leans down, lips brushing my ear. "Do not leave my side."

"Wasn't planning to," I whisper.

"Good," he murmurs. "Because if you stray too far..." His fingers brush my hip in a slow, burning drag. "...I won't be able to stop myself."

Heat coils in my stomach.

And all around us, the Ninth Realm watches — not hungry, not desperate — but with the sharp, predatory curiosity of creatures sensing the beginning of something they have no precedent for.

Something ancient... dangerous... something *destined*.

# CHAPTER 16

The Ninth Court glows like a cathedral carved out of dusk—gold-veined marble, black stone, and drifting motes of starlight that pulse in time with the Realm's heartbeat.

Piper walks at my side, chin lifted, curls wild, blue eyes flicking everywhere they shouldn't. She has no idea how many creatures would kill for that glow clinging to her throat. I lean down just enough for my breath to brush her cheek. "Remember what I told you."

She mutters, "Don't bow, don't stare, don't touch, don't breathe. Got it."

I stifle a laugh. "That is not what I said."

"You said a lot of things very fast."

I slide my hand to the small of her back—not to steer her. To keep idiots from getting close enough to smell her magic. "You'll be fine."

Her scowl says she does not believe me. Fair. She shouldn't.

A servant stops in front of us, offering a chalice smoking with red mist. Piper reaches for it, and I snatch her wrist before she can touch the stem. "No."

Her eyes widen. "I was being polite."

"That is a binding oath. Drink that, and you belong to whoever poured it."

She yanks her hand back so fast the servant flinches. "Why would ANYONE serve that at a party?!"

I murmur, "Because this is Hell, sweetheart. We don't host cookie exchanges."

A noble drifts toward us—tall, obsidian skin dusted with gold, eyes like molten brass.

Piper's gaze flashes to hers. Full. Direct. Warm. In Hell, that's practically an invitation.

A beat of silence ripples through the surrounding air. The noble smiles viciously. "How sweet."

I step between them before Piper realizes she's made a mistake. "Walk away."

Her expression sharpens. "I wasn't addressing you, Athalar."

"I'm aware, and I don't care. You can leave now."

She tilts her head, assessing Piper like a rare gem she'd like to break.

"What are you, little witch? A gift? A promise? A—"

"Enough." My voice cracks through the air like a blade.

The noble's grin fades. She backs away with a lingering look at Piper—one I'll burn out of her skull if she tries it again.

Piper whispers, eyes wide, "Was that—did I—"

"Yes."

She winces. "*Fantastic.*"

Then, as if things couldn't get any more dramatic. A familiar ripple of magic rolls through the ballroom—rich, old, edged in steel.

*Draven.*

My brother has always been a storm given shape. Dark hair, lighter eyes than mine—winter green instead of forest—and a beard shadow that makes half the Court reconsider their alliances.

He steps through the crowd with a predator's confidence and a scholar's precision. I smirk. He always did enjoy an entrance. His gaze locks on Piper first, pupils flaring. Then his eyes dart to me. "Slade," he drawls, "you're causing a scene."

"I'm preventing one."

"Mmm," he hums, circling Piper with his gaze the way a hawk circles something shiny. "This is her?"

Piper blinks. "Her who?"

Draven smiles—sharp, lethal, entertained. "Your mate."

Piper goes bright pink, averting her gaze quickly.

I growl quietly. "Draven."

He holds up both hands as if innocent. "I'm only observing."

A rustling of fabric catches my attention. And I realize a noble behind Piper brushes past too close—*deliberately*. Testing. I grab the back of the noble's collar and yank him backward. "Try that again," I murmur, "and I'll break your fingers."

He turns pale gray and scurries away.

Piper hisses under her breath, "Is it this dangerous everywhere here?"

"This?" Draven says, gesturing around with mild amusement. "This is the *polite* part of the evening."

Piper visibly stops breathing. I step in front of her again, lowering my voice. "You're safe with me."

She lifts her chin—a spark of bravery or pure stubbornness. "Good, because I have absolutely no idea what I'm doing."

Draven grins. "Then this will be fun."

I shoot him a warning look. He only smirks back, delighted.

The Ninth Court fills around us like a storm waiting to break. And Piper Bellamy—glowing, nervous, rebellious—stands at the center of it.

My *mate*.

Hell help anyone who thinks they can touch her.

***

The banquet hall unfurls before us like a spell cast for spectacle. Obsidian floors polished to liquid shine. Firelight trapped in crystal globes. A long table set with plates that shift colors depending on who looks at them.

Piper inhales softly. I feel the ripple through our bond—curiosity, nerves, and the smallest thread of awe.

Too many people notice. I position myself closer. Just enough to warn the Court... *mine*.

Draven falls into step beside her because of course he does. "First time at a Hell banquet?" he asks, voice dripping charm.

Piper shoots him a tight smile. "Is it that obvious?"

"Yes," Draven and I say at the same time.

She rolls her eyes and mutters something about "overgrown demon men and their commentary," but she walks straighter. Gods, she doesn't even realize how her determination glows.

We reach the table just as the herald announces the seating. "By decree of the Ninth King," the herald booms, "Lady Piper Bellamy shall sit at the right hand of Lord Slade Athalar."

A susurration spreads across the hall. Piper turns her head toward me, whisper-shouting, "I'm a *lady* now?!"

"No," I say. "But they're calling you one so no one attempts to court you."

Her cheeks flush. Then quieter, "Is that a thing here?"

"Yes."

"Oh." She swallows, but doesn't argue. Good. She takes her place beside me. I move her chair in—too close, but I don't care.

The bond hums with approval, brushing across my ribs like warm static. Draven drops into the seat across from her, smirking. "Try not to say anything idiotic," I warn him.

"I never do," he lies.

Piper snorts, rolling her eyes, just as a servant places two glasses before her. One clear, one faintly shimmering with gold.

She reaches for the gold one. I catch her wrist under the table. "Not that."

She glances at me. "Why?"

"That one reveals your deepest secrets aloud."

She yanks her hand back and whispers, horrified, "Why is that ON THE TABLE?!"

Draven grins. "Entertainment."

Piper shoots him a glare that could curdle wine. I feel my mouth twitch again, and fight to keep the smile off my face.

She really *is* magnificent.

I'm forced to take my eyes off her when I feel the shift ripple across the room.

The hall goes quiet—heavy, reverent, electric—as Lucifer rises from the head of the table.

He lifts his goblet in greeting.

"Welcome, guests of the Ninth."

Piper, being Piper, lifts her own cup instinctively and chirps, "Um—hi?"

The entire hall freezes. A single fork hits a plate somewhere down the table. Draven chokes. I inhale very, very slowly.

Lucifer's smile spreads—sharp, delighted, dangerous. "Hello, little Bellamy."

Piper blanches. "Oh God. I wasn't supposed—"

"No speaking," I murmur under my breath.

Her eyes are huge. "You said that too late."

Lucifer chuckles. "Let her speak, Slade. I find her refreshing."

Every creature in this room hears his interest. It rolls across the table like a breeze made of knives.

I slide my hand beneath the table until my fingers brush Piper's knee. Steady. Grounding. Possessive.

*Mine.*

Lucifer raises a brow, amused at the gesture but not challenging it—for now. "Proceed," he says, settling again.

Piper sinks two inches in her chair.

Draven leans forward. "I like her," he whispers to me.

"I'm aware," I whisper back. "Don't."

He smirks. "No promises."

The first course appears—literally appears—in front of us in a shimmer of smoke and candlelight. Piper's plate is filled with something golden and delicate. She leans in cautiously. "Is it safe?"

"For you?" Draven says. "Probably."

She gives him a dry look and lifts her fork anyway. Brave. Foolish. Very Piper. She takes a bite—and her eyes widen.

"Oh my God," she says, forgetting the rule again. A hundred gazes snap toward her. She claps a hand over her mouth. "I—I mean—your Majesty, sorry, that was—uh—really good—"

Lucifer laughs. Not a polite laugh. A full, delighted, amused sound that ripples like thunder. "Slade," he says, "your mate is *extraordinary*."

I grit my teeth. "I know."

Piper goes bright crimson. The curse pulses between us—warm, sharp, intimate. My blood heats instantly in response.

Draven watches me like he's seeing something unfold he's waited centuries for. "She's unraveling you," he murmurs.

I don't deny it. Because my pulse is loud. My magic is sharper. And Piper—gods, Piper is sitting beside me glowing like she's the only thing alive in this hall of ancient predators.

And every one of them sees it.

The bond crackles under my skin like a warning—or a promise.

Either way... Tonight will not end peacefully.

***

The Ninth Court's dinners are never relaxed, but this one feels tight as a drawn bow. Piper sits beside me, trying very hard to pretend the room full of demons isn't dissecting every shift of her breath. The glow of her curse is behaving like flickering candlelight—subtle, unpredictable, catching the attention of anyone who cares to look.

And too many are looking.

She lifts her fork carefully, eyes on her plate, shoulders squared with a kind of determined grace... until a noble three seats down stands and raises his glass.

"Bellamy," he says, voice smooth and rehearsed, "your ancestor used to open Ninth Court feasts with a verse. A tradition from her line. Perhaps you would honor it."

Piper freezes. Her fork clinks softly against her plate. I feel the drop in her stomach through the bond before she even looks at me.

"A verse?" she whispers.

The noble smiles in that serpentine way demons have perfected over millennia—courtesy wrapped around hunger. "A simple invocation. A greeting. A phrase carried through your bloodline. It's customary."

Lucifer doesn't intervene. He doesn't need to—his interest is obvious in the stillness of the room.

Piper sits a little straighter, but her pulse kicks under her skin. She tries to find something—anything—appropriate to say, but the curse reacts to the attention long before she does.

I feel the swell of magic rising through her like a tide, ancient and instinctive. She doesn't even know she's doing it. Her lips part. A whisper escapes—quiet, tremulous, but saturated with power. "*Veda'ren.*"

The entire banquet hall goes still over a single invocation. One spoken like a name and a command, answering itself through five centuries.

The floor responds first. Sigils buried beneath obsidian tiles ignite in a gold-patterned spiral beneath Piper's feet, rising in delicate lines around the base of her chair like vines made of starlight. Nobles recoil from the table's edge, their instincts older than their manners.

Piper startles and grips the table with both hands. "Slade—"

"I've got you," I murmur, placing a grounding hand at her spine as the air vibrates with pressure. "Just breathe."

But the invocation is already unfurling, pulling threads older than memory straight through her skin. Draven, two seats down, pushes back from the table and circles behind us. "You didn't tell me she was carrying a Bellamy Memoriam," he mutters.

"She isn't," I snap.

"She is *now*."

Piper looks between us, terrified. "What's happening?"

Before I can answer, the air above her begins to condense—mist, light, shadow, memory—forming the faint outline of a woman wrapped in winter-pale garments and moonlit authority.

Not alive. Not dead. A record with its own heartbeat.

Veda Bellamy's echo lifts its head. Nobles stiffen. A few rise from their chairs. One whispers a prayer to a deity that hasn't answered in ages. And the apparition speaks directly to Piper, "*Find my grimoire.*"

The words ripple through the hall—soft but sharp enough to cut the silence into clean ribbons.

Piper flinches like she's been struck. I feel the echo hit her through the bond—cold, bright, demanding.

Draven moves too close. "We need to break the line before someone binds it—"

The magic reacts badly to his interference. A blast of energy cracks across the table, toppling goblets, extinguishing the floating candles overhead, sending several nobles reeling backward.

Piper cries out and presses her palms to her ears as the chandelier above swings in a violent arc.

Draven curses under his breath and jumps back, shaking his hand. "That's not an invocation. That's a call-through. She opened a channel."

Piper gasps, trembling. "I didn't mean to."

"It wasn't choice," I murmur, cupping her jaw to turn her face toward mine. "The curse used your voice."

The silhouette flickers once, twice—then dissolves into a shower of fading gold. She sags forward, panting. Around us, the nobles are already recalculating. The dangerous ones inch closer, sensing opportunity.

Lucifer doesn't move. Doesn't speak, or even fucking blink. He simply watches.

Draven leans close and murmurs, "We need an exit. *Now.*"

He's right. I rise smoothly from my chair and place a steadying hand at Piper's back. "We're leaving," I say.

She nods, dazed, gripping my sleeve.

Draven gives a sharp grin—half apology, half enjoyment—and raises his hand. Blue fire erupts along the far wall, dramatic and harmless but enough to send half the court gasping and recoiling. It's all the distraction we need.

I guide Piper out of her chair and toward the side corridor. The chandelier steadies above us, the plates settle, the room stirs and recovers. But Piper doesn't. She looks up at me, eyes wide, voice barely audible. "Slade... what did I just do?"

"Not... *what*," I say quietly as the corridor swallows us in deeper shadow. "*Who*."

Her breath shivers.

And I tell her the truth she already fears. "You answered the first Bellamy."

# CHAPTER 17

*Piper*

The corridor swallows us whole—quiet, dim, lined with flickering lanterns—and the second the banquet doors close behind us, my legs go watery. I yank my arm free of Slade's grip and press my back to the wall, dragging in breath after uneven breath. "I didn't mean to say *anything*—" My voice breaks. "I don't even know *what* I said."

Slade steps in close, one hand braced beside my head, the other steady at my waist—keeping me upright, keeping me from spiraling. "You didn't choose it," he murmurs. "The curse chose for you."

"That is NOT comforting!"

Footsteps echo sharply behind us. They sound like a warning. Draven appears, half storm, half smirk, his formal jacket slightly singed from whatever diversion he caused. He looks between me and Slade, eyes bright with disbelief.

"Well," he exhales, "that was catastrophic."

I groan. "Great. Love that word. Really calming."

Draven points at me. "Do you have any idea what you just invoked?"

"I already said NO!"

He scrubs a hand through his hair. "Slade, you want to explain, or should I?"

Slade's jaw tightens. "You'll embellish."

"I always embellish." Draven folds his arms. "I'm delightful that way."

"Tell her," Slade growls.

Draven's grin fades. He steps closer, his expression turning unexpectedly serious. "Piper... what you spoke wasn't an invocation. It wasn't even Bellamy spellwork." He pauses. "It was a summons."

My stomach plummets. "A... a summons for WHAT?"

Draven lifts a brow. "You mean... *Who*."

Slade murmurs, "Veda Bellamy."

I shake my head violently. "No—no no no. That was—she was—she's a MEMORY. A ghost. An echo."

Draven snorts. "Well, she's certainly not echoing anymore."

Slade's hand tightens on my waist when I sway.

Draven leans against the opposite wall with a sigh. "Piper, you didn't just awaken her echo.

You reopened whatever she sealed. Whatever she bound. And that—" he flicks a finger toward the banquet hall—"is why the court lost its collective mind."

My skin prickles. "But why would they care?"

"Because," Draven says, "Veda Bellamy was the witch who nearly brought the Ninth Realm to its knees. And then disappeared before anyone could kill her or recruit her. Which, in demon politics, is very rude."

I stare at him. "She—she WHAT?"

Slade answers quietly. "She threatened every house here. Every bloodline. Including mine."

Draven nods. "And when a Bellamy speaks her name in the Ninth Realm... five hundred years later..."

He whistles low. "That's chaos incarnate."

I slide down the wall until I'm half crouching, half clinging to my own hair like that will stop the panic buzzing under my skin. "So what do I do now?" I whisper.

Slade kneels in front of me, taking my hands—slow, grounding, careful. "We find the truth. We go to the archives. Tonight."

Draven pushes off the wall, adjusting his sleeves. "Before another house decides they want to 'escort' you themselves. And trust me, their idea of escort is either kidnapping or marriage. Sometimes both."

"Oh my GOD."

Slade stands and extends a hand to me. "You're safe with me."

I want to say I don't believe him. But the bond thrums like a heartbeat. I place my hand in his, and the faint buzzing under my skin settles.

Draven claps once. "Excellent! Emotional crisis complete. Now let's move before someone realizes Slade's missing and assumes you two ran off to consummate the bond."

I choke. "DRAVEN."

He winks. "Hey, I'm rooting for you buddy."

Slade gives him a look that promises violence.

Draven lifts his hands innocently. "What? I'm being supportive."

"We're going," Slade says through his teeth. He pulls me close, guiding me down the corridor. Draven strides ahead, checking corners like this is a heist and he's having way too much fun. My pulse is still frantic, my head spinning.

But one truth rings louder than everything else... If Veda Bellamy called out to me... If she wants me to find something...

The archives might be the only place left in any realm to tell me why.

And I'm suddenly *terrified* of what I'll learn.

***

The deeper we move into the palace, the thinner the air feels—like the entire Realm is holding its breath, waiting for me to slip, or speak, or accidentally resurrect another long-dead witch. Slade keeps me tucked against his side with infuriating ease, while Draven prowls ahead like a very smug, very dangerous tour guide.

We reach a pair of enormous obsidian doors etched with sigils that shimmer like frost.

Draven glances back at me. "Welcome to the Restricted Archives. No mortals allowed."

Then to Slade, "And technically no demons either unless they're authorized, but when has that ever stopped you?"

Slade gives him a sharp look. "Open it."

Draven smirks, taps the sigil at the center, and the doors sigh open—slow and ominous, like they're deciding whether or not I deserve entry.

Inside, the temperature drops. A cathedral of dark stone and spiraling glass shelves stretches into shadow. Books float in slow circles. Candles burn without flame. Magic hums in the air like distant music.

Slade guides me in first. "Stay close," he says softly.

I don't argue. Not when the air tastes like old magic and older secrets.

Draven snaps his fingers, sending a ripple of light racing across the shelves. "We're looking for Bellamy artifacts. Veda's things should be catalogued under ancient coven disputes, broken alliances, and general calamities."

I blink. "Filed under... *calamity*?"

"Oh yes," Draven says. "Alphabetically."

Slade searches the far shelves while Draven probes the enchanted lockboxes, muttering something about "archaic organization systems" and "who the hell files bloodline curses next to horticulture texts."

A soft glow catches my attention from a high, narrow alcove. "Slade," I call quietly.

He's at my side in a breath. "It's reacting to you," he murmurs.

The glow pulses again—faint, golden, a heartbeat waiting for mine to sync. I reach up. The artifact responds instantly. A small velvet box drifts from the shelf as if carried by invisible hands. Slade tenses, and Draven jogs over, suddenly cautious.

"Careful," Draven warns. "Objects tied to Veda were known to be... unpredictable."

Slade covers my hand with his. "Let me."

But the box doesn't respond to him. It shies away. Then nudges harder toward me. My stomach twists. "It wants me to open it."

Slade's jaw works as he takes half a step back—far enough not to interfere, close enough to catch me if the thing decides to bite. I lift the lid. Inside rests a ring. It's simple, ancient, gold brushed with faint runes that look like they're sleeping. A Bellamy crest is etched on the inside.

Draven inhales sharply. "That... is Veda's binding ring."

My breath turns to glass. "Binding... to who?"

Slade meets my gaze, something dark and heavy settling behind his eyes. "My ancestor," he says quietly. "Lord Aresh Athalar."

"Oh." The word falls out of me like a stone.

Draven gestures for the box to flip its inner compartment open. "There should be—aha."

A scroll unfurls across the air, shimmering with aged magic. I brace myself as Slade reads aloud. "Union of Athalar and Bellamy to neutralize the realms' volatility...Bellamy heir chosen by prophecy... balance of power bound through sacred bond..."

Slade goes rigid.

Draven swears. "You've got to be kidding me."

The scroll continues... "But Veda refused the binding. She severed the accord and sought another path to power—one unnamed, one *forbidden*. She vanished before judgment could fall."

I grip the ring harder. "So she ran?"

"Yes and no," Slade says, voice low. "She chose something. Something dangerous enough to threaten both our lines."

Draven nods grimly. "And whatever that choice was... it's what you woke up at dinner."

I shake my head. "But why me? Why now?"

Slade glances at me, eyes burning a deeper green than I've ever seen. "Because you're the first Bellamy born with the right magic. Strength. The right resonance even." His fingers brush the ring. "You're the one Veda's unfinished work recognizes."

Cold trickles down my spine. "So Veda really *did* create the curse," I whisper.

Slade doesn't deny it.

Draven whistles. "Well. This is a nightmare."

But Slade's gaze never leaves mine. "It doesn't change anything," he murmurs. "You're not her. And I won't let anyone—past or present—claim you."

My pulse stutters, as the ring pulses. Somewhere deep in the archives, a book slams shut on its own.

Draven clears his throat. "We should leave before the archives start answering her presence. They have a tendency to... animate."

Slade takes the ring from my trembling hand, tucks it into his jacket, and gently pulls me toward the exit. The corridors feel tighter on the way out. The ring calls to me from Slade's pocket. And I can't shake the truth crawling under my skin...

Veda didn't disappear. She left a trail.

And it's leading straight to me.

# CHAPTER 18

*Slade*

The moment we step out of the archives, the air changes. Not the realm—her. Piper's magic hums under her skin, bright and trembling, like a tether pulled too tight. The bond claws at me, stretching between us in a low, electric current I feel deep in my bones.

She stumbles, falling into my arms. And the bond nearly snaps into place.

Her breath brushes my cheek. Her body fits against mine as though molded for me. Her pulse is a frantic, beautiful rhythm calling to every ancient instinct I possess. I lower my head—her eyes flutter, her lips part...

And then—Draven groans loudly behind us. "For the love of hellfire, get a room."

Piper jerks back like she's been splashed with cold water.

I turn slowly, *very* slowly, eyes blazing with pure fury. The spineless little—

Draven holds his hands up. "What? I didn't realize this was Three Seconds Till Destined Mating Time."

I step toward him.

He steps back. "Slade—"

"You interrupted us." My voice drops into something rough and primal. "You interrupted *her*."

"Oh please," he scoffs, "you'll have centuries to—"

I lunge. He vanishes in a swirl of shadow—reappearing ten feet down the hall. "Slade," Piper hisses, grabbing my sleeve, "please don't murder your brother in the middle of Hell."

Draven draws himself up, smoothing his jacket. "Listen to your mate."

I snarl. "Shut—"

But the bond pulses. Piper swallows. Draven smirks like he knows exactly what just happened. "Let's go before someone else in the court decides to test their luck."

Reluctantly, I let her guide me toward the portal chamber.

The air crackles around us all the way home.

***

The moment the portal flickers out behind us, something feels... *wrong*.

Lights on. Scent of cinnamon. A faint thump from the living room.

Piper stiffens. "Rhea's here."

I blink. "Already?"

She rounds the corner—and stops dead.

Rhea stands in the middle of the room with her hands on her hips, hair a wild halo around her face, wearing an expression that can only be described as done. Newt sits beside her in what appears to be a tiny cat-sized corner of shame. Rhea jabs a thumb toward him. "Your fuzzy demon gremlin clawed my four-hundred-dollar curtains. FOUR. HUNDRED. DOLLARS. PIPER."

Newt meows loudly. Zero remorse.

Piper's face softens. "Oh, baby—"

But Newt leaps straight into my arms. He curls there, purring like I'm his chosen deity.

Piper's jaw drops. "*Excuse me.*"

I stroke the cat's head. "He likes me."

"He liked me FIRST."

Draven wanders in, looks at the scene, and snorts. "Gods above, the creature has taste."

Rhea turns sharply, eyes narrowing at him. "And... Who are *you*?"

Draven's smirk blooms instantly. "Draven Athalar. And you are?"

"Done with today," she snaps. "And apparently with your face."

He clutches his chest dramatically. "You wound me."

Piper mutters under her breath, "Oh, fuck—*hell no*. Absolutely not—"

I set Newt down, and the traitor immediately twines around my legs. Rhea glares at him. "*Traitor beast.*"

Draven watches Rhea the way a python watches a spark—interested, surprised, maybe even a little baffled. "Fiery," he murmurs.

Rhea shoots back, "*Annoying*."

They lock eyes. The tension sharpens. Piper drags a hand down her face. "I am too tired to deal with a hate-flirt right now."

I step closer to her, steadying her by the elbow. "You're exhausted."

She leans in—just for a moment—and the bond tugs again, hungry, eager, electric. I lower my voice. "If that invocation had been any longer, you would have collapsed."

She exhales shakily. "I know."

Rhea looks between us, eyes widening. "Oh. Oh gods. This is worse than I thought."

Draven folds his arms like he's settling in. "You have *no idea*."

Piper shoots him a murderous glare. "Don't you start."

Draven lifts his hands. "Fine. But we need a plan. Because the entire Ninth Realm felt what happened tonight."

Newt hops onto the couch, kneads a blanket, and stares at all of us with the disdain of a creature who survived nine of his own lives already.

Rhea plops into a chair. "First order of business? Food. Second? Sleep. Third? Slade explaining literally everything he didn't tell you."

Draven grins. "Oh, this will be fun."

I growl. Piper groans, and Newt purrs loudly. And Rhea? She glares at Draven like she's already planning his burial. Draven, of course, leans into it—folding his arms, lifting a brow, swagger in every inch like he's inviting the challenge.

*Idiot.*

Rhea ignores him entirely and sweeps her attention back to Piper, curls bouncing with each step as she moves into strategist mode—a mode she clearly lives in. "Okay," she says, pointing at the coffee table like it's on her shit list. "Let's get organized. I have contacts. *Real* ones. Not your witchy-woo, bullshit, crystal social media influencers."

Piper snorts. "I don't follow any—"

Rhea cuts her off. "You follow two. They cry on live and sell moon water. I worry about the amount of brain cells you're losing watching that drivel."

Draven chokes on a laugh. She spins on him. "*You*. Shut it."

He raises both hands in surrender. "I'm merely observing excellence."

Rhea blinks—momentarily thrown—then snaps back to me. "Slade. Tell me everything."

I fold my arms, meeting her gaze with equal intensity. She has Bellamy steel, that's certain. A kind of brash confidence most witches fake. Rhea wears it like perfume. "We found Veda's ring," I tell her. "The one meant to bind her to my ancestor, Lord Aresh Athalar."

Rhea's expression sharpens—calculating, quick. "That would explain why the curse latched onto your line specifically. If Veda broke the bond, the magic could've... rerouted? Mutated?"

"Corrupted," Draven offers.

Rhea nods slowly. "That too."

Piper wraps her arms around herself. "And the scroll said she vanished before anything could be discovered."

I continue, "She sought power elsewhere. Something unnamed. Something hidden."

Draven adds lazily, "Something the archives themselves tried to wake up the minute your girl here opened her mouth at dinner."

Rhea winces. "Yeah, I felt that blast from three blocks away. Piper, my Christmas cactus bloomed in the middle of the night. In *December*. Do you know how *cursed* that is?"

Piper groans. "I didn't mean to—"

"Oh, I know. That's the problem." Rhea paces, tapping thoughtfully at her cheek. "Okay. I have someone. A historian—well, more like a magical antiquarian with questionable morals and a penthouse in Prague—but she owes me a favor. She can dig. Deep."

Piper brightens. "Really?"

Rhea nods. "But don't get too excited. She's *not* cheap, and she's definitely not stable. She once tried to resurrect a library."

Draven looks impressed. "I like her already."

"You would," Rhea mutters, rolling her eyes.

Piper sinks onto the couch, Newt crawling instantly into her lap, *traitor*, eyes softening with equal parts hope and exhaustion. "So we'll contact her?"

Rhea nods firmly. "I'll handle it. But I need everything you two know." She points between Draven and me. "Including the part where Piper accidentally summoned the ghost of a five-hundred-year-old Bellamy matriarch in front of the fucking Prince of Hell."

Piper buries her face in her hands. "Please stop reminding me—"

"No," Rhea says sweetly. "I want you to suffer."

Draven grins. "I *like* her."

Rhea shoots back, "I *don't* like you."

Their eyes lock. A spark—sharp, violent, magnetic—crackles between them. Piper's head snaps up. "Uhm."

I agree. "Fuck no."

Newt meows dramatically. Rhea tosses her hair. "We'll talk tomorrow. I'll call my contact tonight."

Draven adds smoothly, "I'll escort you home."

"I'd rather chew glass," Rhea replies. But she still grabs her purse.

Piper blinks. "Wait—are you two—?"

"NO," they say in unison. Then immediately glare at each other again.

Piper whispers, "Oh gods. This is going to be... *feral*."

I watch them walk toward the door—Rhea storming ahead, Draven gliding behind her like a patient predator—and sigh. Piper leans into my shoulder, soft and sleepy, her magic curled like embers around us both. "You okay?" I ask quietly.

She nods. "Just... overwhelmed."

She meets my gaze. I feel the bond tremble again, desperate and hungry. *Soon*. But not tonight. "Get some sleep, Piper," I murmur.

She nods, rising, Newt trotting after her with a final disdainful flick of his tail in my direction.

And as the door shuts behind her, I'm left staring into the quiet—ring burning in my pocket, curse stirring, and the knowledge that Veda Bellamy's shadow is only beginning to wake.

# CHAPTER 19

## *Piper*

Morning settles over my shop like warm fog—gold filtering through frost-dusted windows, cinnamon incense curling upward in sleepy spirals, and my enchanted kettle rattling impatiently on the back counter because it hates being ignored.

The moment I open the shop door, a gust of cold air slides around my ankles, nibbling at the hem of my black velvet skirt. My crescent moon earrings jingle softly, catching the light. My hair—clipped back on one side with a silver star pin—spills over my shoulder in a glossy cascade that smells faintly of lavender oil.

The amethyst pendant at my throat thrums once. A quiet warning, signaling the curse is awake.

"Great," I mutter. "Good morning to you too."

Inside, everything looks exactly as I left it—shelves lined with amber bottles and herb bundles, jars of glitter that absolutely do something, a candle wall flickering like a rainbow of tiny spirits, spellbooks stacked neatly beside agate bookends, and potted evergreens decorated with enchanted ornaments that occasionally blink.

Underneath all of it, I feel the pulse of my magic the way some people feel the weather changing—low, insistent, tugging at the edges of my ribs.

I shrug out of my coat, hang it on the antler hook by the door, and go about flipping open blinds. The sunlight catches dust motes and makes them glow.

My magic stirs—hearth magic, warding magic, the kind of power meant for protection and binding and keeping the world stitched together in invisible seams. Unfortunately, it also likes to flare under stress... react to attraction... misfire around Christmas decorations... and occasionally summon demons into my living room.

So. You know. A mixed bag.

I smooth the front of my charcoal-gray top, tuck a stray curl behind my ear, and whisper to the room, "Let's please avoid any disasters today."

The garland above the counter rustles—*mockingly*.

And I just know, I'm in for a long day.

***

By ten a.m., the kettle whistles and I have a mug of rosemary-black tea warming my hands. I walk the shop floor barefoot—and check the wards, soft socks be damned. The wood floors vibrate better with skin contact.

A faint shimmer curls around the doorway. *Good*. The shelf of moon salts hums contentedly. *Great*. The enchanted mistletoe stays in the drawer where I sealed it. *Excellent*.

Then the front bell chimes, and Mrs. Alderberry floats in on a wave of peppermint perfume mixed with faux-fur dignity. "My dear Piper," she says, taking one long look at me, "you're positively glowing my dear."

I pinch the bridge of my nose. "For the love of all things holy..."

"Oh don't be dramatic. It's a nice glow. Like candlelight and secrets."

"Perfect," I mutter. "I always aim for secrets."

She buys lunar tea and asks zero suspicious questions, which might be the most alarming thing she's ever done. The rest of the morning drifts by in slow ripples, questions about potions, requests for charms, curious tapping on the enchanted snow globes.

Nothing levitates, or bursts into flames. Nothing sings at me. For two blissful hours, life feels... *stable*.

Then it hits me. A hum beneath my skin, followed by a tightening just behind my sternum. Heat blooming across the bond like a sunrise.

*Slade.*

I whisper, "Of course."

The bell rings, and there he is.

Slade Athalar fills the doorway like something carved out of shadow and old myths—tall, sharp, wrapped in a dark charcoal coat with obsidian buttons, hair tousled in that unfair way that says he probably just raked a hand through it and moved on with his life. His forest-green eyes find me instantly. My pendant warms, and my magic sparks. A jar shivers in response to the connection between us. He steps inside, the air bending around him—heat first, then ozone, then something sweetly dangerous.

I hate him. I *hate* that I *don't* actually hate him.

"Morning, gorgeous," he murmurs, voice low, like he's allowed to say things like that.

I lift my chin. "You're early."

"You look ravishing, little witch."

"STOP SAYING THAT."

His mouth curves slowly, wicked. Delighted, even. He moves through my shop with the fluid confidence of someone born to walk marble halls and make mortals lose their minds. Customers stare openly, some blushing, one nearly dropping a jar of enchanted sugar.

Slade ignores all of it. He stops in front of me, fingertips brushing the counter. "You felt it," he says.

"Of course I did," I snap. "My magic is basically a hazard light right now."

"The Ninth Court is whispering about you."

My pulse stutters. "Me?" I squeak.

He leans closer. "Your invocation. The bond. The archives. Veda. They felt everything."

The lights flicker. The snow globes hum a chord of disapproval. My pendant heats until I swear it leaves a violet glow on my skin. I exhale shakily. "This was supposed to be a normal day."

Slade's eyes soften—just enough to make my stomach swoop. "For you, normal is gone."

And as my shelves tremble with quiet magic and the curse winds tighter around my ribs, I realize... He's right. Normal is gone. And something in the air is shifting—toward danger, toward truth, toward him.

And toward whatever the hell Veda Bellamy awakened last night.

***

Slade lingers in the shop long after the last customer leaves, leaning against my counter like the room was built around him. I'm very aware of how I look under his gaze, my black velvet skirt brushing my knees, my curls clipped back on one side and tumbling down my back, and the damned amethyst pendant warming against my skin—*again*.

*Too* aware.

His voice slips under my guard. "Come with me."

"No."

"Yes," he says, narrowing those gorgeous verdant eyes in my direction.

"I am *working*."

"You're done," he says simply. "And you haven't eaten."

I open my mouth—but the truth is, my stomach betrays me first, rumbling like I swallowed thunder. He smiles—slow, knowing. "We'll go to the market. You choose what you want. I'll cook."

That should *not* sound sexy. It absolutely does. I try to put steel in my spine. "Why do you want to cook for me?"

His answer is maddeningly simple. "Because I want to feed you."

Oh gods. My magic flickers along my ribs, reacting before my mind catches up.

And maybe it's the curse. Maybe it's the bond. Or, maybe it's simply the fact that my entire world has been breaking open for days.

But I close the shop early. And Slade looks at me like I just handed him something precious as we walk out the front door.

The winter air hits us first—crisp, pine-tinged, full of chiming bells from the Christmas stalls lining the square. Lanterns flicker along the walkways, casting a honey-gold glow over wreaths and rows of seasonal vendors. But everything around us shifts subtly as we walk.

Lights flare brighter. Shadows curl away from him. People part without thinking.

Slade isn't doing it on purpose. Power just... *moves* for him. I shouldn't find that attractive either. But I *do*. Gods, I do.

He takes a basket from a stall, offering it to me without ceremony. "Start picking."

I try. But every time I reach for something, he plucks a better version from the display.

"You're impossible," I mutter.

"And you have terrible tomato instincts," he counters.

I grab a bundle of basil. He replaces it with one fuller, fresher. "*Stop interfering*," I hiss.

"I'm helping."

"You're *bossy*," I argue, biting back laughter.

"You like it."

I nearly fling a package of pasta at him. Instead, I grab the homemade fresh noodles—soft, flour-dusted, smelling faintly of rosemary. He approves with a low, pleased sound.

We walk the aisles like this—bickering, bantering, brushing hands more times than either of us acknowledges—until the basket is filled with rich reds, deep greens, warm spices. It feels strangely intimate, and dangerously normal.

On the walk home, Slade walks close enough that the heat of his body melts every chill before it touches me.

I pretend I don't notice. He pretends he doesn't know that I noticed.

Which... makes for a *very* quiet but charged walk home. Snow starts falling, little trickles of flakes at first, that somehow seem to get thicker and denser the closer we get to the apartment.

By the time we cross the threshold of the small alcove the building manager has the audacity to call a lobby, it's coming down really hard.

Slade takes the lead, and I follow him up the stairs trying to ignore how right this feels. The moment we step inside my apartment, Newt rockets across the floor like a sentient puffball and vaults onto the kitchen island.

He stares at Slade. Then meows—*twice*. And if that wasn't bad enough, the brat rubs his entire face against Slade's forearm.

"Unbelievable," I say.

Slade scratches under Newt's chin. "He has impeccable judgment."

"*Traitor*," I whisper at the cat.

Newt blinks slowly. Translation? *You're welcome.*

Slade rolls up his sleeves—forearms cut from marble, faint runes glowing under the skin like embers—and starts cooking with terrifying competence. He moves like the kitchen belongs to him. Oil sizzles. Garlic blooms fragrant and golden. Tomatoes soften in the pan until they release a sweet, bright steam. He even slices basil with the kind of precision that suggests he's gutted a demon using similar technique.

I lean against the counter, trying not to stare and failing miserably.

"You're watching," he says.

"You're cooking," I counter. "Maybe, I'm checking to make sure you didn't poison the food."

He grins, "Liar." He scans my face. "And you're flushed."

"It's warm in here."

"It isn't."

I shove him with my eyes. He laughs—the deep, dark kind that curls into my spine. "Sit," he says.

I obey.

He plates the tortellini delicately, drizzles something intoxicating over the top, and places the steaming dish in front of me with all the gravity of a vow. I take a bite. It's sinful how good this is.

It's like fucking magic.

Slade leans his hip against the counter, watching for my reaction. I hate how my eyes flutter closed, how a tiny sound escapes my throat, and how he *hears* it.

He comes closer. His voice a low rasp. "I like watching you eat, your expression always shows exactly what you're thinking. It's... *sexy*."

"Stop saying things like that," I groan, flushing from head to toe all over again.

"Why?"

"Because they work."

His smile burns all the way through me.

We eat by candlelight, close enough that his knee brushes mine under the table, close enough that the bond hums with every uneven breath I take. Talking comfortably for what feels like hours. He tells me tales of what it was like growing up in hell—news flash, it's no picnic—and all the embarrassing shit you usually save for your fourth or fifth date. You know, like a *month* of dating.

After dinner, we rinse and soak the dishes, laughing and joking like it's the most natural thing in the world.  When we're finished, I insist on a movie.

Slade insists on sitting beside me. Newt insists on sitting in Slade's lap. *Traitor.*

We settle on *The Holiday* because I refuse to lose that battle and Slade refuses to admit he enjoys watching Jude Law be charming.

Halfway through, the room shifts. Warm. Quiet. Lights twinkling across my walls in soft gold. My curls falling forward until he gently sweeps them back behind my shoulder.

His fingers linger. My magic sparks — soft, pink-gold, fluttering beneath my skin. The garland above the window rustles. The lights flicker in a low pulse.

Slade notices. Of course he does. "Your magic's responding," he murmurs.

"I can't help it."

"You don't want to." I turn my head to argue, but he's already watching me. *Really* watching me. Like I'm somehow heat, gravity, and inevitability all wrapped into one.

His hand lifts, brushing the curve of my jaw—slow, reverent, with a restraint that shreds me. "Tell me to stop," he whispers.

I can't. I don't. So he kisses me. And gods—it's nothing like the accidental first kiss. The charged, frantic thing we clung to between worlds.

This kiss is *deliberate.* Slow enough to unravel me. Deep enough to ruin me.

He kisses like he knows exactly how I'll taste. How I'll melt. How I'll *feel.* Slade's mouth coaxes heat out of my bones, his hand cupping the back of my neck, thumb stroking the line of my throat.

I gasp. Slade swallows it.

My magic surges—lights flaring, ornaments shimmering, the whole room tuning itself to the sound of my pulse.

When he finally draws back, my chest is rising too quickly, my cheeks flushed, my lips tingling, my pendant blazing hot against my skin like a warning I want to ignore.

Slade rests his forehead against mine. "You let me in tonight," he says softly.

I want to deny it. I can't. "Maybe," I whisper instead.

His mouth curves—a dark, devastating smile. Newt meows impatiently, reminding us he exists.

I laugh shakily at his rudeness. Slade chuckles against my cheek. And for the first time since this curse began, I feel something warm, steady, dangerous—*hope*. Want... Trust.

And maybe I *am* just a little bit... *his*.

# CHAPTER 20

*Slade*

Piper is still asleep. Curled on her side, hair a dark spill across her pillow, her amethyst pendant resting against her throat like a star that forgot it should be cold. Newt sleeps on her ankles, paws twitching in feline dreams. The room hums faintly—her magic smoothing the air in slow, rhythmic pulses.

She looks... peaceful. Which is a lie. I can feel the curse moving under her skin, restless even in slumber. It beats against my senses like a second heartbeat, faint but insistent.

Piper's phone vibrates on the nightstand. It's Rhea—calling from Prague. At dawn. This can't be good.

I step out of the bedroom and shut the door behind me.

"Piper," she snaps the moment I answer, "*wake up*. We have a problem."

"We have many," I murmur. "Clarify yours."

"You're not Piper," Rhea says with mild curiosity. "Where's Piper?"

"Asleep." I answer, tone clipped. I'm impatient, beyond ready to hear what is so... *problematic*.

She sighs heavily, "Fine. I suppose you'll have to do. I met with my contact."

That gets my attention. The antiquarian witch with a penthouse full of cursed books and very few survival instincts. If Rhea reached her at all, it means she's already pulled favors that cost her something.

"What did she find?" I ask.

Rhea exhales—a blend of excitement and real fear. "The Bellamy curse isn't limited to Christmas."

Ice pours into my veins. "Explain."

"It wasn't just Veda," she continues. "There were five sisters. Five bloodlines." A rustle of papers. "They tied themselves—willingly or not—to the old pagan rites."

"Which rites?"

"All of them," she says sharply. "Lupercalia. Ostara. Summer Solstice. Samhain. Yule."

A cold, heavy truth settles in my chest.

"Five pillars," I say quietly. "Five rites. Five sisters."

"Yes." Rhea lowers her voice. "And every sister reacted differently to the original... event."

Event. That word does not comfort me. "What event?"

"That's what we don't know yet." Rhea's voice tightens. "But the curse wasn't a single spell gone wrong. It wasn't an accident. It was a pact. A ritual. A sacrifice. Something they bound themselves to."

I pace the living room, fingers flexing, magic simmering just under my skin.

"And Veda?"

"Veda wanted power," Rhea says. "More than the others. Enough to sever her intended bond—with your ancestor. Enough to choose something darker."

I stop pacing. Because darkness has a cost. It always has. "What did she choose?"

Rhea hesitates—*way* too long for my liking.

"Rhea," I warn.

"We don't know... yet," she finally admits. "But whatever Veda bound herself to—it didn't stay with her. It spread. It tied itself to every Bellamy born from those original sisters. *All* of them."

The living room lights flicker.

Piper reacts even in sleep—her magic flaring, pulsing up through the floorboards, brushing against the edges of my senses. Rhea hears the silence. "Oh gods," she whispers. "Slade. She's reacting, isn't she?"

"Yes. She's reacting," I admit quietly.

Rhea swears under her breath. "Slade, this isn't just a Christmas curse. Or some holiday cycle. This is the entire wheel of the year. Every season. Every rite. Every ancestral thread that's tied to the original sisters."

My jaw tightens. This curse is bigger than her. Older than her. Hungrier than anything a mortal-born witch should ever have been asked to carry.

"What about Veda's disappearance?" I ask. "Any record?"

"Just fragments," Rhea says. "But one thing is clear... Veda didn't simply vanish. Something took her. Or she willingly went to something no one else would follow." She takes a shaky breath. "And Piper is the *first* Bellamy of our family to find her true mate."

The lights surge. A low hum vibrates through the apartment. Piper shifts behind the closed door—half-asleep, sensing the rise in magic.

I force my own power down. "You cannot tell her all of this at once," I say. "She's not ready."

Rhea scoffs. "She's more ready than any of us."

"No," I snap. "She's powerful, but she's untrained. And if Veda's darkness touched every sister's bloodline, then the thing Piper awakened last night is not just ancient—it's *adaptive*."

Rhea goes silent. Then, softer, "She needs you, Slade."

The words hit harder than they should. Because they're true. The bond knows it. I know it. And now Rhea knows it. "I won't let anything take her," I say.

Rhea exhales. "Good. Because the next part is worse."

"Rhea."

"Your ancestor's journals had an entry," she continues. "A prophecy fragment. It said the Bellamy witch who reawakens the line will be the one who—"

Static crackles across the line. Interference? Something magical, maybe? "Rhea," I say sharply. "Repeat that."

The noise grows—"...the witch who—" .... "...balance or break—" .... "...Veda's choice—" .... "...Slade, someone's trying to—"

The call cuts. I stare at the phone, fury sharpening through my chest. Something—or someone—doesn't want that prophecy spoken aloud.

The apartment door creaks open behind me. Piper stands there, sleepy, curls tousled, pendant glowing faintly against her throat. "What happened?" she whispers.

The curse hums. The bond pulls. And for the first time since she summoned me—I'm truly afraid of the thing waking inside her blood.

She feels it. The shift in the house, tension in the air, and the curse stirring like a creature rolling over in its sleep.

I don't soften my voice. I can't. "Rhea called," I say. "From Prague."

Her brow furrows. "Is she okay?"

"Yes." No. Not really.

"She found answers," I continue. "And we need to talk."

Piper crosses her arms, chin tilting in that stubborn angle I'm already half in love with. "Talk about what?"

"The curse."

Her breath catches, and I gesture toward the living room, toward the couch she likes to bury herself in when she's overwhelmed. She doesn't move. She's bracing herself. "I'm fine right here," she says.

Of course she is.

She wants walls. Distance. Time to prepare. But... There's no time for any of that.

"Piper," I begin carefully, "the curse... it didn't start with Veda alone. There were five sisters—"

She cuts me off with a sharp, incredulous laugh. "Five? As in... *more* than one crazy ancestor making bad decisions?"

"They weren't decisions," I correct. "They were rites, the old ones. Pagan, the ones bound to the wheel of the year."

"That makes absolutely no sense."

"It makes perfect sense," I say. "For an ancient curse. For a bloodline that keeps producing witches powerful enough to attract attention—human and otherwise."

Her jaw tightens. "What are you saying?"

"I'm saying this isn't *just* a Christmas curse, Piper. It never was."

She stares at me like I've kicked her chair out from under her.

"Rhea said the curse is tied to every major rite, every holiday our covens celebrate," I continue. "Lupercalia. Ostara. Solstice. Samhain. Yule. All of them."

She pales. "Meaning...?"

"Meaning your *entire* bloodline—every branch descended from those sisters—is bound. Not just you."

Piper takes a slow step back. "My whole family," she whispers. "All of them. All these years."

"Yes."

Her hands shake. She hides them in her sleeves. "And Veda?" she asks, voice tight. "What happened to her?"

"No one knows. But whatever she chose... it consumed her."

Piper closes her eyes, shoulders trembling once. "I can't do this," she says softly. "Not right now."

"You don't have a choice," I say. "We don't have a lot of time."

"*Great*," she snaps. "So I'm on some cosmic timer?"

"You are."

She glares at me. "Slade. You're supposed to lie in moments like this."

"I don't lie." Not to her.

Before she can argue, the front door unlocks—of its own accord. A swirl of frost-scented air sweeps through the apartment. And Rhea strides in. Hair wild from travel. Coat dusted with snow. Eyes sharp with knowledge she looks desperate to unload.

"How," Piper croaks, "are you already HERE?"

"Private portal," Rhea says simply. "I wasn't going to trust that call to finish." She sets her bags down and marches straight to us. "I heard the interference," she says to me. "Someone does NOT want this prophecy spoken out loud."

Piper swallows. "Prophecy?"

Rhea turns to her, expression fierce, almost protective. "You have until Christmas Eve."

Piper freezes. Completely. "Until Christmas Eve to what?" she whispers.

"To decide," Rhea says, voice low, "whether you accept the bond."

My entire body goes still. Rhea continues, undeterred. "If you accept Slade—if you let the bond click into place—it will break the curse."

Piper's lips part. No sound comes out. "And if I don't?" she finally manages.

Rhea's expression darkens. "Then the curse will move on," she says softly. "For another hundred years. Another cycle. Another generation of Bellamy witches."

Piper stares at her cousin like the world is tilting sideways. "You're telling me," she says slowly, "that I have three—three weeks—to decide if I'm going to mate myself to a demon lord to stop an ancient bloodline curse?"

"Technically two and a half," Rhea corrects.

Piper looks at me. And I feel the bond surge—raw, hot, too aware of her fear.

I take a step forward. "Piper," I say gently, "this isn't about forcing a bond. It's about protecting you. Your family. Your power. Your life."

Her eyes shine—not with tears, but fury. "Don't," she whispers. "Don't make it sound noble."

"It is."

"It's *convenient*," she snaps. "You show up in my living room, tell me I'm your mate, then surprise—if I don't agree by Christmas, I doom my family for another century."

"It's not convenient," I say. "It's cosmic alignment. Bloodline fate. A choice only *you* can make."

"And if I choose wrong?"

"You won't."

My certainty only makes her angrier.

She storms past both of us, pacing the living room like she wants to rip the walls apart. Rhea watches her carefully, then shoots me a sharp glare—like she's silently telling me not to make this worse. Finally Piper stops, breathing hard.

"So let me get this straight," she says. "I either let an ancient curse ruin *another* generation of Bellamy's... OR I give in to a fated bond I didn't ask for?" She looks between us, scrunching her nose in frustration when she realizes we're not contradicting her. "Some Christmas this turned out to be."

The curse hums through the apartment—sympathetic, agitated, alive.

And for the first time... I see the moment Piper fully grasps the weight of what she carries. The moment she realizes fate isn't something happening to her. It's something demanding... *from her*.

And the worst part?

She might choose to walk away from me to spare herself the burden.

The lights flicker. The damned amethyst at her throat glows. And the morning begins with one truth beating through my chest...

She will choose. And I will not survive it if she chooses wrong.

# CHAPTER 21

*Piper*

Two days.

That's how long I've been avoiding him—long enough that the air in the apartment feels stretched thin, as if even the walls are waiting for us to speak to each other again. I pretend it's because I'm busy with the shop, or because

I'm tired, or because the curse still hums through my blood like an unsettled dream. But the truth presses much closer to the surface. I don't know what to do with everything Slade told me. And everything Rhea added. Or everything I felt at the ball that I'm still trying very, very hard not to think about.

Newt is furious with me. Which is impressive, considering he's a twelve-pound cat. He sits perched on the arm of the couch—Slade's side—tail curled primly around his paws, eyes narrowed in a perfect imitation of parental disappointment. Every time I pass, he flicks his tail like he's pushing me toward the hallway where Slade has been staying.

"You're being dramatic," I mutter while bottling rosemary for the apothecary shelf.

Newt blinks with the slow, offended patience of an ancient god.

"I'm not apologizing." Another blink. "And you can stop trying to guilt trip me with the silent treatment."

Newt flicks his tail harder.

I sigh. "Fine. Maybe I should apologize."

He hops off the couch with a triumphant little chirp and trots down the hall toward the guest room—Slade's room—pausing once to glance back at me as if saying, *See? You know what to do.*

"Traitor," I mumble. But he has a point.

The apartment still smells faintly of cinnamon, lavender, and lingering magic from the Christmas-tree flare-up. Every charm feels like it's waiting to activate. Every candle flame leans toward whatever direction Slade happens to be in. The air thickens simply because he's in the same room as me.

And for the first time since I summoned him, he hasn't pushed. Not with words, or touch. And definitely not with that wicked patience that feels like a promise every time he looks at me.

He's quieter now—present, but giving me distance. It's the distance that hurts.

In the end I avoid it. Because that's what I do best when I'm stressed.

Instead, I try to focus on the small tasks in my apartment—the mundane ones I usually love. Refilling herb jars. Straightening my shelves. Rearranging the earrings on my dresser as if their placement matters more than the storm building behind my ribs.

But my attention keeps drifting to the long linen-wrapped parcel waiting on the kitchen island.

It arrived an hour ago, delivered by a courier witch who looked far too relieved to hand it off and disappear. The moment my fingers brushed the string-tied edge, I felt it—an old pulse beneath the wrapping. Not alive, but attentive. As though whatever rests inside has been listening through centuries of dust, waiting for someone with my blood to wake it.

The tag reads:

**FROM: Archivist Lyudmila, Prague.**

**FOR: Piper Bellamy.**

No note. No warning. Just the weight of something carved out of my family's past.

I haven't opened it. I'm not sure I'm ready to.

A subtle shift of air behind me tells me Slade is standing in the doorway long before he speaks. The room warms the way it always does when he enters, shadows stretching around him as though he's the gravitational center of even the light.

When I turn, snow melts along the shoulders of his coat. His hair is wind-tousled, eyes dark and steady, carrying that quiet heaviness I've been trying—and failing—to ignore.

"Not opening the shop today?" He asks, voice low and even.

"I didn't sleep well," I answer, shaking my head, and fussing with a jar that needs no fussing. "Or at all."

"That makes two of us."

It lands deeper than it should. He doesn't sleep—not in the human sense—but the way he says it makes my chest tighten.

"Slade..." My voice softens. "About the other night. I shouldn't have snapped at you."

"You reacted to fear," he says gently. "There's nothing to apologize for."

"But I hurt you."

His gaze shifts—steady, open, unexpectedly unguarded. Something inside me stumbles at the look. "Piper," he murmurs, "you didn't hurt me. You frightened yourself. And that unsettles me far more than anything you said."

My fingers curl against the counter, grounding myself in the familiar warmth of polished wood. "I wasn't frightened."

"You were." His tone is calm, not accusatory. "And there's nothing wrong with that. But ignoring it doesn't stop the curse from moving."

My eyes drift, almost of their own accord, to the parcel on the island. He follows the motion.

"What's inside it?" he asks quietly.

"I don't know. Rhea's contact sent it." My voice drops. "She said she'd found something connected to the curse."

Understanding flickers through him. He steps closer, slow and deliberate. "You're afraid to open it."

"I am not afraid." The lie rings clear the moment it leaves my mouth.

His expression softens—not pity, not triumph, just understanding. "You don't have to be ready," he says. "You only have to stop treating the truth like it's something waiting to hurt you. You're stronger than you think."

The words settle in my chest with a warmth that feels like both comfort and challenge.

I reach for the parcel. My hand hesitates, then brushes the linen. The fabric yields as if warmed by countless hands before mine. Something hums beneath it—soft, patient, aware.

"Piper," Slade warns quietly, "whatever is inside will recognize you. Your blood. Your magic. You won't be able to undo that."

"I know."

"Do you?" His voice deepens—not ancient, not fearful, just thoughtful. "Because this isn't Bellamy spellwork. It's older. Wilder. Whatever Veda reached for when she turned from my ancestor—this may be the first clue to what it actually was."

My breath cools in my lungs.

"Do you think she bound herself to something?"

"I think she reached for a force she didn't fully understand," he says. "Something outside the coven. Outside the realms. Something primal. And whatever it was... we won't know until we read what she left behind."

The word primal hangs between us like a distant storm.

I loosen the string and fold back the linen. Inside rests a journal—simple, cracked, softened by time. The moment my fingertips make contact, the faint pulse beneath the leather quickens in recognition.

Magic answers. Not violently—purposefully. The floorboards hum, candles brighten, and Newt lets out a startled sound from the bedroom as though jolted awake.

Slade steps closer, placing himself between me and whatever memory is rising from the past.

The journal warms beneath my palm, as though the centuries have been waiting for this exact moment. A presence stirs—not a voice, not words, but intent, brushing against my senses like the echo of a name.

Recognition moves through me in a slow, pulsing sweep.

*Bellamy.*

Not spoken, not heard—felt.

My breath stutters. I pull back instinctively, but Slade steadies me with a firm hand at my elbow. His voice is quiet, measured. "It's responding to your lineage."

I swallow hard. "Slade... what is this?"

He holds my gaze, thoughtful rather than fearful, the steadiness in him grounding the unsteadiness in me.

"We don't know yet," he says. "It could be a memory. A spell. A remnant of whatever pact Veda made. But it isn't demonic, and it isn't anything I've seen before."

A low hum rolls through the journal again, warm and patient, almost like acknowledgment.

Slade's expression shifts, the severity in it tempered by something gentler. "Whatever Veda offered herself to," he says, "we'll find out together."

The journal pulses once more beneath its wrap—soft, deliberate. And for the first time, I realize—the danger here isn't Slade. It isn't even the curse.

It's the story Veda left behind. And the truth waiting inside that journal has been reaching for me across five hundred years.

***

The journal—or what I thought was a journal—lies on the island between us, its leather cover warm beneath my fingertips. The pulse inside it has steadied, no longer a sharp summons but a deep, rhythmic insistence, like a heart that has waited far too long to be heard.

Slade stands beside me, close enough that I feel the heat of him along my arm, but he doesn't touch me. He's watching the grimoire with the kind of patient intensity that feels almost tender, something threaded between worry and restraint.

"It's not just a journal, is it?" I whisper.

"No," he agrees quietly. "It's her book of shadows."

The air thickens in response, as if the name alone shifts the atmosphere. A subtle weight presses against my skin, not threatening—simply present. A presence that has been trapped between pages long after its author vanished from the world.

I open the cover.

The grimoire opens easily beneath my hands, the leather soft with age, the pages sighing like they've been waiting to breathe again. There's no glow, no dramatic flare—only a warm thrum under my fingertips, a pulse that answers something in my blood.

Slade stands beside me, close but not touching, as though he knows I need room to take in whatever waits inside these pages.

The writing is elegant, dark, a script that curves with emotion and precision all at once. I expect a story. A diary. Maybe a warning.

What I find instead steals the breath from my lungs.

The page pulls me straight to Veda's most painful memory. She begins with the night everything changed—the night she believed would bind her to love and power forever. Christmas Eve. The old rites. The winter solstice still humming in her veins. That was the night Lucifer promised eternity. The night he told her she was his chosen, the one who would stand beside him as queen of every realm that touched shadow and dawn.

Slade stiffens when he sees Lucifer's name scrawled in her looping hand, but he stays silent.

I read on.

Veda had loved him. Not blindly—boldly. Fully. Enough to let him shape her magic into something sharper. Enough to share the power he offered her. Enough to accept his request when he asked for a child—a *son*—to anchor their union. She believed their bond was real. She believed he was her mate.

I feel my throat tighten. "She really thought he loved her."

Slade's jaw shifts, a dark, controlled movement. "Lucifer can make anyone believe anything he wants. It doesn't make it true."

Veda writes of the moment everything shattered. She bore him a daughter instead of a son. Instead of holding her, instead of claiming them both, Lucifer tore the bond apart without hesitation. Not gently. Not quietly. He rejected her daughter. Rejected her. And because their magic had intertwined, because she had opened herself so completely, the rejection ripped through her soul like a blade.

The pain of it nearly killed her.

Slade's voice softens behind me. "A broken bond like that... it would have felt like being torn out of herself."

I swallow hard, eyes blurring over the next lines.

Veda describes how she screamed. How the bond snapped like a star dying. How everything she had built, everything she had believed, collapsed beneath the weight of Lucifer's rejection.

And how she tried—desperately, recklessly—to use the very power he had given her against him.

Not a foreign force, or an unknown entity. His *power*.

She called upon the rites he taught her, the magic he'd anchored in her veins, the bond that still thrummed with the remnants of what they had shared. She reached for the shape of him inside her blood and tried to tear it out, to rip every part of him from her soul.

But she didn't strike him. The backlash struck *her*. Her sisters, their daughters—*everyone* tied to Bellamy blood.

Her grief twisted the magic wild, and it turned inward, snapping tight around the family line like a snare designed by heartbreak itself.

Slade exhales, the sound long and steady. "It wasn't Lucifer's curse. It was the consequence of trying to use his power to wound him."

I turn the page slowly, my fingers trembling. Even the parchment feels warm now, like it remembers the moment Veda wrote these words.

The next entry is frantic, the ink pressed too deep. Veda writes that she tried to sever the bond by sheer force, to cut out the magic he planted in her, to make him feel the devastation she felt. But Lucifer's power was older than she realized, tied to laws she didn't understand, and when she tried to shatter it, the magic recoiled.

Slade's voice lowers, almost a whisper. "This is the moment everything shifted."

"She was still bound to him," I murmur. "Even after he rejected her."

"Yes," Slade says, expression grave. "The power he gave her didn't vanish just because he broke the bond. She wielded magic that wasn't hers to control."

I swallow, eyes drifting to the next lines.

Veda writes that she begged the magic to take back what she had given. She begged it to punish him, to sever him as he severed her, to tear him from her the way he tore himself away. But Lucifer's magic didn't answer to her desire. It answered to its own laws.

"I don't think she understood the power she was using," I whisper. "Or the cost."

Slade nods, slow and grim. "Lucifer's magic obeys Lucifer's rules. She tried to weaponize a bond that was already broken. It couldn't strike him... so it struck everything connected to her instead."

The grimoire warms again beneath my hand—not ominous, but aware. As though it recognizes me. A Bellamy descendant finally reading the truth its pages have held for centuries.

My voice softens. "Slade... if this really started because she used his power..."

"Then we need to understand the bond she had with him," he finishes quietly. "Because whatever magic she shattered—it's still echoing through your line."

The grimoire pulses once beneath my touch. Warm... Patient... Intentional. And I know this is only the beginning of what Veda left behind.

The curse isn't just a wound. It's a history of love twisted into ruin. A story of a bond misused, broken, and turned inward until it swallowed generations.

And now?

It has finally opened its eyes for me.

# CHAPTER 22

*Slade*

The summons arrives the way all hell-summons do—burned into reality itself.

A thin ribbon of smoke unfurls near Piper's windowsill, coiling through the morning light. The scent hits first—silver, ash, and a faint sweetness that always clings to Lucifer's magic. The parchment materializes a heartbeat later, embossed with the Ninth Realm sigil, humming faintly as though it has its own pulse.

Piper freezes mid-step, eyes wide. I feel her magic contract, a startled inhale beneath her skin.

"Don't touch it," I say immediately.

She touches it anyway. The scroll warms under her fingers, then unravels itself with a dramatic flare I know Lucifer added purely to irritate me.

Her eyes flick back and forth as she reads. Her breath tightens. Her jaw sets.

I step closer. "What is it?"

She holds it out with two shaking fingers. "He knows, this letter confirms it," she whispers.

A rush of heat spikes low in my spine. "And?" I ask, realizing she isn't telling me everything.

"He wants me to come to the Ninth Realm," she says softly.

"To question you." My voice turns colder than winter steel. "About what you touched. And what you read."

Her gaze lifts toward mine—uncertain, but not afraid. I think she stopped being afraid of hell the moment she opened Veda's grimoire. I wish I could say the same.

"He can't hurt me, right?" she asks.

The truth rises like a blade I wish I didn't have to hold. "He won't," I say. Not that he can't. Because he absolutely can. But he won't, not while I fucking breathe. "Get your coat," I murmur. "We're going."

She hesitates only long enough to slip her boots on. Then, she stands, her curls spill down her back like dark fire as she pulls on her jacket.

I watch her. I always watch her, because I can't stand to miss a single second. And the curse watches me, pulling us closer every time she breathes.

We step into the hall, taking the back exit and descending down several flights of stairs to the basement entrance. I don't hesitate, hand waving as my magic calls to the Ninth Realm of Hell.

The portal opens with a low groan of stone and stars. The Ninth Realm presses in the moment we step through—warm, luminous, humming with the kind of magic mortals aren't built to feel all at once.

Lucifer waits for us at the foot of the obsidian bridge like he's been expecting a parade. Tall. Effortlessly regal. More starfire than man. His smile is an insult. "Slade Athalar," he says with that smooth, infuriating silk he's perfected over millennia. "And *little Bellamy*."

Piper bristles. "Don't call me that."

He ignores her entirely, eyes sliding to me. "She opened the grimoire."

I step in front of her without thought. "That is *none* of your concern."

He tilts his head, his burning with fury. "Everything involving Veda Bellamy is *my* concern."

Piper stiffens behind me. I feel it like a tremor through the bond—anger, grief, the lingering ache of a wound given to her bloodline five hundred years before she was born.

Lucifer smiles faintly, amused by the tension. "She has her ancestor's fire. Veda used to get that same look when she wanted to burn down the world."

That does it. Piper slides out from behind me, chin lifting with a fury that crackles like embers. "You would know," she snaps. "Since *you're* the one who broke her."

Lucifer goes utterly still. The entire bridge seems to hold its breath. I step forward, prepared to end this with violence if I have to. But he... *laughs*.

A low, indulgent sound. Feral at the edges. "Oh, little Bellamy," he says, leaning back with infuriating grace. "Veda wasn't broken. She was misguided. And I am not responsible for her choices."

Piper's voice trembles with rage. "You rejected her."

"She offered me a son," Lucifer replies, bored. "She gave me a daughter. The bond snapped because it was *meant* to snap."

Her eyes burn, the sconces flickering in response. "You *used* her."

"She *asked* to be used," he answers simply. "Power was the only thing she worshipped more than me."

I feel Piper's fury rise like a storm. Her magic flashes through the air, bright and sharp—wards sharpening around her, the pendant at her throat glowing like a star about to burst.

I step in close, voice low. "Piper. *Enough.*"

"*No,*" she hisses. "He destroyed her life. He *ruined* an entire bloodline. He—"

Lucifer raises a hand, stopping Piper in her tracks. She glows. The curse hums like a living thing, hot and alive beneath her skin. My own magic snarls in response, coiling protectively, furious at the pull radiating off her.

"Slade," she whispers, "why is he looking at me like that?"

Because he sees the bond tying itself between us—feels the curse responding to her anger. Because she's too much like Veda in all the ways that mattered—and none of the ways that would have saved her.

Lucifer steps closer. This time I don't let Piper slip past me. My arm snakes behind her, drawing her against my side, my aura flaring high and sharp.

"That's close enough," I warn.

Lucifer lifts a brow. "You shield her more fiercely than any mate I've ever seen."

"She doesn't belong to you," I say.

He grins. "She looks at me like she wants to stab me. Veda looked at me like that too."

Piper lunges, and I catch her around the waist, pulling her back against my chest. She shakes with fury. "Say her name again and I swear I will—"

"You will do *nothing*," Lucifer interrupts, voice soft and razor-sharp. "You came into *my* realm. You rifled through *my* archives. You stirred old magic. You owe *me* an explanation."

"You owe my *family* an apology."

Lucifer considers her for a moment—really looks at her. The curls. The stubborn chin. The curse coiled around her ribs like a serpent waiting to strike. "...No," he says finally. "I don't."

She lets out a breathless laugh of disbelief, anger spiking so hot the air warps. He steps back with a lazy shrug, dismissing us with a wave. "You may go."

I blink. "Just like that?"

"For now." His smile dips wicked. "But you will return."

Piper crosses her arms. "Why would I ever come back?"

"Because the next rite nears," Lucifer says. "Lupercalia. A delightful celebration of passion, blood, and bonding. I expect to see you both." His gaze drags over her slowly, insolently. "In *or* out of clothes."

Piper's magic detonates in a flare so brilliant the bridge lights up.

I snarl and take a step forward. "You don't speak to her like—"

Lucifer lifts a hand, amused. "Calm down, Athalar. I'm not inviting her to my bed. I'm inviting her to her birthright."

Her breath stutters. "My *what*?"

"You'll understand in time," he says. "But for now—*leave*."

Piper is shaking when I guide her back through the portal. Not from fear. From fury. From betrayal that isn't even hers—but burns through her blood as though it is.

When the portal seals behind us, she sags into my chest, breath trembling. I hold her, one arm banded around her waist, my magic wrapping her like a shield. "He's a bastard," she whispers.

"Yes," I murmur into her hair. "But he can't touch you."

She tilts her face up to mine. "He already has," she says softly. "He touched Veda. And that means he touched every one of us."

My jaw tightens. Because she's right.

And because I would burn every realm—hell included—before I let him do it again.

# CHAPTER 23

*Piper*

I've been pretending the world didn't tilt under my feet the moment I opened Veda's grimoire. It's been two days since I learned the curse wasn't some Bellamy mishap—it was heartbreak weaponized. Since Lucifer looked at me like history had found its favorite puppet again. And two days since I let Slade hold me while I shook apart.

I've avoided him since. Not because I'm angry—because I'm terrified of how safe I felt in his arms.

The apartment hasn't forgiven me for the avoidance. The lights flicker with attitude. Newt keeps knocking shit off counters like I personally hurt his feelings. And I swear the Christmas garland sighed dramatically this morning.

Slade has kept his distance, like he thinks he's done something wrong, which somehow makes everything worse. His silence presses against the room like a missing heartbeat.

I'm pacing the living room, hair flowing down my back, dressed in a purple sweater, a black corduroy skirt, dagger earrings brushing my neck, and my familiar amethyst pendant warm against my skin, trying to calm down after closing shop for the day. Nothing is working.

I've already put on my favorite Christmas slippers—Jack and Sally will *always* be superior—thinking the familiar soft and plush goodness would be the ticket.

I'm on my third turn about the room, when the air shifts—warm, shadow-sweet, unmistakably Slade—and I freeze.

He stands in the doorway, hands in his coat pockets, shoulders tense like he's bracing for impact.

"We need to talk," he says.

"I know." I fold my arms. "I'm just... not ready."

"Then we talk when you are." He turns slightly, giving me the option to step away.

Something in my chest twists. This—this gentle consideration—is exactly why I've been avoiding him.

Before I can reply, magic ripples across the room like someone dragging a hand through water.

Draven steps through the veil. Of course he does.

He doesn't knock—doesn't greet. He gives me a long once-over and clicks his tongue. "Bellamy, you look like you're deciding whether to adopt a puppy or commit a homicide. Honestly? Either works."

I blink, then scowl. "*Why* are you here?"

"To check your pulse," he says. "Slade's been sulking so hard the Ninth Realm developed a weather pattern."

Slade growls. "*Draven...*"

"What? I'm helping," he says with a fake pout.

He's not helping.

Before I can answer, the apartment door opens and Rhea breezes in wearing designer jeans, a cashmere sweater and a winter coat that probably costs more than my monthly rent. She holds two bottles of wine and something that smells like cinnamon and mischief.

She sees Draven, he sees her, then they stare. The air between them all but crackles with mutual disdain.

"Oh," Rhea says flatly. "The problem child."

Draven smirks. "Sunshine."

"Don't call me that."

"Then stop glowing when you're angry."

"I don't glow."

"You're glowing now."

And I know—with a certainty that terrifies me more than the curse—they're *next*. Not now. Not today. But eventually? Absolutely.

Rhea marches past him, setting the wine on my counter. "We're doing dinner. A distraction. You need one. He—" she flicks her chin at Slade "—needs one. And this one—" she glares at Draven "—needs supervision."

Slade's shoulders relax, only a fraction, but enough to cut through my guilt. He wants to stay.

He's giving me space only because he thinks it's what I need. My chest tightens. "Fine," I whisper. "Dinner."

His eyes soften in a way that makes my knees warm.

***

Slade cooks, and I swear it's because he's secretly a top chef.

The man who can tear open portals with a flick of his hand now stands barefoot in my kitchen, sleeves rolled to his forearms, sautéing garlic and basil for spaghetti like sin has its own culinary school.

The scent is intoxicating—warm, rich, threaded with heat and something darker underneath that is unmistakably him. If desire had a kitchen, this would be it.

Rhea has already made herself at home, leaning one hip against the counter as she uncorks the second bottle of wine with a flourish that suggests she's uncorked far more dangerous things in her life. "You realize," she says, eyeing the pot Slade is stirring, "that you're setting unrealistic expectations for mortal men everywhere."

Slade doesn't look up. "I'm *not* mortal."

Draven drags a chair out, flips it backward, and straddles it like he's starring in a demonic boy-band audition. "Oh please. Stop flirting with her through food. It's embarrassing."

Slade's reply is calm, elegant, and deadly. "You're only mad because you'd burn water."

"I can cook," Draven says indignantly.

"You can heat," Slade counters dryly.

"Heat *is* cooking," Draven says with mock shock.

Rhea snorts into her wine. "Heat is combustion, sweetheart. Cooking is chemistry."

Draven shoots her a look. "Are you implying I lack finesse?"

"I'm outright declaring it."

They glare at each other with enough friction to power a city grid. The room hums around them—my garland twitching, the ornaments chiming softly like little traitors delighted to witness whatever's happening between those two.

Newt curls at Slade's hip, tail flicking as though he's claimed the demon lord as his new favored scratching post. When Draven reaches for a piece of freshly grated cheese, Newt launches a paw swipe so aggressive it would have taken a finger if Draven hadn't yanked his hand back.

"Your familiar is broken," Draven mutters.

"He just has impeccable taste," Slade answers without missing a beat.

Something in my chest warms. The apartment itself seems to agree, because the lights brighten and dim in a soft pulse—like a pleased exhale.

Dinner ends up being ridiculous and perfect. The table is warm with candlelight. The spaghetti, of course, is sinful. Rhea tells a story about accidentally turning an ex-boyfriend's hair bright pink during an argument. Draven counters with a tale involving a stolen carriage, a banshee choir, and absolutely no shame.

Slade watches me more than he eats, every glance low and lingering, like he's memorizing the way I laugh. And I—I can't stop smiling. I forgot what that felt like.

The curse hums through the apartment, but nothing lashes or sparks. Instead, it feels almost... *indulgent*. As if it approves.

After dinner, Rhea slams her palms on the table. "We're playing Santa Shots."

Draven groans. "Why must mortals corrupt their own holidays?"

"Because we deserve it," she chirps. "Now, pick your damn cup."

She lines up shot glasses shaped like tiny Santa boots, each filled with a mix of peppermint schnapps and something suspiciously glittery.

The rules are simple. Draw a card. Do what it says. Or drink.

Mine says: **TELL THE TABLE WHO YOU'D KISS UNDER THE MISTLETOE.**

My pulse stutters, palms sweating, stomach churning as I flush from head to toe. Rhea grins like a wolf at me, and Draven lifts a brow. Slade tilts his head slightly, gaze never leaving mine.

"I'm drinking," I declare.

Rhea cackles. "*Coward.*"

Slade's smirk is infuriating. "Interesting choice."

I glare at him over the rim of my glass. "Drink if you think you're subtle."

He lifts his own cup without hesitation. "I'm very aware I'm not."

Rhea howls, Draven chokes, and Newt chirps like he's judging both of us. The next card goes to Draven.

It reads: **COMPLIMENT SOMEONE AT THE TABLE WITHOUT INSULTING THEM IN THE SAME BREATH.**

He stares at it like he's positively flabbergasted by the request. "I can't do that."

"You absolutely can," Rhea says.

"I physically can't!"

Slade gestures at the shot. "Drink."

Draven drinks.

Rhea's card says: **REVEAL YOUR HOLIDAY WISH.**

She doesn't hesitate. Her eyes flick to Draven for half a second—so quick I almost miss it—and then she downs the shot.

Draven splutters. "You can't just—what was that look?"

"What look?" she says sweetly. "You must be hallucinating."

"I saw it," he says sternly.

"No you didn't," Rhea smirks.

"Yes, I did," Draven counters with a frown.

"Oh, look at that—your ego grew three sizes. Very Grinch-core," Rhea says, giggling over her joke.

They bicker until Newt climbs onto Slade's shoulder and steals the attention back to himself by meowing loudly.

Eventually, we migrate to the couch with wine, movies queued up, and blankets that smell like cinnamon and old magic. Rhea claims the armchair. Draven takes the floor, muttering about mortal furniture. Slade sits next to me—close enough that our legs brush every time I shift.

We put on a Christmas movie. I have no idea which one. My awareness narrows to the warmth of his arm against mine, the steady rise and fall of his chest, the low rumble of his chuckle when I mock the acting. When I lean forward to grab my wine, his hand steadies my knee—not intentional, not seductive, just instinctive.

But the curse reacts anyway. The room brightens, ornaments sway, and the damned garland shivers like it's sighing happily. I feel it inside my ribs too—warm, alive, tugging gently toward him.

And Gods help me... I let myself lean into the moment.

For the first time in days, the weight in my chest loosens. The fear dulls. The world feels possible again. And I realize, with slow, inevitable clarity—I don't want to lose this.

Any of it.

Not the laughter. Not the chaos. Not the demon lord who cooks like seduction is a language.

I'm falling.

*Fast.*

And the only thing scarier than the curse in my blood is the way he's waking something in my heart.

# CHAPTER 24

*Slade*

The apartment is quiet without her.

Not empty—Piper has never left a room empty in her life—but quiet in a way that feels wrong. No soft humming while she brews potions. No clatter of jars. No gentle, restless buzz from her magic. No Newt yowling like the world revolves around him.

Just the hush of morning light sliding through the curtains and the faint scent of lavender clinging to the air from where she slept.

Three days until Christmas.

Three days until the deadline hanging over her head like a blade.

Three days until she must choose me—or walk away and let the curse devour another century of Bellamy women.

She left early, dressed in a soft winter sweater that clung in ways my hands have memorized, crescent-moon earrings catching the light, curls pinned back on one side so her throat was exposed just enough to tempt the darkest pieces of me. She kissed Newt goodbye, ignored how long she lingered looking at me, and walked out before she could talk herself into staying or I could talk her into never leaving again.

And now I stand in her kitchen, hands braced on the countertop, staring at the space she usually occupies like a man teetering on the edge of something sharp and inevitable.

Tonight, I'm done holding the line.

If she's going to decide, she deserves to do it with the whole truth in front of her—not just the curse, not the fear, not the weight of a five-century wound.

She deserves what the bond feels like when it is not twisted by grief. She deserves me without restraint, deserves pleasure so consuming it silences doubt and drowns hesitation.

Tonight, she will know exactly what it means to be mine.

The planning starts slowly. Then consumes me.

The first step? Atmosphere.

I move through the apartment with deliberate care, letting my magic rise in quiet ribbons of shadow and warmth. Candles light at a gesture—hundreds of them, soft gold and deep crimson, flickering like stars fallen into her home. Their glow settles gently, casting warmth on the walls, softening edges, turning the entire living room into something intimate and low-voiced.

Then the rose petals.

Human tradition, yes—but there is something deeply satisfying about the softness of them spilling in a path from the front door to her bedroom. A trail meant only for her eyes, her steps, her anticipation.

The scent of roses mixes with candlelight and the faint winter-cold air drifting through the cracked window. It smells like desire waiting to be touched.

In the bathroom, I draw a bath.

Warm water fills the tub in a slow, steady cascade, steam rising in curling tendrils. I infuse the water with enchanted salts—Bellamy-safe herbs woven with my power, crafted to soothe her magic, loosen tension in her limbs, and coax every last flicker of doubt into quiet submission.

The foam rises thick and velvety. The air smells of jasmine, bergamot, and heat. I imagine her sinking into it, sighing as the water kisses her skin.

Magic stirs low beneath my ribs. I continue.

Food comes next. A seduction in its own right.

I dice garlic, listening to the soft scrape of the knife against the board. The aroma blossoms instantly—warm, rich, honeyed with butter. Basil bruises beneath my fingers. Tomatoes simmer, while I grill the chicken. I choose a dish mortals have always equated with romance because they are not wrong. Cooking for someone is an act of devotion. Cooking with intention is an act of claim.

By the time the creamy cheese sauce thickens, the kitchen smells like promise.

Newt pads into the room, tail flicking, gaze narrowed in deep feline suspicion. He circles my feet once. Twice. Then bumps his head into my shin with a sound that clearly means, *if you screw this up, I will pee in your shoe.*

"I'm aware," I tell him.

He meows again, louder.

To avoid further criticism, I pull out the small collection of gifts I acquired for him earlier. A plush bed he will ignore. Toys he will pretend to disdain. Treats he will inhale. I set them near the tree, where several wrapped boxes already wait—some for Piper, some for her cousin, one questionable one for Draven.

Newt inspects his pile with grave importance, then sits directly on top of the softest blanket like he has just accepted the throne he deserves.

Only one thing remains unfinished.

The tree.

I step toward it, and the ornaments hum—responding to Piper's presence even without her here. I breathe out, letting my magic thread through the branches. Lights brighten gently, glowing like embers. Snowflake charms sway. A single glass star shifts into place at the top, catching the candlelight and spinning the reflection into soft halos around the living room.

When I step back, the room feels transformed. Warm. Sensual. Inviting. Like the inside of a heartbeat. Like a place where a choice could be made.

A soft pulse moves through the apartment—Bellamy magic responding to mine. The curse, sensing intention. Not flaring. Not resisting. Simply watching.

It knows something is coming. So do I.

I check the clock.

Piper will close her shop soon. She'll lock the door, pull her coat tight around her shoulders, tuck her curls behind one ear, and walk toward home with the exhaustion of the season weighing on her.

But tonight—tonight she'll open the door to warmth, to candlelight, to rose petals, to a bath drawn just for her, to food waiting on the table, to a demon lord ready to worship her without hesitation or restraint—and she'll understand exactly what choosing me would feel like.

Not a demand, or command. Not a bargain.

A truth. A promise. And if she lets me—if she steps into my hands willingly—the bond between us will not just hum.

It will ignite.

I glance at the window again, at the soft snow beginning to fall, at the faint glow of holiday lights outside, and I feel something dangerous unfurl in my chest. Something close to anticipation... desire... hope.

"Come home, Piper," I murmur to the empty room. "Let me show you what you've been running from."

Behind me, Newt hops into one of the gift bags and rustles around like a gremlin. I let him, because it's adorable and I'm tired of fighting him to stay out of them. It doesn't matter anyway.

Everything is ready.

And when she crosses that threshold... she will never doubt the bond again.

***

The lock clicks. It's a soft sound—barely a whisper of metal—but my entire body answers it like a command written into bone.

Newt perks up on his velvet blanket-throne, ears forward, tail curling. The candles flicker in the living room. Even the tree seems to pause, lights pulsing once in quiet anticipation.

Then the door opens, and Piper steps inside.

She doesn't notice me at first.

She just stands in the doorway, holding her tote bag, curls tossed by the winter wind, cheeks flushed from the cold. Her sweater is dusted with snowflakes that glitter under the warm candlelight, and her amethyst pendant glows faint-ly—reacting to the magic suspended in the room.

Her lips part. Slowly. Barely breathing.

She sees the rose petals first. Then the soft glow. Then the faint steam coming from the bathroom. Then the table—set for two. And the tree—haloed in gold.

Her eyes soften in a way that hits me like a blade slid between ribs. "Slade," she whispers, so quietly I almost miss it.

I step forward from the kitchen. Her gaze snaps to mine, pupils expanding in a single dizzying heartbeat.

"Welcome home," I murmur.

She doesn't move. She just stares at me, breath trembling, as though every carefully stacked defense she built this week is threatening to slide apart all at once. "What... what did you do?" she manages.

"Everything," I answer. And it is the truth.

Her fingers curl tighter around her tote strap. Piper's throat bobs. Her magic rushes to the edge of her skin—soft, warm, curious—brushing against me the way a candle tests the air before catching flame.

She takes one step toward me. Just one. But it's enough to make heat coil at the base of my spine.

"I made dinner," I say quietly. "A bath is drawn. And the rest..." I gesture around us. "The rest is simply because you deserved to come home to warmth instead of dread."

Her breath catches. "I—Slade, you didn't have to—"

"I wanted to."

The truth hangs between us, warm as the candlelight.

She looks at the rose petals leading to the bathroom, at the table set with soft linen and wine, at the ornaments swaying lazily on the tree as if held aloft by the hush settling over the room.

Then her gaze drifts back to me—slow, deliberate, burning.

"What is all this?" she asks.

"A seduction," I say simply. Her pulse jumps, I see it in her throat, and the way she darts her eyes. "But only if you want it."

The air thickens with longing—not frantic or wild, but deep and certain, like a tide drawing her toward me.

I extend a hand. She doesn't take it. Piper steps closer instead. Her sweater brushes my knuckles. Her breath warms my throat, her magic pressing against mine, shy but insistent.

She lifts a hand and touches my cheek, barely—just the edge of her fingertip, feather-light as a promise she's afraid to speak aloud.

The single point of contact makes my power roar through me so fiercely I clench my jaw to keep myself from dragging her into my arms.

Her voice is soft, but not uncertain. "Show me."

*Gods*, she will undo me.

I take her hand gently, letting my thumb trace the line of her palm.

"Dinner first," I whisper, because if I don't maintain some kind of order, I will take her against the nearest wall without hesitation.

She blushes, color blooming beneath her pale skin in a way that makes my control strain. "I can eat after," she murmurs.

"No," I say, stepping closer until I feel the warmth of her body against mine. "You're going to sit at that table, and I'm going to feed you, and then—when your guard is soft and your mind is quiet and you're drowning in how much I want you—*then* I'll take you."

Her breath shudders. "And if I want it now?" she whispers.

I inhale sharply, fighting every instinct urging me to claim her. "Then you'll wait," I say, voice dropping, "because I'm going to savor every moment of you—not rush through it."

Her eyes darken. "Slade..."

I press a gentle hand to her lower back and guide her toward the table. The rose petals crush softly beneath her boots. The candles respond to her presence—brightening, warming, leaning toward her as though reaching for their witch.

When she sits, her curls spill over her shoulders, her lips parted in a small, breathless shape that makes desire curl deep in my gut.

I pour red wine into her glass—she watches my hands. I sit the plate in front of her—she tracks the way my mouth moves. I go to take my seat, and her eyes greedily roam over my body.

The curse stirs, not in warning, but in something almost like approval.

I take a slow sip of wine, letting my gaze drift to her throat, her collarbone, the faint rise and fall of her chest. "Eat," I murmur.

Her fork trembles slightly when she lifts it. Every time she takes a bite, her eyes flick to mine, like she can feel how much I want to devour her instead. By the end of the meal, her cheeks are warm from wine, her defenses softened, her aura loose and glowing.

Newt hops onto her lap, curls into a ball, and purrs as if sealing my victory. She sets her fork down, breath unsteady. "What now?" she asks.

"Now," I say, rising from my chair and offering her my hand, "you let me take care of you."

She slides her fingers into mine. Newt hops off her lap, offended of course, but returns to his perch. The bond stirs—rich, heavy, thrumming like a heartbeat between ribs.

I lead her toward the bathroom.

The scent of jasmine and bergamot welcomes her, steam drifting lazily from the full tub, lilies floating on the surface, candles lining every edge of the room.

She sucks in a breath. "Slade..." Her voice breaks. Emotion—soft, aching, vulnerable—rushes through her aura like a tide.

I step close behind her, letting my fingers skim her waist, then her hip, gentle but certain. She shivers. "You deserve beauty," I murmur against her ear. "You deserve softness. And you deserve a night where nothing hurts."

Her head tips back slightly, exposing more of her throat. "And you?" she whispers.

"I deserve to worship the woman fate carved for me."

She trembles. I reach for the hem of her sweater, brushing my knuckles along the warm skin beneath—her breath shatters.

"Slade... I want this."

I take her chin gently, turning her face toward mine. "I know," I whisper, before I kiss her.

And this kiss—this one is not hungry or rushed or desperate.

It is slow. Deep. Certain. A kiss meant for a mate. A kiss meant for a woman I intend to kneel for as much as I intend to ravish.

Her fingers curl into my shirt—her body leaning into mine.

Her magic flares and melts and folds around me like a sigh. And as I lift her into my arms, carrying her toward the bath, one truth settles into place with absolute clarity...

Tonight, she won't run from the bond. Tonight, she'll feel exactly what it means. And when she chooses—she'll choose *me*.

# CHAPTER 25

*Piper*

Slade's mouth on mine feels like a slow unraveling—careful, deep, coaxing, as though he's learning every way I could possibly break and choosing instead to piece me together. His hands guide me with a steadiness that makes my pulse trip over itself.

When he lifts me, my breath catches. My arms wind around his neck on instinct, curls brushing his jaw, my pendant glowing faintly between us. He carries me with a certainty that shakes something loose inside my chest—something hopeful, and dangerous.

He sets me at the edge of the tub. Steam rises in soft coils. Candlelight glows against the water, petals drifting like tiny spells waiting for touch. I whisper, "Slade... what is all this?"

His gaze drags over me, slow and warm. "Something you deserve."

The words settle under my ribs like heat blooming. I reach out—fingers trembling despite myself—and brush them against his cheek. His breath stutters almost imperceptibly. "Show me," I murmur.

He takes my hand and lifts it to his lips, kissing the center of my palm with devastating gentleness.

Then he helps me undress—not rushed, not hesitant. Just deliberate. Learning. Mapping.

Worshipping every inch of skin revealed under candlelight.

When he lowers me into the bath, the water wraps around me like silk. The enchanted salts melt into my tense muscles, releasing a sigh I didn't realize I'd been holding for days.

Slade kneels beside the tub and rolls his sleeves to his forearms. It shouldn't be erotic, but gods—it is. His power hums, the room thickening with warmth and something darker, possessive but held carefully under the surface.

He dips his hand into the water and pours it over my shoulder. The heat trails down my collarbone. I shiver.

"Relax," he murmurs, thumb brushing the hollow beneath my throat. "You don't have to be anything here. Not brave. Not ready. Just you."

My voice wavers. "I didn't know I could feel this calm."

His fingers trace the line of my jaw. "You're safe."

The bond stirs beneath my skin—not violently, but like a heartbeat searching for another. The water ripples. The candles sway closer. Even my magic softens, reaching toward him.

I exhale shakily. "Slade... what is happening?"

He cups my cheek, leaning close enough that his breath warms my lips.

"We are."

I drag him into a kiss—not careful, not shy. A kiss that answers a question I never let myself ask. His hand slides into my hair, tilting my head, deepening the contact until the world dissolves around the heat of his mouth.

The bond surges—heat rushing across my skin, the air crackling, the ornaments chiming a soft, high note like bells in winter wind. He pulls back only far enough to breathe, his forehead against mine, lips brushing as he speaks. "If we take this further," he whispers, voice thick with strain, "the bond will snap further into place."

My heartbeat thrums like a drum beneath my ribs. "Then why stop?" I ask.

His eyes darken—not with refusal, but desire held painfully tight. "Because I don't want the bond to choose for you."

Something inside me softens—aching, warm, terrified. "Slade," I whisper, "I'm not running from you."

His breath shudders, and he kisses me again—deeper, slower, a promise pressed to my mouth.

Water sloshes softly as he braces a hand beside me, the other sliding along my jaw. My fingers move into his hair. His thumb grazes the swell of my breast beneath the water. A gasp slips from me, swallowed into his mouth.

The bond flares hot. Magic curls around his wrists like ribbon. He breaks the kiss with effort—real effort—breathing unevenly.

"Piper," he rasps, "I want you. Gods, I want you. But not because the curse pushes or the bond demands. I want your yes when you're clear. When you're steady. When you're choosing me, not a destiny handed to you."

My chest tightens, full and aching. "I'm not choosing destiny," I whisper. "I'm choosing *you*."

Something raw flickers in his eyes. Hope. Hunger. Devotion. He leans in, brushing his lips to mine once more—soft, reverent, almost breaking. "Then I'm not going anywhere," he murmurs.

And he stays—kneeling by the tub, kissing me slow, steady, worshipful—until the water cools and my skin hums with warmth that has nothing to do with magic.

Until there is no doubt left in me... I am falling. And the bond isn't the thing pulling me over the edge.

*Slade* is.

Steam curls around me as Slade lifts me from the bath, his hands sure, steady, possessive in a way that feels like worship disguised as restraint.

The towel is warm when he wraps it around me, but his hands are warmer—slow against my hips, guiding me back into the bedroom where candles flicker like they're bowing to him.

He doesn't rush—doesn't speak. He just watches me in that molten, hungry way that makes something inside me unspool completely.

When he reaches me, he takes his time unwrapping the towel from my body, letting it fall soundlessly to the floor. His gaze drags down the length of me like he's memorizing every inch, and his breath deepens—barely noticeable, except I'm watching him as closely as he's watching me.

"Come here," he murmurs, voice low, velvety, and threaded with something darker. Something inevitable.

He backs me toward the bed with unhurried steps, his fingers brushing up my sides as if he's checking that I haven't changed my mind—without actually asking. I don't pull away. My body knows exactly what it wants.

He sits on the edge of the mattress and pulls me forward by the hips, guiding me to stand between his knees.

Then his hands slide behind my thighs. And the shift in him is immediate. His voice drops, roughened by want. "Piper... I'm done waiting."

The words melt straight through me. Heat blooms across my skin. Every nerve stands awake.

Before I can answer, he leans in and kisses the inside of my thigh—slow, lingering, reverent. His fingers flex against my hips, urging me just a little closer.

Another kiss, higher. Another. Then his breath ghosts over the very place I'm aching.

I grip his shoulders automatically, my knees threatening to give out. "Yes, Gods, I want this." Slade groans—a low, broken sound like tasting me is the first relief he's had in centuries. And then he drags his tongue against my heat.

My breath hits the air in a sharp cry. I feel him smile against my skin, dark and pleased and utterly undone. "Slade—"

"Lie back," he murmurs without lifting his mouth. "Now."

The command threads through me like a spell, and I obey without thinking, sinking onto the bed as he pulls me to the edge, hands strong under my thighs.

Then he tastes me again. And again. Slow at first—deep, unhurried strokes that pull helpless sounds from my throat—then more insistent, more claiming, like he knows exactly how long he's wanted this and has no intention of pretending otherwise.

His grip tightens when my hips arch.

"Good," he breathes against me. "Don't hide from me. Let me feel you."

The dominance isn't sharp. It's velvet wrapped around steel. It makes me want to melt into him, to open for him, to offer more without being asked.

His tongue circles me, deeper this time, and my hands fly to the sheets, twisting. I'm shaking by the time he finally pulls back, his mouth wet, his pupils blown wide.

He wipes his thumb along his lower lip, tasting me there too. "Piper," he says quietly, intensely, "I've wanted that since the moment you summoned me."

He crawls over me, caging me in without touching me fully, his breath warm against my cheek.

"And now," he whispers, voice like dark silk sliding over my skin, "I'm going to give you what you've been wanting." He kisses me—slow, deep, tasting of me and hunger and the promise of what comes next. "And you're going to take it," he murmurs against my lips. "Every. Last. Bit."

The room tilts, my pulse stumbling under the weight of him. Slade finally lowers his full body over mine, his arms locking mine above my head into place.

He nudges me apart with his knees, leaning back, spreading my legs wider before seating himself at my entrance.

I whimper, reaching to touch him—only to receive a sharp smack to my thigh.

"Tsk, tsk. I haven't given you permission yet, little witch."

I snarl, and he grins, running his hands along my body, cupping my full breasts before teasing the nipples with feather-light flicks that make my breath stutter. I squirm beneath him, crying out when he pinches one, then smacks the other.

"Yes," he murmurs, satisfaction dripping from every word. "Let me hear you."

I lift my head, eyeing his dick—because I absolutely did hit the luck department with Slade. I bite my bottom lip, and he instantly tracks the movement like it's a spell cast just for him.

"Piper, be a good girl," he warns, taking his thumb and circling my clit once in a motion that steals my breath. His tone drops to something dark and dangerous. "Or I'll withhold your second orgasm."

I gasp as he slams into me, crying out in pleasure when he moves again—his hips finding a rhythm that has me seeing stars.

"Slade!" I cry out, arching my hips to meet his.

He growls, leaning over me, pumping harder, faster, securing my hands again above my head as if I might break apart without his hold. Slade leans down, kissing my neck, biting across my chest, claiming every inch, kissing me again until I'm breathless and filled with nothing but pleasure and need.

The pressure keeps building, the sensation growing too big—too much.

"Slade, I—"

"Come for me, Piper. I want all of the Ninth Realm to hear you become mine," Slade says, voice low, husky, and thick with desire.

I detonate, crying out his name over and over as my release takes me. The first orgasm was bliss, but *this*—this is something else entirely.

It still trembles through me, rolling in slow, powerful waves, when Slade groans—a sound pulled from somewhere raw inside him. His body tightens above mine, muscles straining as if holding himself back.

I drag my hands from his grip and cradle his face—finally touching him—and the moment my palms meet his skin, something shatters.

A pulse erupts between us. Soft at first. Then... blinding.

Heat unfurls from where our bodies join, a molten ribbon of magic threading through me like liquid light. Shadows curl up his spine, coiling around my hips, my ribs, sliding beneath my skin as though searching for a place to anchor.

Slade freezes, eyes widening—dark green irises glowing with an inner gold I've never seen before.

"Piper," he breathes, voice breaking, "the *bond*—"

It snaps further into place. Not like a chain, or a cage. Like a star collapsing inward and reforming around us—a fusion of heat, desire, recognition, and something older than either of our bloodlines.

His power surges, sweeping through me in a warm, shadow-soft tide. My own magic rises to meet it, bright and wild, flooding out of me in a flare of heat that prickles across my skin like embers waking after centuries of sleep.

The moment they touch—our powers don't collide.

They converge.

Shadow melts into light. Light sinks into shadow. A perfect, impossible symmetry.

I feel him. Not just his body, or his desire. His fear. His reverence. His aching, desperate hope that I'll choose him. His vow—silent but absolute—that he will burn the realms before he lets anything touch me.

The depth of it steals the air from my lungs.

"That's you," he whispers, forehead falling to mine as he thrusts again, slower now, deeper. "All of that—gods, Piper, that's you."

The pleasure swells again, threaded now with emotion so potent it makes my eyes sting. Every movement he makes sends another ripple of power through the bond, another strand weaving into place, tightening, anchoring.

His shadows curl around my wrists, gentle where they had once been firm. My magic flows into his chest with every breath. Our hearts sync—first by accident, then by instinct, then because the bond demands it.

His voice thickens. "I'm inside you everywhere."

And he is.

Inside my mind, my magic—my soul in a way that feels terrifying and holy.

I cling to him, legs tightening around his waist as he thrusts deeper, the bond tightening with every push, pulling us closer, closer, until I can't tell where my magic ends and his begins.

The world narrows to heat. To shadow. To the man above me who feels like home and inevitability.

The pressure builds again—a rising, spiraling pull that gathers at the center of my chest and between my thighs all at once. The bond flares—and I break. Pleasure tears through me like the sky splitting open, bright and consuming. I cry out, the sound echoing through both our bodies as Slade follows, groaning my name into my neck as he spills into me.

Magic explodes outward in a burst of gold and black. Candles flare. Lights hum. The air itself ripples, bowing to the force of what we've become.

Slade collapses onto me—not heavy, but holding me, grounding me as the last threads of pleasure ripple through the bond, locking into place like a final, perfect stitch.

His breath warms my shoulder. My heartbeat pulses against his chest. Our magics curl together like two flames choosing the same wick.

"Piper," he murmurs, voice hoarse, reverent. "You're *mine*."

I slide my fingers into his hair, tugging him close. "And you," I whisper, breath trembling with the truth of it, "are *absolutely* mine."

The bond settles between us like a constellation.

Alive... and *waiting*.

# CHAPTER 26

*Slade*

The first thing I feel is her. Her warmth curled against my chest. Her breath brushing the hollow of my throat. Her magic—now permanently braided with mine—thrumming in soft, molten pulses across my skin.

The second thing I feel is the bond. Alive. Settled. Purring through every nerve like satisfaction incarnate.

The third thing is a realization that hits me slowly. Then, like lightning. I *slept*. For the first time in over a century.

I open my eyes to find her still sleeping, lashes brushing her cheek, lips parted in a breath that ghosts warm across my collarbone. Her curls spill over my arm, soft and wild, as though the night remade her in its image.

I press a kiss to her temple—because I can. Because she's *mine* now. Because the simple act feels like worship.

She stirs, stretching like a cat before blinking up at me with sleep-heavy eyes that make something deep in my spine tighten. "Morning," she whispers, voice rough and sweet.

I brush my thumb along her lower lip. "Good morning, little witch."

"Did you… did you rest well?" She asks, unsure how to phrase the question.

"I slept," I say quietly, a sense of wonder filling me. "And I believe… It's because of *you*. And our bond."

Piper's eyes widen, understanding flooding her, and I feel it the moment she realizes the curse really is broken. Her cheeks warm, and the bond gives a pleased thrum—like it approves, like it wants more.

So do I.

The first kiss of the day begins soft, slow, almost reverent… and ends with her beneath me again, fingers gripping my shoulders as if she never intends to let go. Her legs wrap around me, and the moment our hips align, the bond sparks, bright and consuming.

I grind into her, languidly exploring her. She's sore from last night, I can feel it in every shift of her body, but it doesn't stop her from wanting. "Slade," she murmurs, pressing a kiss to my throat.

Her arms are wrapped around my neck, fingers threading through my hair, tugging gently as I claim her mouth with another deep kiss.

I pull back, breaking the kiss, and run a hand down her exposed chest. I love her perfectly fluffy stomach, those beautiful stretch marks and curves, all the way to the aching center between her legs. She's ready for me, soaking wet. "Such a good girl," I groan. She cries out when my fingers circle around her clit in three quick successions.

The sound is music to my ears, and I sink into her without another thought, thrusting with deep strokes that claim another growl from my throat.

Breakfast doesn't stand a chance.

We end up in the kitchen twenty minutes later, both flushed, breathless, Piper wrapped in my shirt like a lure designed by the gods themselves. I cook because she's smiling and watching me with warmth in her eyes she does not yet realize she's wearing.

Her knees brush mine under the table, her toes trace my calf. Piper's laughter spills bright into the room—and the bond hums like a second heartbeat.

After breakfast, we end up on the rug with Newt.

The cat immediately claims her lap, glaring at me as if I'm the interloper in my own conquest. Piper pets him with one hand and plays with my hair with the other, absentminded and warm, and the sensation drags a groan from my chest.

She tilts her head, amused. "You like that?"

"Like," I repeat, running my hand along her thigh. "Try 'unable to think straight.'"

Her laugh is silk and sunlight, and I kiss her before I can stop myself—hard, hungry, grateful.

The couch doesn't survive us.

She ends up straddling me, curls draping down like dark ribbons across my shoulders, her lips swollen, her breath shaking every time my hands slide beneath her shirt. The bond crackles between us, eager, pulsing, begging us to keep go-ing—so we do.

And I've never been more thankful for a fuck-ing shirt. I slide her underwear to the side, and Piper frantically works at my sweats. In seconds I'm inside her again, and Piper is riding me with an agonizing pace.

Slowly, deeply, until she's trembling and I'm groaning her name into her throat. She works her hips, and I nip at her neck, sliding a hand up to claim her throat. I give it a gentle squeeze, arcing my hips up to meet her thrusts, and she cries out when the orgasm hits. It doesn't take me long to follow.

Lunch happens sometime after. *Barely.* We eat on the floor with Newt curled smugly between us, purring like he invented intimacy.

The afternoon drifts around us in quiet con-tentment.

Piper curls against my side on the couch, tracing the lines of my chest with lazy fingers that make my thoughts scatter like sparks from fire. She plays with the hem of my shirt, and I play with her hair. Neither of us says much because we don't need to.

The bond fills all the empty spaces with warmth and truth and a kind of peace I didn't think existed for demons like me.

I kiss her again before dinner. And during dinner. And after dinner.

By the time I carry her to bed, she's breathless and flushed, laughing against my throat as if her heart never learned what fear felt like.

And when she slides her hands into my hair and pulls me down to her, whispering my name with the kind of want that makes my entire body bow toward her—I know with absolute certainty.

I could spend a thousand lifetimes like this. Touching her... Feeding her... Holding her... Loving her...

Over and over. As many times as she'll let me.

Because the bond is no longer a tether. It's a *promise*.

And I intend to honor every breath of it.

# CHAPTER 27

*Piper*

The shop smells like winter and possibility. Cinnamon bark simmering in the cauldron-shaped diffuser. Orange peel drying on the racks. Juniper sprigs tucked inside tiny glass bottles that catch the sunlight in jeweled flashes.

Two days before Christmas Eve, the place always hums with magic and human excitement in equal measure. Today, though? The air feels warmer. Softer. Threaded with something I recognize now without thinking—Slade's presence.

He moves through my shop like he was always meant to be part of it—setting out trays of enchanted soaps, straightening bundles of protective sachets, tying ribbons around herb packets using a skill that makes customers stare at his hands more than they should.

He doesn't seem to notice their stares. But I do. So does the bond—quiet but pleased, warm as a candle flame flickering between our ribs.

When the morning crowd thickens, he steps easily beside me, handing me bags, answering questions, lifting boxes, and murmuring calm instructions that make my pulse skip. We work in tandem, like a practiced duo instead of a witch and a demon lord learning how to be something together. Every time our hands brush, a subtle spark sweeps up my spine, warm and intimate, like the universe nudging us together just a little more.

By noon, the shop is full of familiar faces—locals who've been coming to *Bellamy's Hearth & Home* since my grandmother ran it.

Mrs. Hanley points openly at Slade as she leans across the counter. "And who is that tall drink of trouble?"

I flush. "He's... helping."

"Helping?" She squints at me over her glasses. "His helping looks a lot like hovering."

She waves her cane toward him. "You! Tall one!"

Slade turns with the patience of a saint—or a very determined predator. "Yes, ma'am?"

Mrs. Hanley studies him like a hawk assessing a shiny new offering. "Are you kind to our Piper?"

He opens his mouth, but I beat him to it.

"He is," I say quickly, unable to stop the smile that pulls at my lips.

The smile is what gives me away. Everyone sees it. Everyone reacts to the way I practically glow, coming alive from within.

Mrs. Hanley beams. "Good. Because we'll tear you limb from limb if you break her heart. Understand?"

Slade gives her a solemn nod. "Perfectly."

I swear the bond purrs at his seriousness.

The next customer—a college girl who's been buying anxiety charms for three years—gives Slade a long, appreciative once-over before turning to me. "Piper... is he your...?"

I feel my cheeks warm again. "Something like that."

Her grin could power a small city. "He's *gorgeous*. And he just scared off that creepy guy who always asks if you have sage 'for personal use.' You're living my dream life."

Slade overhears exactly none of this and exactly all of it, judging by the faint smirk tugging at his mouth as he organizes crystal grids like he was born doing it.

Through the afternoon, women come and go—mothers, grandmothers, teenagers, coven members, solitary witches—all giving Slade variations of the same warning:

"If you hurt her…"

"You better treat her right…"

"She deserves the moon, demon boy…"

Each time, he nods, replies politely, or simply stands a little closer behind me, presence protective but not oppressive.

He never once looks irritated. If anything, he looks… proud. My chest does strange, fizzy things about that.

Near closing time, the door jingles and Rhea sweeps in, smelling like peppermint lattes, snow, and trouble. Sweeping between customers with the confidence of someone who has hexed more than one person for standing in her way. "Okay, move," she announces, waving her hand in a grand arc. "I have news."

Slade stiffens beside me—just enough that I feel it in the bond—and I raise a brow.

Rhea wiggles her fingers at him. "Relax, Lord Broody. It's good news. The world isn't ending yet."

"That's debatable," Slade mutters.

I cross my arms. "What kind of news?"

"The *best* kind." Rhea plants her hands on her hips, grinning like the cat who stole Christmas. "The Bellamy Yule Ball is officially happening this year. On Christmas Eve because of course everyone had to be difficult, but it's no matter. OH! And you're both attending."

My heart leaps. "Really? Elle will be there?"

Slade looks confused. "Elle?"

"Maristelle," I explain. "Rhea's older sister."

"That's not my sister's name today," Rhea snaps. "Her name is Elle. Nobody calls her—" She glances around the shop and lowers her voice to a whisper. "—the *full* thing. It's basically a slur."

I laugh, and the sound bursts out of me too bright to stop. Slade turns sharply, eyes softening in that warm, hungry way that still makes me melt.

"Anyway," Rhea continues, pretending she isn't flustered, "Elle is flying in tomorrow, and she already asked if you're alive or if you've been eaten by possessed garland."

"Reasonable," Slade murmurs.

Rhea ignores him with expert precision and hops onto the counter like she owns the place. "Formal attire. Gold and evergreen theme. Try not to embarrass us."

Slade folds his arms. "I don't embarrass."

Rhea smirks. "I've met your brother."

Slade's eye twitches. "What does Draven have to do with anything?"

"Ohhh," I say, leaning in. "Draven's going to be there?"

Rhea freezes. Actually freezes. Neck, cheeks, tips of her ears—every inch turns sickly shade of red.

Slade glances at me like we've just uncovered an ancient secret. "Interesting."

Rhea points a threatening finger at him. "Shut it."

He tilts his head. "You're flushed."

"I am not flushed."

She is very flushed. I bite back a smile. "Was he invited?"

"He invites himself everywhere," Rhea snaps. "Like a very sexy fungal infection."

Slade's brows rise. "Sexy?"

Rhea's eyes go wide. "I mean—*no*—well—he's—*shut. up.*"

Slade leans closer to me, voice low. "She's adorable when she panics."

Rhea glares, amber eyes glowing like candle flames about to leap from their wicks. "I am not panicking. I simply refuse to acknowledge that demon-shaped problem until absolutely necessary."

"So he's coming," I say sweetly.

She groans like she's dying. "Yes. He grew out of 'too good for mortal gatherings' sometime around 1870 and now he attends everything. Including this."

Slade smothers a smirk. "Should I tell him you expect three dances?"

"Do it," she threatens, "and I *swear* I will hex your tailbone."

He opens his mouth—probably to ask if I want to place bets on the day she finally snaps and kisses Draven senseless—but I elbow him before he can instigate. Rhea smooths her hair back, eyes bright with that Bellamy mischief that always seems one wink away from trouble. "Formal attire," she reminds us, then shakes her head like she thought of a better idea. "Actually I'll send over something for you, Pipes. Something bold, dramatic... witchy!"

I raise a brow. "That's vague and unhelpful."

"It's perfect," she corrects, waving off my accuracy. "And Piper?"

"Yeah?"

Her expression softens in a way that hits unexpectedly deep. "You *belong* at this ball. You always have. You weren't just invited—you are *expected*. *Wanted*."

A small breath catches in my chest. Because it's true. Even after my parents' deaths, even after I drifted from gatherings I couldn't handle, even after the curse made holidays feel unpredictable and heavy—my family never closed its doors.

Rhea says it like a reminder, one I didn't know I needed.

Like a *welcome home*.

The shop seems to warm at her voice. Afternoon light settles along the shelves, turning the jars into stained-glass mosaics. The air smells like chamomile, clove, and something faintly sweet from the batch of enchanted wax melts curing near the register.

Slade finishes tying up an order and steps behind me, presence falling into place like it was always meant to be there. His aura brushes mine, subtle yet solid—a warm, steady tether. Rhea notices instantly, her grin blooming slow and victorious.

"Oh, that's adorable," she mutters. "You two are disgusting."

I elbow her lightly.

Slade pretends he didn't hear, though the corner of his mouth twitches.

"Aunt Lyra's going to weep when she sees you two walk in together," she says. "She's been *begging* the universe for a Bellamy Christmas miracle."

My cheeks heat, but Rhea's teasing isn't sharp—just affectionate, warm, threading through the hollow places grief used to live.

Slade shifts fractionally closer, his magic brushing my skin in a slow, quiet sweep. He doesn't touch me—not here, not in front of customers—but I feel him like a heartbeat beside my own.

Anchoring. Reassuring. *Mine.*

Rhea sees it—all of it. And her smile softens into something understanding and knowing.

I've already chosen him—*us*—the bond.

I just haven't made it officially... *official.* Not yet, not when so much still hangs over the coming days. But the decision thrums quietly between us, warm and steady as the magical thread pulling us together.

The shop glows in the last stretch of afternoon, dust motes drifting like tiny enchantments. Newt sprawls across a display of faux snow and refuses to move for anyone but Slade. Customers linger, laughing, whispering that they "approve of this one."

Rhea nudges me with her shoulder. "Elle is dying to see you," she says. "Don't make her wait."

My chest tightens—not with fear this time, but anticipation... belonging. A future that suddenly feels possible.

Slade steps close enough for his body heat to slip under my skin, and when my eyes meet his—dark, warm, full of unspoken devotion—I feel the truth settle deeper.

I'm ready. I've *been* ready. And this Yule ball... it isn't just a family tradition.

It's the night *everything* shifts.

And I can't wait.

# CHAPTER 28

*Slade*

Piper sleeps late the morning before the Yule Ball—curled around Newt, hair a dark river across her pillow, face soft in a way that makes something fierce and tender rise in my chest. I watch her breathe for a moment longer than I should, then slip out quietly before the bond tempts me to stay with her all day.

I need to think.

And more importantly—I need to plan.

By the time I make it outside, the winter air is sharp with frost and pine. Piper's neighborhood glitters beneath a thin veil of snow, as if the world itself is dressing up for tomorrow. I summon a small transport sigil and let it pull me toward the city center, hoping movement will quiet the restless pulse under my ribs.

It doesn't.

Because I'm nervous.

Not about the ball. No—I am nervous because tomorrow, I want to ask Piper Bellamy to marry me.

The thought alone is enough to make my steps falter. Me. Slade Athalar. Demon lord of the Ninth Realm. A creature carved from ancient fire and darker instincts. *Nervous.*

I've led armies. Broken curses. Faced horrors that would hollow a mortal mind.

And yet the idea of Piper looking at me with anything less than joy when I ask her—It tightens something under my ribs.

I reach for my phone and call Rhea.

She answers on the second ring with the force of a spell gone sideways. "Slade? Is Piper okay? Where are you? What did you—oh gods, did Draven break something?"

"Rhea," I say slowly, "I need your help."

There is a sharp inhale. A pause. And then—"Oh my gods," she breathes. "You're doing it tomorrow, aren't you?"

I close my eyes briefly. "Yes."

The shriek is loud enough to startle a flock of pigeons off a nearby lamppost.

"Oh THIS IS THE BEST DAY OF MY EN-TIRE LIFE—DRAVEN, GET OVER HERE NOW—SLAAAADE IS PROPOSING!"

"Rhea," I warn, not even bothering to ask what the hell Draven is doing with her.

"Nope," she chirps. "You're stuck with us now. Where are you?"

"I'm on my way to the shopping district," I groan, knowing damn good and well this is about to be a nightmare.

"Perfect! Be there in a second."

The line goes dead, and I instantly regret my life choices.

They arrive within minutes—Rhea in a coat made of emerald faux fur and unearned confidence. Draven in a black wool trench coat, expression somewhere between amused and resigned.

Draven folds his arms the moment he sees me. "Well, congratulations, little brother. Took you long enough."

"Draven," I mutter.

Rhea smacks his chest. "Be nice! He's trying to do something romantic!"

"Romantic?" Draven lifts a brow. "He's a demon lord. The last romantic thing he did was burn down a plane of existence because someone insulted his cat."

"That was *one* time," I say.

Rhea waves her hands dramatically. "*Focus*! We have jewelry to find. We're not getting Piper Bellamy a mediocre ring."

She marches toward the first boutique like a general leading troops.

Inside, it's warm and glittering—rows of enchanted jewelry humming quietly under the lights. The air smells like polished stone and dark magic, the kind used for warding wealth and protecting secrets. Rhea drags me from case to case, discarding dozens of rings with the efficiency of a woman who has extremely high standards.

Draven mostly stands behind me, hands shoved into his pockets, offering the occasional commentary like, "She'd never wear that... Too fragile.

Piper would snap that in a week...That one looks like something our mother would curse."

Finally, Rhea stops. Her breath catches, amber eyes widening a fraction. "There," she murmurs, pointing at a ring nestled in a velvet tray.

My chest tightens—it's perfect.

A deep, dark green stone—almost black until the light hits it just right—set between two black diamonds that glimmer like nightfall. The setting is elegant and wicked all at once. The band—blackened gold or some metallurgic equivalent used by witch artisans—spirals with subtle runes, old ones meant for protection, devotion, longevity.

"It's..." I struggle for the word. Too soft, too inadequate.

Draven supplies it. "Her."

Rhea looks at me, eyes shining. "This is the one, Slade. This is Piper."

I nod slowly, reverently.

"Yes," I say. "It is."

She claps once, giddy. "Good. Now let's get you a tux."

Rhea ushers us to the register, and the clerk supplies an old fashioned looking ring box that's set in deep emerald. It's exactly what I imagined for this ring. After a few moments of interaction, I've placed an order for a custom matching wedding band, and we're off and onto the next stop.

Shopping with Rhea amounts to being bossed around an upscale menswear boutique while Draven offers sarcastic color commentary.

Rhea rifles through fabrics and cuts like she was born in a runway show. "She's wearing deep evergreen velvet with gold accents," she informs the tailor. "Off-the-shoulder, sweetheart neckline, slit up the left—no, Slade, you cannot see it. You'll survive."

I try to look unimpressed, but the truth is—my heart gives a sharp, anticipatory kick at the thought of Piper in a gown like that. Curves, velvet, gold against her skin—

Rhea snaps her fingers. "Eyes up, demon. Let's get you something that won't clash."

She picks a black tux with a subtle evergreen sheen when the light hits it, paired with a dark satin tie and obsidian cufflinks etched with old sigils.

Draven nods, approving for once. "You'll match without looking like an ornament."

"Thank you, Draven," I say dryly.

"He means that as a compliment!" Rhea beams. "This is perfect."

I touch the ring box inside my pocket. *Tomorrow.*

Tomorrow at the Yule Ball, I will ask Piper Bellamy to be mine—not just by bond, but by vow, by name, by every realm that exists.

Rhea squeezes my arm. "She's going to say yes," she whispers. "She's already there without even realizing it."

I know. I feel it every time she looks at me like I'm something more than the monster she summoned. Every time her magic curls around mine with quiet trust. Every time her breath catches when I touch her.

The bond hums, deep and steady. My future rests in a small velvet box in my pocket. And for the first time in my long life, the unknown does not frighten me.

We leave the boutique in good spirits—Rhea humming like she's choreographing a wedding march already, Draven muttering about how sentimental mortals and their lovers make him feel old, and me... feeling something I haven't let myself feel in centuries.

Hope.

The box in my pocket feels heavier now, not with dread but with promise. A future wrapped in velvet and dark gold.

Before we part, I step back into the tailor's shop on the pretense of checking the tuxedo's final alterations. Rhea raises an eyebrow, but she lets me slip inside alone. The tailor bows low when he recognizes me.

"It will be ready by morning, my lord," he assures, smoothing the sleeve reverently. "Pressed, warded, and delivered to Miss Bellamy's residence."

"Perfect," I say. "And the enchantments?"

"All set. It will react to her magic as well as yours."

Good.

I need everything tomorrow to feel as if the realm itself is acknowledging my bond with Piper—even if she hasn't said the words out loud yet.

When I step back outside, Rhea eyes me knowingly. "You're nesting."

I scowl. "Demons do not nest."

Draven smirks. "You just checked your outfit three times in one hour."

"Because tomorrow is *important*," I say sharply.

"Oh, we know," Rhea sing-songs.

I ignore both of them and teleport home—well, our home now, though Piper doesn't quite realize it yet—and send her a message before I do anything else.

**SLADE:** *Running errands. Be back by evening. Don't lift anything heavy at the shop. And drink water.*

Three dots appear almost instantly.

**PIPER:** *You make it sound like I'm fragile.*

**SLADE:** *You are precious. That's worse.*

Her reply is a single heart emoji and a threat to send me a picture of Newt sitting in my tuxedo bag when it arrives at the apartment. I smile—actually smile—as I step into the Ninth Realm.

My estate sits at the edge of the Ninth, built across obsidian cliffs and waterfalls of molten light. Most beings think the Ninth Realm is fire and brimstone, but that is only what Lucifer shows outsiders. The truth is far older—lush, radiant, balanced by creation and destruction both.

And my home reflects that.

White stone veined in black gold. Balconies that overlook star-fed rivers. Windows framed in iron roses that bloom in moonlight. Rooms full of art and ancient scrolls and relics collected over lifetimes.

I've never cared for any of it. Never needed it. Or intended to share it.

But today?

I walk through each room imagining Piper in it.

Her laughter in the atrium. Her curls spilling across my pillows. Her magic weaving itself through the hallways like warm, wandering light. Her tiny, judgmental cat claiming the marble sun lounge as his throne.

The thought does something strange to my chest.

I make arrangements with my staff—wardens and housekeepers who manage the estate in my absence.

"Prepare the east wing," I tell them. "And the gardens. And refresh the wards around the balcony. Not defensive—harmonic."

They blink, then bow. "Yes, my lord."

"And put flowers in the master suite," I add before I can stop myself. "Something fragrant. She likes soft scents."

Rhea would call it adorable. Draven would call it pathetic. I call it... necessary.

If Piper says yes—if she allows the bond to settle into something that is not just magic but devotion—I want her to step into a home prepared for her. A realm that has been waiting for her. A future built with her in mind.

A place she can choose for herself.

I walk through the garden last.

Glowing vines twine up marble columns. White blossoms shaped like crescent moons open as I pass. The night sky here mirrors the mortal one but deeper, sharper, starfields layered upon starfields.

This is where I'll bring her someday.

To show her the realm she unknowingly runs through my blood every time she breathes my name.

And tomorrow... Tomorrow begins that path.

If the Yule Ball doesn't fall into chaos first.

I glance toward the horizon—a sweep of molten silver and aurora fire. A good omen, some would say. I reach for the ring box again, thumb brushing the velvet. "Yes," I murmur quietly into the warm Ninth Realm wind. "She'll say yes."

And for the first time in centuries, I let myself imagine a future.

A real one—with *her*.

# CHAPTER 29

*Piper*

The Yule Ball arrives wrapped in frost and gold.

I wake to the sound of soft tapping on my window—snowflakes catching in the early glow of morning, drifting down in slow spirals as if the whole world is holding its breath. Even my apartment feels different today, warmed by soft enchantments humming in the corners. The bond thrums quietly under my skin like a heartbeat that isn't mine alone.

Newt stretches at the end of the bed and gives me a look that's equal parts judgment and approval, as though he's finally accepted that I'm choosing Slade.

The dress arrives just after noon.

Rhea sends a text before it does—*Don't freak out. Seriously*—and she's right, because when I open the garment bag, the breath leaves my lungs in one long, stunned exhale.

Rhea oversaw every alteration. And now, seeing it finished, I understand her warning.

The gown is a deep evergreen velvet that looks nearly black until the light catches it. The sweetheart neckline curves gently upward, balanced by the off-the-shoulder sleeves that frame my collarbones. The bodice is fitted in a structured corset, hugging my waist and lifting my chest just enough to make me blush at my own reflection.

The mermaid skirt clings to every curve before flaring softly near the floor, a high slit on the left side revealing a tantalizing sweep of leg.

But the belt—that's what steals my breath.

A gold heirloom snowflake, wrought in a Bellamy filigree pattern no jeweler could replicate, inlaid with tiny diamonds that catch even the dullest light. It's delicate and ancient, the metal warm under my fingertips, humming with the protective magic my ancestors wove into every family piece.

There's a small note, pinned to the garment bag. *"For you, your mother used to wear it every Yule. Mom wanted you to have it. Try not to ruin your makeup, - R."*

I swallow thickly, admiring the belt before swatting away tears.

Getting ready feels weightier than usual. I shower, letting the warm water settle the nerves dancing beneath my skin. I curl my hair in soft spirals, pin one side back with a shimmering gold comb, and let the rest fall freely. I swap out my everyday jewelry for gold—thin layered necklaces, delicate hoops, a bracelet that sparkles like frost. My heels are gold as well, strappy and elegant.

Gold eyeshadow dusts across my lids. A soft shimmer brightens my cheeks, and my lips flush a warm rose. My perfume—amber, vanilla, and winter citrus—settles around me like a memory wrapped in warmth.

When I'm done, I stand in the mirror and almost don't recognize the woman looking back. Not because she looks different—but because she looks whole.

A soft knock at the door breaks the moment.

Slade waits on the other side, devastating in a black tux with an evergreen sheen, subtle runic embroidery catching each shift of light. His hair is sleek, his jaw clean-shaven, his shoulders impossibly broad.

But when his eyes land on me, everything inside him stills. "Piper," he breathes, voice touched with awe, "you are... *unforgettable*."

Heat blooms across my cheeks. "So are you."

His gaze roams slowly down the dress, lingering on the heirloom belt. Understanding softens his expression. "That belonged to your mother."

I nod. "Rhea found it in her collection. She said... Aunt Petunia wanted me to have it."

Slade steps closer, his voice dropping into something soft and reverent. "She would be proud."

The words hit deep—deeper than I expect.

He offers me his arm, and I take it, waiting for his magic to open the portal.

The portal to the Bellamy estate opens in a swirl of silver and evergreen light, carrying us into an expansive foyer strung with floating candles and garlands enchanted with frost. Warmth spills over everything—gold light reflecting in polished floors, hearthfires glowing green with witchfire, distant music drifting through arched doorways.

We step into the ballroom and my breath disappears entirely.

A canopy of starlight glitters across the ceiling. Green and gold ribbons float lazily overhead. Crystal centerpieces shimmer like winter constellations. The Bellamys—my loud, magical, chaotic family—move through the candlelight in a blur of velvet and warmth.

Aunt Lyra sees me first. Her gasp is theatrical enough to summon a breeze. "Piper Bellamy," she calls out, sweeping toward me in lace gloves and dramatic sleeves, "you look like Yule itself decided to take human form."

I laugh—a bright, genuine sound—and Slade glances at me like he wants to memorize every note.

Lyra hugs me tight, then pulls back to inspect Slade with narrowed eyes. "And this must be the infamous demon lord. You're taller than I imagined. Congratulations on surviving this long."

Slade chuckles, bowing his head slightly. "I'll take that as a compliment."

Before I can reply, Rhea bursts into view in a whirl of emerald silk, eyes alight with mischief and pride.

"You look perfect," she announces, grabbing my hands and giving me a once-over. "Elle is going to lose her mind."

"Where is she?" I ask.

"Being dramatic," Rhea sighs fondly. "You know. Existing."

Right on cue, Maristelle—Elle to everyone who wants to live—glides down the curved balcony stairs like she was born in moonlight.

Her gown is liquid gold, catching the light in long, fluid sweeps as she moves. Her hair—lighter brown than Rhea's, straight as a blade and glossy as polished bronze—is swept up into an intricate braided twist, tendrils pinned with tiny gold snowflake clips. Her amber eyes, a paler shade than her sister's, warm instantly when they land on me.

"Pipes!" she squeals, voice ringing through the ballroom like a bell. She rushes the last few steps, practically launching herself into my arms.

I laugh as she squeezes me tight enough to wrinkle the velvet. "You look incredible."

She pulls back, offering me a full once-over. "Oh please. I look like a festive Oscar statue. You—" she grabs my shoulders and shakes me lightly, "—look like Yule royalty. The belt? The dress? Piper Bellamy, you are going to slay tonight."

"Rhea oversaw the alterations," I admit.

Elle snorts. "Of course she did. She's been vibrating about it *all* day long."

Rhea, hovering dramatically behind us, flips her hair. "I have excellent taste, thank you."

Elle rolls her eyes in that perfect younger-sister way and then her attention shifts—sharply, curiously—to the demon standing solidly at my side.

Her gaze drags slowly up Slade, from the embroidered evergreen sheen of his tux to the crisp lines of his shoulders, to the way he holds himself like a fortress carved out of shadow. Her expression shifts. Approving. Calculating. A little dangerous. "And this," she says, voice velvet-edged, "must be *him*."

"It is," I say, biting back a smile.

Slade inclines his head with a quiet grace that still knots heat low in my belly. "Slade Athalar. A pleasure to finally meet you."

Elle's eyes narrow—not in suspicion, but in the kind of scrutiny only a Bellamy woman can pull off without blinking.

Then she smiles. Sharp. Beautiful. *Entirely* Bellamy. "Good," she says. "Because if you hurt her, I will turn you into a garden ornament. A tasteful one, but still."

Slade's mouth curves—just barely. "That seems to be a theme as of late."

Rhea chokes on her drink. "Elle, for gods' sake, he hasn't committed a crime."

"*Yet*," Elle mutters. "But I like to set expectations early."

I snort, and Slade rests his hand at the small of my back, thumb brushing warm circles through velvet—a grounding, steady touch that sends a shiver down my spine.

Elle notices. Of course she does.

"Oh saints, you two are disgusting already," she says, but her smile softens. "It suits you."

"The ballroom looks exquisite," I say, trying to change the subject.

Rhea sidles in, linking her arm with mine. "Elle helped oversee the decor this year. Don't encourage her ego too much."

"You mean my mastery?" Elle counters. "My artistic genius? My contribution to holiday magic?"

Rhea mutters, "Your relentless need to micromanage," under her breath.

Elle gasps, scandalized. "I do not micromanage."

"Elle, you rearranged the centerpieces six times," Rhea deadpans.

"They weren't speaking to the theme," Elle huffs. "Gold. Evergreen. Legacy. Family. I refuse to apologize for having vision."

The sisters bicker, warm and familiar, their back-and-forth settling around me like a quilt I didn't realize I'd been cold without.

New couples slip onto the dance floor. Candles drift overhead. A soft haze of gold magic hums along the walls. Every part of this estate breathes Bellamy history.

Elle turns back to me, expression suddenly softer, more earnest beneath the glamour. "It's good to have you *home* tonight, Pipes."

Emotion tightens in my throat, unexpected and sharp. "It's good to *be* home."

She squeezes my hand, just once, then whispers, "I'm so happy for you," before stepping aside to greet someone calling her name.

Slade's hand slides into mine.

The orchestra swells, violins threading through the air like ribbon. The ballroom glows with Yule warmth—family laughter, clinking glasses, enchanted garlands twinkling with frostlight.

And for a moment, just one shimmering breath of time, everything inside me settles.

The curse still coils beneath my skin. The choice still waits. Danger still hums like a distant storm.

But surrounded by Rhea's fierce loyalty, Elle's bright warmth, my family's chaotic love, and Slade's steady devotion—I feel something I haven't felt in a very long time.

Not fear, or even dread. Nor the weight of my family's legacy.

But... *belonging*.

Slade leans down, brushing a kiss to my temple, his breath warm against my skin. "Ready?" he murmurs.

I look around—the glowing room, the swirling magic, the people I've always loved—and then up at him.

"Yes," I whisper, heart steady.

Because for the first time, I know without hesitation...

I am exactly where I'm meant to be.

# CHAPTER 30

*Slade*

The Bellamy estate glows like it remembers what joy feels like.

Warm candlelight drifts through garlands of evergreen and gold ribbon, each strand humming faint pulses of old magic—Bellamy magic, familial and bright. Frostlight charms hang like suspended stars above the ballroom, casting shifting halos across velvet gowns and tailored suits.

And for the first time in centuries, I am surrounded by witches who are not afraid of me.

Not because they misunderstand what I am—oh, they know *exactly* what I am—but because tonight, I am *hers*. Piper's. And they see that as something worth celebrating.

My fingers brush her waist as we move through the crowd, her evergreen gown clinging lovingly to every curve. She glows under the lights. The gold snowflake belt at her waist catches every flicker of candlelight, throwing little sparks across the room like she's wearing a constellation.

"Are you enjoying yourself?" she murmurs, eyes bright.

More than she realizes.

"Yes," I say simply, because anything more would spill into poetry I'm not ready to embarrass myself with. "Your family is... overwhelming."

Piper laughs, the sound slipping down my spine like warm wine. "Oh, trust me, they're on their best behavior tonight."

Best behavior involves three different aunts trying to charm protective spells into my pocket, a group of cousins debating whether I shed, and Uncle Rowan loudly asking how many wings I can summon at full power.

So yes. *Best* behavior.

Music swells—a string ensemble swirling into a traditional Yule reel. Couples pull toward the dance floor. Others drift toward the hearth at the far end of the room, where the Yule log burns in a huge stone fireplace, flames tinted gold and green by Bellamy rites.

Piper squeezes my arm. "Want to join the reel?"

I look at the dancers spinning in intricate patterns designed for witches with precise footwork and impeccable balance.

"No," I say dryly.

She grins. "Coward."

"Accurate," I reply.

She rewards me with a soft kiss at the corner of my mouth that almost makes me reconsider humiliating myself in front of her entire lineage.

*Almost.*

Instead, we join Rhea and Elle near the dining tables, where platters of roasted chestnuts, spiced meats, glazed carrots, berry-wines, and Yule cakes fill the air with warm sweetness. Rhea's plate is stacked like a small hill. Elle's is an artfully arranged miniature painting. Piper collects a mix of both, because she is chaos wrapped in elegance.

We talk, eat and laugh merrily as the time goes by.

I watch her move through the room like she was always meant to be at the heart of it. I watch her mother's side of the family beam when she smiles. I watch magic circle her like a loyal, eager thing, humming softly as if it recognizes her strength now.

The bond between us pulses—not demanding, not forceful. Just present. Certain. Waiting.

I swallow against the weight of what I have in my pocket.

The ring rests against my chest beneath my jacket—a dark green stone caught between black diamonds, set in a band forged from hellforged obsidian alloy. A promise crafted by hand. By intention.

I plan to ask her during the Yule Blessing, after the log blessing is spoken and the spell of renewal is cast.

It will be perfect.

Until—"Attention!" a cheerful voice booms across the ballroom, amplified by magic.

Aunt Petunia.

Piper stiffens. Rhea mutters something unrepeatable about their mother. Elle looks like she's witnessing a train crash she can't stop.

Aunt Petunia stands at the front of the ballroom, cheeks rosy with wine, raising her glass high. "Everyone, gather round! I have wonderful news!"

The room hushes. I inhale, bracing for impact.

Petunia beams at us—the kind of smile only an overeager aunt can manage.

"I'd like to congratulate Piper," she announces grandly, "on finally finding a man who is tall, handsome, and not a complete disaster. And Slade"—she gestures broadly with the grace of a tipsy goddess—"we are delighted to welcome you into the family!"

The ballroom erupts in applause. Piper flushes scarlet. Rhea's eyes widen in horrified delight. Elle chokes on her wine.

And I... stand there with a ring in my pocket and every ounce of thunder stolen from me by a woman in sequins and sheer enthusiasm.

Petunia continues, unfazed. "Now, before we begin the Yule Blessing, I think it's only right that Piper say a few words about the person she—well—*clearly* loves."

The crowd murmurs with eager anticipation. Piper's hand tightens in mine. She looks up at me—not nervous, not overwhelmed.

Sure. Certain. Ready.

And something inside my chest loosens under the weight of her choice.

She takes a slow breath, steps forward, and the room quiets without a single spell.

"Thank you," she says, voice steady. "Truly." She looks over her family, her eyes softening. "This year has brought a lot I didn't expect," she continues. "Some difficult things. Some terrifying things. But it also brought me someone who stood by me even when I didn't know what I wanted. Someone who stayed. Someone who fought for me. Someone I—"

Her voice catches. She turns toward me fully, and the world narrows to just her. "Someone, I *choose*."

Heat thunders through my chest. The bond pulses—soft, then stronger, then burning bright and wild.

She steps toward me. "Slade," she whispers, "I accept the bond."

The rush hits us both at once.

Magic pulls taut between us—then surges, brilliant and unrestrained. Her power rises like a tide, luminous and warm, blooming against my shadows as if they've always belonged together.

A wind sweeps through the ballroom—not harsh, but cleansing—carrying the scent of pine and spellfire.

The curse *shatters*.

Not slowly. Not gently. But like a chain breaking under the force of her choice.

A soft gasp ripples through the room as golden sparks lift from Piper's skin, swirling upward like freed fireflies.

Her eyes glow. My chest burns. The bond seals with a final, perfect snap—an ancient lock finding its missing key. She exhales, swaying slightly, and I catch her before her knees give.

Around us, the Bellamy family bursts into joyous noise—cheers, laughter, applause, warm magic sweeping the room in waves of relief and celebration.

The curse is broken. She chose *me*. And I realize, holding her against me, that this—this exact moment—is the truest magic I've ever witnessed.

I lean down, brushing a kiss to her forehead. "Piper Bellamy," I whisper, "you've just rewritten the fate of your entire line."

Her smile wavers, soft and luminous. "We did it together."

Aunt Petunia dabs at her eyes dramatically. Rhea hoots. Elle fans herself like she's overheated.

The room returns to joy and celebration as the orchestra swells into a jubilant Yule hymn.

And I stand there, holding the woman who just broke a five-hundred-year-old curse with nothing more than her heart...

While the ring in my pocket burns quietly, patiently, waiting for the moment I will finally ask her to be mine forever.

***

The applause is still echoing in my ears when I take Piper's hand and guide her away from the center of the ballroom. She's glowing—literally glowing—her skin lit from within by the bond, by her choice, by the new magic settling into place inside her blood.

I can't breathe in this room anymore.

Not when every instinct in me screams to taste her gratitude on my tongue. To feel her in my arms without half the Bellamy family watching like happy vultures.

I lead her down a quiet corridor lit by floating candles, the noise of the ballroom fading into a warm, distant hum. Evergreen garlands wrap the banisters. The air smells like pine and winter berries. The enchantments woven into the walls hum with old magic.

Piper laughs breathlessly. "Slade—people are going to notice—"

"Let them," I murmur, pulling her gently but insistently until her back meets the wall. "You just broke a curse older than your bloodline. They can indulge me for five minutes."

Her breath catches when I step closer. The light from the candles glints off her skin, her gown, the gold snowflake belt around her waist. My fingers find her hips instinctively, fitting there like they've belonged there from the beginning.

"You're radiant," I whisper against her throat, brushing my lips along the place where her pulse flutters unevenly. "I felt every part of that bond settle. Every piece. Every breath you took."

She shivers—beautifully, uncontrollably. "You felt all of it?" she whispers.

"All," I murmur, trailing my mouth higher. "Every thought. Every doubt melting away when you chose me. Every ounce of your power rising to meet mine."

Her hands slide into my hair, tugging me closer, her lips brushing my jaw. "Slade..."

I tilt her chin up with a single finger, the gesture gentle despite the heat simmering under my skin.

"I need you to hear this," I say, voice rougher than I intend. "I need you to know it." Her eyes lift to mine—soft, shining, full of the trust she never had at the beginning. "I love you, Piper Bellamy."

The words settle between us like a vow. Not dramatic. Just certain. Steady. True.

Her breath trembles. "Slade...I—"

"I love you," I repeat, brushing my thumb over her lower lip. "Not because of the bond. Not because of fate. I love you because you walk into hell itself and dare it to blink. Because you face everything afraid and still choose to stand. Because you choose me—every time."

Her eyes brim with something I want to drown in. She pulls me down into a kiss—not desperate, not rushed. Slow. Intentional. Deep enough that the room spins around us.

Her fingers curl around the lapels of my jacket, pulling me closer until our bodies align perfectly. My hand glides along her thigh, up to the slit in her dress, brushing warm skin as her breath hitches.

I whisper against her mouth, "Five minutes isn't nearly enough."

She smiles against my lips, wicked and soft all at once. "Then take your time."

I do.

I kiss her like the night is ours alone, like the bond glowing under her skin is a living thing calling to every part of me. Her magic hums against mine, brushing, teasing, curling around my senses like warm silk.

My mouth finds her throat again. Her fingers tighten in my hair. The world narrows to us—heat, breath, magic—

"ARE YOU TWO SERIOUS RIGHT NOW?" Rhea's shrill voice cracks through the air like someone fired a spell into the wall.

Piper jolts. I drop my forehead to her shoulder and inhale very slowly to keep from vaporizing her cousin on instinct.

Rhea stomps down the corridor in heels that absolutely shouldn't allow her to storm in any capacity. Her gown swishes behind her like a furious comet.

"It is time for the Yule Closing," she huffs. "The elders are lighting the final candle, Mom is seconds away from telling the entire room how she delivered Piper as a baby, Elle is placing bets on whether Slade can blush, and *you two*—" She gestures at us with outrage. "—are making out behind the druidic blessing alcove like horny teenagers."

Piper covers her face with both hands. "Rhea—"

"Nope. No arguing." Rhea points at Piper. "You look perfect. Stop ruining your lipstick." Then she points at me. "You. Stop being six and a half feet of temptation. Now come on. They're waiting."

Piper snorts into her hands. I straighten my jacket, fighting the smirk threatening to break free. "You have impeccable timing."

Rhea glares. "I take pride in ruining emotional moments."

"Accomplished," I say dryly.

She flips her hair. "Thank you."

Piper threads her fingers through mine, cheeks flushed, eyes bright. When she looks up at me, the bond hums again—warm, settled, certain.

"You said five minutes," she murmurs teasingly.

"And you," I murmur back, brushing her knuckles with my thumb, "were worth every bit of getting caught."

Rhea groans dramatically. "Oh my GOD. Move."

Piper laughs, tugging me forward, and we walk back into the light and sound of the ballroom—hand in hand, magic settled between us like a promise.

The Yule closing waits. Everything ahead of us waits.

And for the first time in centuries, I'm looking forward to all of it.

# CHAPTER 31

*Piper*

Christmas morning in my apartment smells like cinnamon, cloves, and the faint sweetness of the spell-protected pine tree glowing in the corner. For once, the holiday doesn't feel like a loaded gun pointed at my head.

Slade is in the kitchen humming an old Ninth Realm winter song—quiet, low, a melody that curls along the edges of my skin like warm smoke. Newt sits on the counter beside him, acting as foreman, occasionally smacking Slade's hand away from the mixing bowl like he's afraid he'll ruin breakfast.

I'm dusting powdered sugar across the cinnamon rolls when—KNOCK KNOCK KNOCK!!!

"OPEN UP! IT'S CHRISTMAS, YOU HAG!" Rhea yells.

I unlock the door and she flies in wearing an emerald peacoat, amber eyes sparkling like she swallowed mischief for breakfast.

Elle appears behind her—in a red sweater dress, black leggings, and winter boots, her honey-brown hair straight and tucked behind her ear. Her lighter amber eyes brighten when she sees me.

"Pipes!" she squeals, hugging me tightly. "You look adorable."

"You look like a holiday goddess," I laugh.

Elle steps aside so someone behind her can enter.

A tall man with bronze-tousled hair and warm hazel eyes fills the doorway. He carries a tin wrapped in holly-patterned paper and smiles like he was born charming.

Before I can ask—another knock, smooth and deliberate.

Draven strolls in wearing a deep green coat and a scarf that looks like he bullied someone for it. Snow melts in his dark hair. His eyes flick to Rhea—and they both freeze.

She goes rigid. He goes still. The air tightens. Elle mutters behind her hand, but it's so low I miss it.

The hazel-eyed newcomer—steps forward with a grin and extends the tin toward me. "Draven said you might appreciate some homemade fudge," he says warmly. "I'm Caelan Athalar. Cousin to these two."

He gestures at Slade—who has just stepped into the room—and then at Draven, who nods in greeting before returning to staring at Rhea like she's become an unsolvable riddle.

I smile, taking the tin. "Thank you. Welcome."

Rhea finally finds her voice—sharp, brittle. "You didn't tell me you were bringing someone."

Draven shrugs. "You didn't ask."

Elle elbows her. "Be nice."

Caelan's grin widens, completely unbothered. Slade crosses the room, brushing a kiss against my temple, his presence curling protectively behind me. "Cousin," he says to Caelan. "You get dragged here willingly, or did Draven bribe you?"

"Bribed," Caelan says. "Five minutes of peace. I haven't seen him this tense in years."

Rhea scoffs loudly. "I'm sure he isn't *tense*."

"*You* are," Elle whispers.

Rhea shoots her a murderous look.

Everyone spills into the living room. Presents gather under the tree like a constellation of bright paper and ribbons. Cinnamon rolls warm the table. The entire apartment hums with magic—gentle, festive, almost content.

We settle on the couch and floor, exchanging gifts we'd bought for each other.

Slade unwraps a leather-bound cookbook from Elle—full of witch-approved, familiar recipes.

Draven gets enchanted socks from Rhea that warm themselves automatically. He pretends he hates them. He absolutely doesn't. Rhea unwraps a gold tarot pendant from Elle. Elle receives a starlight hair comb Rhea "totally didn't spend a fortune on." Caelan gets a charmed flask that refills with mulled wine from Draven. I open a delicate gold bracelet from Slade—its charm shaped like a crescent moon engraved with my initial. My throat tightens.

Elle is knee-deep in wrapping paper, humming off-key and wielding ribbon like a weapon, when she suddenly blurts at full volume, "Rheadora Aureline, hand me the scissors!"

The room freezes. Slade stills mid-stir. Caelan's fork stops halfway to his mouth. Newt lifts his head, ears twitching like he knows some serious shit has just went down.

I blink once. Twice.

Draven... Draven looks like someone just slapped him with destiny.

Rhea goes red from collarbone to scalp. "ELLE," she snarls, "I swear on *all* Bellamy secrets—"

Elle yelps, clapping her hands over her own mouth. "Oops! I panicked! The tape was stuck and—"

I'm already laughing. "I *always* forget your full name exists."

Rhea shoots me a look that could curdle milk. "It *doesn't* exist. We do not say it. We do not breathe it. We do not acknowledge its presence in mortal planes."

Draven murmurs the name under his breath like he's testing it on his tongue. "Rheadora..." Rhea freezes. He continues, slower this time. "Rheadora Aureline. That's—"

"Don't," she warns.

His lips curve. "Beautiful."

Rhea throws a bow at his head hard enough to qualify as a threat. "Choke."

Caelan cackles. "Oh, I like *her*."

Slade leans in close to me, voice warm against my ear. "Your family is... extraordinary."

"You mean chaotic," I whisper.

He kisses the corner of my jaw. "That too."

Dinner turns into exactly the kind of warm, loud, borderline-dysfunctional feast I always wished my childhood had included. Rhea complains about Elle's wrapping technique. Elle complains about Rhea's control issues. Caelan steals garlic knots off everyone's plates except Slade's. Draven and Rhea bicker so intensely it might actually be flirting. Newt sprawls in the middle of the table like he's the centerpiece.

The air smells like roasted herbs, melted butter, cinnamon sugar, and the faint spark of magic that always hangs around a Bellamy celebration.

At some point, Rhea nudges Slade and demands he "stop brooding and pass the cranberries." He does with surprising grace.

Draven tells a story about a demon noble who once accidentally cursed himself into speaking only compliments for a week. Rhea snorts wine out her nose. Caelan applauds like we're on Broadway.

Elle sighs dramatically. "Isn't this nice? A calm, peaceful Bellamy Christmas."

Rhea shoots her a look. "Don't say 'peaceful.' That's how you summon disaster."

Elle shrugs. "Too late. Pass the stuffing."

The laughter, the teasing, the clatter of forks and crystal—it all turns warm inside my chest, settling in places I didn't know were empty until now.

Slade brushes a hand along my thigh under the table. Not demanding. Not claiming. Just... there.

And in the soft glow of the tree lights, with my chosen family bickering around me, I realize tonight feels like a promise.

A future wrapped in warmth and wickedness and the kind of love that doesn't ask permission. A future where Slade Athalar fits beside me like he was built for that place all along.

And when he kisses my temple softly, reverently—I know I'm not wrong.

This is *home*.

***

The warmth of the apartment finally starts to feel heavy, the rich scent of dinner giving way to the faint smell of melting wax and pine needles. Draven, who has been locked in a low-volume, hostile-flirting discussion with Rhea about the merits of enchanted holiday lighting, finally stands up, stretching his intimidating height.

"Right. My work here is done," he announces to the room at large.

Rhea scowls. "What work? Being irritating?"

"Achieving peace," Draven counters, his dark eyes sparkling with something too close to satisfaction. "And delivering this one safely home." He gestures to Caelan, who is still eating a stolen garlic knot and laughing at Draven.

Caelan claps Draven on the shoulder. "Good luck with your brooding, cousin. Thanks for the wine, Piper."

Draven nods. "Thank you for the meal, Piper. Though I suspect you poisoned the gravy, it was surprisingly tasty."

"It's a Bellamy recipe," I say sweetly. "Only works on demons."

He gives me a half-smile that is actually genuine. Rhea stands up, dusting crumbs off her emerald coat. Elle scrambles over to her, grabbing her arm.

"Rhea, I am so sorry about the name!" Elle whispers frantically. "It just came out!"

"It better not come out again, or I'll curse your entire wardrobe to turn beige," Rhea snarls.

Elle laughs. "Got it."

Rhea turns to me. "I suppose I should go before I accidentally stab someone with a dessert fork."

Elle hugs me tightly. "Happy Christmas, Pipes!"

"You too, you beautiful bitch," I laugh, hugging her back. "Go enjoy the rest of the day. Get some rest."

"No setting the apartment on fire, Lord Athalar. I like this pine tree," Rhea instructs, her amber gaze flicking over Slade, sharp and assessing.

"I'll try to resist the urge," Slade drawls, his eyes locked on mine.

One by one, they file out. Draven, Caelan, then Elle, and finally Rhea, shutting the door with a deliberate click.

Silence descends, heavy and satisfying. Newt, relieved the chaos is over, simply sprawls out on the rug, a furry, orange sigh.

I turn to Slade, the peaceful, wicked smile I usually reserve just for him tugging at my lips. "Your family is utterly exhausting."

"Mine?" He tilts his head, his eyes deep as shadows in the dim light. "One of yours named me a brooding Christmas hazard."

I cross the room to him, running my hands up his chest, feeling the solid heat beneath his shirt. "She's not wrong. Now, come here, hazard."

Slade's hands immediately settle on my waist, pulling me flush against his hard body. The gentle spell of holiday contentment vanishes, replaced by the familiar, hot surge of desire that always flares between us—a delicious collision of witch and demon.

"I was humming a Ninth Realm love song earlier," he murmurs, his breath warm against my earlobe. "Did you catch the lyrics, little witch?"

"Something about frozen mountains and eternal damnation?" I tease, my fingers tangling in the dark hair at his nape, pulling him closer.

"Close. It was about stealing the sun and chaining it to my hearth, where it would shine only for me," he rumbles, his voice dropping to a seductive whisper.

He takes my mouth, and the kiss is demanding, erasing the lingering memory of the family noise. My hands trace the powerful lines of his back, finding the place where his tension always knots. I dig my fingers in, making him groan into my mouth. He sheds his coat and shirt, casting them to the floor without breaking contact.

He lifts me, setting me on the edge of the kitchen counter. The spiced warmth of the kitchen intensifies. Slade presses against me, his chest solid and hot, the hard muscles under my fingertips radiating pure demonic heat. His hands slide under my dress, smoothing over the bare skin of my thighs. My skin immediately prickles. I feel the magic thicken in the air around us, heavy and demanding.

He pulls my dress up and pushes my underwear aside, never breaking the deep connection of our lips. The cold marble of the counter is a sharp, welcome contrast to the burning heat he generates. He presses into me, a heavy, familiar confirmation of need, and I wrap my legs tightly around his waist, guiding him.

"You are the only chaos I want to control," Slade growls as he enters me with a deep thrust.

He's moving, fast and deep, a primal rhythm that makes the world outside the kitchen dim and meaningless. He pulls my head back, exposing my throat, and his mouth immediately clamps down, pulling hard, a furious, silent claim I welcome with a guttural sound. My nails drag down his back, fueling the intensity.

We're both breathing in harsh, ragged gasps, the frantic sounds muffled by the sheer force of our kiss. Every stroke is a furious, passionate statement, the only language either of us needs right now. Slade never stops, using the power of his hips to drive me toward a desperate, shuddering climax.

I'm lost, utterly consumed by the rhythm and the heat, when his body goes momentarily rigid. I've already climaxed, shaking against him, but he simply holds me tighter, staring deeply into my eyes. The air is thick with the scent of sex—him—*us*.

He lifts his head, pulling his hips back slowly, drawing a long, wet groan from my throat. He doesn't move far, just far enough to part my thighs and rest his hands on my knees. Then he lowers his head, the demon lord bowing to the witch.

The shock is immediate and absolute. His mouth is hot against my clit, skilled, and utterly relentless. He uses his tongue and lips with a dizzying intensity, tasting every part of me. I'm frantic, gripping his shoulders, completely undone by the sudden focus. It's too much, too fast, a furious current dragging me under again. I feel the raw, guttural need building immediately, eclipsing everything else. My hips buck, demanding more, demanding release. The magic in the room sparks like lightning, fueled by the sheer desperation of my second climax. It rips through me, blinding and shuddering, leaving me breathless and weak.

He pulls back, lifting his head, a dark, satisfied look on his face. He looks like sin.

I don't give him a chance to speak. I push him back against the counter, slide off the edge, and drop to my knees. The air is still smoking with our combined magic, but I want to take control. To show him the full extent of my own need. I push his pants all the way down, freeing him fully, and take him into my mouth, deep and worshipful. I use my lips and tongue, tasting the heat, focusing entirely on driving him to the same breathless, feral edge I just experienced. I push my hands up his chest, feeling the ragged beat of his heart under my fingers. I take my time, savoring the slow, building tension.

He groans, low and warning, pulling my head down—a possessive, dominant gesture that makes my core clench—and then he finishes, several strokes later, hot and heavy against the back of my throat.

We stay tangled on the floor for a long, silent moment, breathing in the aftermath, both slick with sweat and desire.

Slade finally pulls me to my feet, settling me back on the counter, his eyes heavy with possession. He starts buttoning his shirt slowly, deliberately, not looking at me—a sure sign that the intense, silent moment is over and the thinking has begun.

I seize the opening before heavier conversations can land between us. "Slade," I begin, smoothing my hands over my jeans like a nervous teenager, "do you remember the Yule Ball?"

His eyes flick to mine, curious, amused. "Hard to forget."

I swallow, heart thumping in that ridiculous way it does whenever I ask him for anything. "Well... Aunt Petunia is hosting something smaller. Just her, Rhea, Elle—and *us*. A little post-holiday gathering. I wanted to know if you'd go with me."

For a moment he simply watches me, and I can almost see the gears behind his eyes—ancient, strategic, forever calculating the next threat in the shadows. But then the tension shifts, melts, and something warm flickers in his expression.

He focuses entirely on me.

A slow, sinfully confident smile curls at the corner of his mouth. The kind that always sends a shiver down my spine.

"I will come, witch," he murmurs, lowering his head until his lips brush mine.

The kiss is quick but devastating—heat and promise rolled into one perfect stroke of his mouth. My breath stutters, my knees wobble, and my core tightens like my body is answering a question he hasn't even asked yet.

When he pulls back, he's still smiling that knowing, wicked smile. And... Suddenly, I have the unnerving sense that agreeing to this family gathering is only the beginning.

And whatever comes next, gods, do I want it.

# CHAPTER 32

*Piper*

My apartment is finally quiet. It's the day after Christmas, and the air still smells faintly of pine, cinnamon, and the lingering, dangerous magic Slade and I whipped up on the kitchen counter yesterday. The chaos is gone, leaving behind only the sticky sweetness of too much sugar and the deep, humming contentment of a battle well fought.

I'm curled up on the sofa, buried under the giant fleece blanket Elle gave me, wearing Slade's massive, soft Henley shirt that smells like pine and ancient leather. Newt, sensing the relaxed atmosphere, has decided my thigh is the optimal place to practice his kneading claws.

Slade is sprawled beside me, looking ridiculously comfortable and out of place all at once. His thick black hair is slightly mussed, and his piercing, dark green eyes are focused—or pretending to be—on the television screen. We're watching a marathon of classic holiday reruns. Right now, some fuzzy black-and-white scene is playing out, completely nonsensical but absolutely hilarious.

"I don't understand why the mortal male keeps trying to convince the child that the mythical beast is real," Slade murmurs, his voice a low, rough rumble.

"It's about belief, and... *consumerism*," I sigh, reaching up to run my fingers through the hair at his nape. My own hair, is a wild mess of curls. It's probably sticking straight up, but at this point... I don't care.

He leans into my touch, a purely instinctual response, and the sight of the demon lord melting over my petting never fails to make my stomach clench.

"Belief is a tool for manipulation," he counters, but he laces his fingers with mine, pressing my hand to his neck. "This is better."

Newt leaps onto Slade's chest and immediately begins batting at the corner of the blanket, clearly bored with the lack of demonic activity. Slade raises an eyebrow at the creature, a silent challenge passing between them, before he gently hooks his finger around the cat's collar and deposits him onto the floor.

"Go hunt a dust bunny," he instructs.

The flickering light from the screen casts shadows across Slade's face, highlighting the strong line of his jaw and the depth of those impossible green eyes. He shifts, pulling me closer until my hip is pressed tight against his hard thigh. The casual contact is anything but. The domestic calm cracks between us, like a dam about to burst.

He doesn't look away from the TV, but his thumb begins tracing slow, deliberate circles into the soft skin of my inner thigh, just beneath the hem of his shirt.

My breath hitches. I know this game. The waiting, that slow, intense build up that's always worth it a million times over.

"You're enjoying this film, aren't you, little witch?" he asks, his voice smooth and deceptively mild.

"No," I manage, my entire focus centering on the heat his touch is generating.

His hand stops, then his fingers curl slightly, finding the sensitive skin at my hip. He finally looks at me, his eyes suddenly depthless and focused entirely on possession. The soft light of the reruns on the TV makes the moment feel stolen and illicit.

"Tell me what you'd rather be doing," he challenges, his thumb pressing lightly into my flesh, demanding an answer.

I bite my lip, leaning into his ear, my voice thick. "I'd rather you remind me who I belong to, *Lord Athalar.*"

That's all the invitation he needs. The demon breaks containment, and I know it's over for me.

Slade rolls onto me, pinning me to the cushions. The sound of the TV vanishes, and all that's left is us.

He captures my mouth in a deep, consuming kiss, pushing me further into the yielding foam of the sofa. This isn't the loving kiss from yesterday. No, this is a demand, rough and immediate. I cling to his shoulders, feeling the power in his grip, the absolute authority of his body over mine.

He tears his mouth away, stripping the borrowed shirt from my body and tossing it somewhere behind the sofa. The air in the room is suddenly hot. His hands are everywhere, rough and practiced, reminding me exactly what it means to be claimed by something ancient and powerful.

He yanks my leggings down, disposing of them quickly, his eyes never leaving mine. I see the hunger there, the need to take and control. He is already hard, a perfect, wicked ridge against my stomach.

"I own this view, witch," he growls, his voice lower than a Ninth Realm threat. He braces his elbows on either side of my head, locking me in place.

I answer by bucking up against him, demanding release.

He smiles—a sharp, triumphant flash of white—and ignores my frantic movements. He runs a single finger down my folds, slow and agonizing, until he finds the wet, aching center of my need.

He doesn't use his fingers the way I might, gentle and seeking pleasure. He uses them to claim. His hand clamps down, firm and dominating, pressing harder against my clit.

"You won't rush me," he dictates. "You'll take exactly what I choose to give you, when I choose to give it. Nod for me, Piper. Show me you understand."

I nod immediately, a frantic little jerk of my head, entirely submitting to his will. The dominance heightens the raw, immediate pleasure to an unbearable pitch. I'm panting already, salivating at the thought of what he's about to do to me.

"*Good girl*," he murmurs. And the praise? The control? It's better than any foreplay.

He shifts, tearing open his own pants and kicking them aside. Then he's over me, his weight settling against mine, his dark green eyes burning with desire. He positions himself, pressing his thick, throbbing length against my pussy.

Slade doesn't hesitate. He drives into me with a single, powerful thrust that steals the air from my lungs and forces a silent scream from my throat. My hands instantly fly to his back, gripping him tightly, accepting the full depth of his authority.

He starts moving, the pace slow and brutal, designed to push me to the edge of sensory overload without letting me cross it. He watches my face, watching the pleasure—and the absolute surrender—flash in my eyes.

"Are you *mine*, Piper?" he demands, his voice a vibrating threat near my ear.

"Yes," I gasp, the word ripped from my chest.

He rewards me with a punishing, desperate series of thrusts, taking me higher and harder until the living room is filled with the sounds of our heavy breathing and the rhythmic creak of the old sofa. I reach my climax in a blinding, silent rush, clawing his shoulders as my body arches high off the cushions.

Slade follows immediately, groaning my name as he buries himself in a final, heavy plunge.

We lay there, utterly spent, breathing each other in. The sounds of the fuzzy reruns play softly in the background, a ridiculous soundtrack to the passionate wreckage we've made of the living room. Newt has returned, settling on the ottoman, observing the proceedings with judgmental curiosity.

Slade presses a gentle kiss to my temple, the dark green in his eyes softened by a deep, satisfied warmth.

He finally rolls off me, pulling me tight against his side under the blanket, the cool air hitting our damp skin.

"That," he says, his voice deep and rough, "is how you put Christmas to bed."

I giggle and snuggle closer, resting my cheek against Slade's chest, listening to the slow, deliberate rhythm of his breathing. The room smells faintly of spent magic, pine wreaths, and the faint ghost of cinnamon that clings to my skin. The credits roll across the TV in soft grayscale, but neither of us is paying attention anymore. My body feels boneless, warm, thoroughly worshipped, and entirely ruined in the best way.

Slade's fingers trace slow, lazy paths down my spine, the motions languid and assured. He kisses the top of my head, then my cheek, then the corner of my mouth, each kiss softer than the last—gentle, affectionate, almost unbearably intimate.

"Piper," he murmurs, his voice still carrying the lazy gravel of afterglow, "you're shivering. Are you cold?"

"I'm fine," I breathe, nuzzling into him. "Just... melted."

He chuckles quietly, a sound that rumbles through his chest like a warm tide. "You melt *beautifully*."

For a long, blissful moment, the world is nothing but his warmth and the faint jingle of the Christmas-themed commercial playing in the background.

Eventually, he brushes a damp curl away from my cheek and presses another soft kiss there.

"Get dressed," he murmurs.

I blink. "For what?"

"For air. For time that isn't limited to couches with questionable structural integrity." His smile curves wickedly. "And because if we stay here, I will not let you walk again tonight."

Heat pools low in my belly again, but he sits up and helps me sit too, wrapping the fleece blanket around my shoulders before I can protest. Newt gives a disapproving chirp, as if we're ruining his evening, then leaps onto the back of the sofa with a dramatic flick of his tail.

Slade stands, retrieving our strewn clothing with casual efficiency. When he hands me my leggings, he brushes a kiss against my knuckles—tender and reverent—before stepping back to pull on his own shirt.

"Come on," he says, offering his hand. "There's a place I want to take you."

I lace my fingers with his, still feeling the phantom of his touch everywhere he claimed me. We dress slowly, stealing kisses between buttons, the quiet kind that taste like promises rather than hunger.

Ten minutes later, we step out into the crisp winter air, the snow still fresh from the afternoon flurries. The street glows with soft holiday lights—warm gold, red, and evergreen, twinkling along rooftops and lampposts. Slade slips an arm around my waist, pulling me snug against his side as he guides me down the sidewalk.

"Where are we going?" I ask, leaning into his warmth.

"To dinner," he answers. "Somewhere quiet. Somewhere I can watch you glow without interruption."

"I'm *not* glowing."

He stops walking. The streetlamp above us casts a halo over the snow. He tilts my chin up with a single finger, his eyes drifting slowly over my face, my lips, the faint flush still coloring my neck.

"You're radiant," he says softly. "You always are. But tonight... it's *different*."

I open my mouth to argue, and... instead, I choose to feel the words in my chest, hot and aching. I tuck myself into him, letting him lead us through the soft winter evening, past frozen storefronts and twinkling trees. The world feels gentle for once—like the universe is exhaling with us.

We arrive at a tiny Chinese restaurant tucked between two older brick buildings, the kind with red lanterns in the window and a hand-painted sign that flickers between OPEN and OPN because the light's been dying since 1998. Warm air rushes out as soon as Slade opens the door, carrying the mouthwatering scent of ginger, garlic, sesame oil, and something fried and glorious.

Slade watches me step inside, but his gaze is already drifting toward the illuminated menu wall like a man approaching a holy relic.

"This is your guilty pleasure, isn't it?" I murmur.

His eyes darken in a way that is both sheepish and unrepentant. "No one must *ever* know," he says solemnly, guiding me in with a hand at the small of my back. "I have a reputation to consider."

I grin at his foolishness.

We're seated in a corner booth—intimate, candle lit by a small electric tea lights shoved into a frosted glass holder that pretends it's fancier than it is. Slade sits beside me instead of across from me, thigh brushing mine, his arm draped behind me as if it belongs there permanently.

The warmth between us is quiet, content—like a soft exhale after too many days of tension.

The waiter arrives with chilled water and a basket of hot, crackling scallion pancakes. Slade tears one open with reverence, steam rising. He dips a piece into the soy-ginger sauce, then lifts it to my lips.

"You're spoiling me," I tease, accepting the bite.

"You *deserve* spoiling," he replies simply. "You deserve more than you know."

I choke back the sudden tears, smiling sweetly and divert the conversation to another topic.

We talk about nothing and everything. Newt's criminal tendencies. Elle's dramatic retelling of their childhood. Rhea's ironclad ability to hex people without technically hexing people. The Yule Ball and how my dress nearly made Slade combust.

He listens like each word I say is part of some ancient instruction manual meant only for him. He asks questions, and tucks each answer away like a treasure.

Dinner arrives—Spicy beef noodles for me, Mongolian chicken for him, and an order of crab rangoons that he absolutely did *not* share evenly. Dessert is sesame balls filled with molten red-bean sweetness, eaten between slow smiles and soft, teasing kisses.

By the time we step back out into the night, my heart feels full in a way that terrifies me and soothes me at the same time.

Snow drifts lazily through the air—soft, delicate flakes melting instantly on Slade's coat. He wraps his arm around me, pulling me flush against his side as we stroll home through the glowing street.

There's no rush.

No fear.

Just us—a witch wrapped in winter layers. And the demon lord who worships her quietly, fiercely, without apology.

As we walk, hand in hand under drifting flakes and twinkling lights, I feel it settle deep inside me.

This is magic too. Not the dangerous kind. Not the cursed kind. The gentle, quiet... *forever* kind.

A magic I didn't know I needed, and one I don't *ever* want to lose.

# CHAPTER 33

*Slade*

Normalcy feels strange.

Not unwelcome—just... *new*. A rhythm I've never known but instinctively fall into, as if the bond has carved a groove between our lives and I simply step into it each morning.

Three days after Yule, the world softens around us again.

Piper wakes tangled in my arms, warm and bright against my chest. She presses a drowsy kiss to my jaw before slipping out of bed, hair a riot of black curls haloed in early light. She brews coffee, and I pretend I don't notice the obscene amount of sugar she adds. Newt claws at my ankles. She curses at her curling iron. I steal her toast at breakfast, and her laugh settles deep within my marrow. Ordinary. Perfect.

After breakfast, our day diverges. She heads to the shop bundled in scarves and determination, and I return to hell.

My estate is already lit with preparations, staff moving like rippling shadows beneath vaulted obsidian arches. The Ninth Realm hums with anticipation and curiosity. Every demon with a tongue is talking about the Yule Ball *or* the witch who shattered a five-hundred-year curse with a kiss and a vow.

I ignore the stares. The whispers. The smug grin on Draven's face when he asks how I'm "enjoying domestic life." I check in with the tailors, confirm the final touches on a few arrangements, inspect the wards around my estate—everything I can do to ensure the night I plan for her will be flawless.

But even here, even surrounded by my own power, my thoughts drift back to her. To the way she smiled when she saw the charmed snowglobe I left on her nightstand, how she whispered I'm yours like it was truth she'd been waiting centuries to say. And my favorite part? The way her magic curls around mine now—quiet, instinctive, content.

By the time I return to the mortal realm, dusk is settling in, painting the city in shades of gold and violet. Piper is in our living room, arranging bundles of crystal towers and cinnamon sticks for winter blessing kits.

She looks up, eyes brightening when she sees me, like light blooming behind her ribs. "Perfect timing," she says, sweeping over and kissing me once, soft but sure. "I *need* you."

Those three words ignite me even when she's not meaning them in the way I'd prefer.

"For what, little witch?" I murmur against her mouth.

She pulls back, rummaging through her tote until she finds her phone. "You, my *very* serious, very intimidating demon lord, are about to help me make social media content."

I blink, totally confused. "I'm sorry, *what*?"

She grins—wicked, brilliant, and completely ir-resistible. "You heard me. Promotional stuff. For the winter sale at my shop. Ya know... For fun."

"I don't... *do* social media," I grumble.

"You'll be great."

"I terrify mortals," I snort.

"You terrify *everyone*." She pats my cheek like I'm a reluctant puppy. "That's part of your charm."

Before I can protest, she drags me into the kitchen, where she's set up a little corner with holiday decorations: candles, faux snow, shiny baubles, and a tiny chalkboard that reads Slade's Spicy Spell Picks in glittering gold handwriting.

"I did *not* authorize that name," I say dryly, arching an eyebrow.

"I did. Now stand here," Piper huffs.

She positions me beside a display of herbs and crystals, fussing with my hair like I'm being prepped for a magazine cover. Newt sits nearby, tail flicking, already judging us both.

"Okay," she says, stepping back. "Look... *powerful*. But approachable-powerful. *Not* I will drag your soul into the void powerful."

"That's... *literally* my only setting."

She snorts and hits record, and we end up filming three videos.

The first is a simple product promo—except Piper keeps accidentally brushing my arm, and each time the bond flares warm and bright, and she blushes so hard the camera picks it up.

The second is supposed to be a tutorial, but Newt leaps into frame, steals a cinnamon stick, and Slade Athalar, Lord of the Ninth, ends up chasing him down the hall while Piper cackles.

The third is a trending audio that Piper insists I participate in—something about "my hotter-than-hell boyfriend doing witchy things." She tries not to grin. She fails abysmally. I stand behind her and wrap my arms around her waist for the final shot, burying my face in her neck.

Her laugh in that moment is soft, breathless, joy distilled to sound.

We spend the next hour editing the clips on her phone, Piper perched in my lap, humming absently every time she cuts a frame or adds glitter text. She shows me the final videos, pride glowing in her eyes.

"See? Perfect," she says.

I kiss her temple. "If you say so."

She turns, cupping my cheek, expression softening into something quieter. "Thank you."

"For what?"

"For being here," she says simply. "For fitting into my life like you've always belonged here."

The bond thrums deep in my chest—warm, steady, anchored. I tuck her against me, nuzzling into her curls. "I do belong here, Piper. With you. Wherever you are."

She exhales shakily, leaning into me, letting the truth settle between us like a vow neither of us needs to speak aloud.

Later, we cook dinner together—her chopping vegetables while I stir the pan, our bodies brushing, bumping, orbiting in a dance that feels instinctual, familiar, effortless. She steals a taste from the spoon; I steal a kiss from her fingers. The apartment smells like ginger, garlic, and sage.

When we finally sit down to eat, Piper tucks her knee against mine beneath the table and smiles at me like I'm one of the only things her heart has room for.

And I realize—this is what eternity is supposed to feel like.

Not fire, or war. Not loneliness, but this. Softness, warmth... *home.*

And as Piper rambles cheerfully about tomorrow's plans, I watch her. Heart full to the edge, knowing one truth with terrifying clarity... I would burn every realm to keep this.

To keep her—keep us. *Forever.*

# CHAPTER 34

*Piper*

I should recognize the look on Slade's face the second he steps into the shop—quietly smug, deliberately composed, carrying that slow-burning anticipation that usually means my night is about to get interesting.

Instead of pouncing or issuing some sinful command, he simply leans a hip against the counter, arms crossed, eyes glinting with intent. "Close early," he says, voice smooth as warm dusk. "We can even dress up. I'm taking you out."

I blink at him, halfway through labeling a jar. "Out?"

A hint of a smile curves his mouth. "Dancing."

That single word sends a spark straight through me. Slade doesn't do crowds. He doesn't do thumping music, mortal nightlife, or even strangers at Lucifer's Ball breathing near me.

"You want to go dancing?" I ask slowly.

"I want to take you somewhere," he says, stepping close enough that the shadows lean toward him, "where the world is loud enough that you forget everything except me."

Well. That's that.

I lock the door, and we head straight home.

By the time I finish getting ready, the sun is gone and the apartment hums with quiet anticipation.

When I step out of the bathroom, smoothing down the shimmering black dress hugging every curve, Slade is waiting in the living room—lounging on the arm of the sofa like temptation sculpted itself and got comfortable.

His eyes drag over me in a slow, possessive sweep.

"Little witch," he says, voice deepening, "you're... devastating."

My pulse trips. Because he's not wrong—he looks lethal in his open-collar black button-down, sleeves rolled up over rune-marked forearms, the sharp line of his jaw begging to be kissed or bit.

"You clean up pretty damn well yourself," I say.

He steps forward, fingers brushing my waist—light, but enough to spark heat down my spine. "Come with me."

***

The place he chooses glows with enchanted neon—gold dust drifting in the air, music pulsing low and dark, weaving magic through the bass. The crowd is warm, the lights soft, the whole room thrumming with spell-infused energy.

Slade guides me through the bodies with a hand at the small of my back, protective even in the chaos.

He doesn't sit, doesn't offer a drink. No, Slade takes my hand, pulls me straight onto the dance floor, and it's like the world tilts.

The music is slow and heavy, almost sin-thick, designed to pull bodies flush. Slade draws me in with both hands—one curling at my hip, the other sliding along my back, each touch deliberate.

"Relax," he murmurs into my ear, lips brushing my skin. "Let me hold you."

I sink into him easily—*too* easily—our bodies finding rhythm like we've been dancing together for years. His thigh slips between mine, and my hands find his shoulders. The bond hums low and sweet, like it approves.

He watches me closely—every breath, every sway of my hips, every bite of my lip. His eyes dip to my mouth, then lower, then rise again with a hunger that coils heat low in my stomach. Slade turns me, my back against his chest, his hands guiding my hips with a slow, devastating precision.

"Careful," he murmurs, voice all velvet and warning. "Move like that again and I'll take you home before the next verse."

"Maybe I *want* you to," I whisper.

His fingers tighten, just enough to make my knees soften.

"We're not done here," he breathes, turning me to face him again. "Not yet."

We keep dancing, bodies sliding into each other with heat and promise. His thumb strokes slow circles against my side, and my pulse stumbles every time he pulls me closer. The magic in the room thickens—cinnamon, smoke, warmth—wrapping around us like a spell.

I don't know how long we dance like that, the two of us grinding against each other with careful precision. It's only when Slade pulls me from the dance floor and toward the front door that I realize I've never felt this alive.

When we finally step outside, snow is falling again in slow and quiet little flakes. Slade wraps an arm around me, pulling me against him as we walk through the near-empty street. The world somehow feels warmer next to him—less dangerous, more possible.

The snow catches in my curls. Slade brushes a thumb across my cheek, everything about him soft, intense, and unbearably mine.

"Piper," he murmurs, voice rough with something deeper than desire. "Let's go home."

There's no hesitation. No fear. Just heat, certainty, and the bond humming between us.

I take his hand. And we walk the rest of the way home.

I don't release his hand until we're inside my apartment and the lock has clicked shut behind us. The air is cold from the snow outside, but the heat Slade generates is immediate and overwhelming.

I turn, ready to be kissed, ready to be taken, but he simply leans back against the closed door, his dark green eyes heavy with a patience that feels like a threat.

"That dance was a declaration," he states, his voice low. "Now, I take the payment."

He doesn't move. He waits. For me to cross the floor, for me to submit to the inevitable. The challenge hums in the air between us.

I walk to him, slow and deliberate, shedding my coat onto the floor as I go. My blue eyes don't leave his. When I reach him, I place my hands flat on his chest, feeling the steady, powerful thrum of his heart.

He still doesn't touch me, letting me feel the weight of my own desire, my own need to be dominated.

"Do you know what you're doing, Piper?" he asks, his fingers hooking lightly under my chin, forcing me to meet his gaze.

"I'm giving you control," I whisper, my voice catching.

"Good girl," he murmurs, and the praise is a coil tightening low in my belly.

This time, he kisses me like he's starving—a kiss of deep possession that sweeps away the cold and the noise and the magic of the nightclub. His hands finally settle on my waist, not to hold me, but to lift me, slamming me against the door with a controlled force that makes my teeth click.

I wrap my legs instantly around his waist. He pushes my skirt up, bunching the fabric at my hips, his fingers finding the edge of my silk underwear.

"Mine," he growls against my throat, the word a deep, guttural sound that vibrates through my bones.

He doesn't waste time. His fingers slide beneath the silk, slick and demanding, and the sudden, intense pressure sends a bolt of desire straight through me. I gasp, arching my back, pressing my mouth frantically to his jawline.

He releases my mouth and lowers his head, his teeth scraping lightly over the sensitive curve of my collarbone, establishing his claim with a lingering, biting intensity. His hand moves, finding the perfect, unrelenting rhythm to drive me wild.

"Look at me," he commands, pulling his face back just enough for me to see the darkness in his eyes. "Tell me what you need, little witch."

"You," I choke out, unable to form anything coherent. "Now."

He laughs—a low, dark sound of triumph. "Now is my command."

He frees himself, his length hot and heavy against my core. He positions me, making me feel every heavy inch of him, and then he drives home in one single, punishing thrust. My head falls back against the wood of the door, and the impact rattles my teeth, but the shock is immediately replaced by agonizing, beautiful pleasure.

He moves with a furious, controlled rhythm, pinning me against the door, my feet dangling, dependent entirely on his strength. He takes me high and hard, dominating the space between us. Dominating every action, demanding every single sound and tremor from my body. I clutch his black hair, pulling him closer, begging without words for him to speed up, to take me past the edge.

He stops abruptly, pulling back halfway, breathing hard.

"Say it," he orders, his voice raw.

"Please," I beg, frantically, my hips twitching.

"No," he shakes his head, watching the desperate plea in my blue eyes. "The other one's."

"*I'm yours*," I gasp, surrendering the final layer of my control.

"Good girl," he rewards me with a deep, shuddering thrust that steals my breath and sends me into a blinding, ecstatic climax, my voice lost to a silent, drawn-out scream.

He follows quickly, burying himself deep, his body going rigid, his demonic magic flooding me in a sweet, heavy wave. He holds me against the door, the only thing keeping us upright, and we hang there, spent and breathless in the aftermath.

Slowly, his grip softens. He lets my feet slide down the door, letting me rest against his chest. He kisses the top of my head, a gentle, possessive gesture.

"We need to get off this door," he murmurs, his tone returning to his normal, rough affection.

We stumble, toward the living room sofa, sinking onto the cushions, tangled and spent. Slade pulls the discarded throw blanket over us. He rests his cheek on my curly hair, his energy settling.

The room is warm in the soft glow of the Christmas lights we never bothered turning off. My breathing evens out, matching the steady rise and fall of his chest beneath my cheek. His arm wraps around me, firm and protective, like he's anchoring us both to this moment.

For a long time, neither of us speaks. We just breathe, tangled together, the quiet intimacy of the night settling around us like a second blanket.

Eventually, Slade exhales—a slow, deep release that brushes the top of my head.

"Piper." His voice is soft, low, rough from everything we just did. "Tomorrow... I want you to come with me."

I blink up at him, still tucked into his side. "Where?"

"My estate," he says, brushing a thumb across my cheek with deliberate tenderness. "There are preparations I need to oversee. It's time you saw it. All of it."

A little spark flares low in my chest—excitement, anticipation, maybe even a nervous thrill.

His estate isn't just a place. It's his world. His history. His home.

"You're sure?" I ask, my voice quiet.

His eyes meet mine—steady, full of meaning he doesn't even try to hide.

"I want you there," he says simply. "Not as an obligation. Not because of what we've been through. I want you there because you're mine. And because I want you to see the place where I learned to be who I am."

My throat tightens. I lift a hand and stroke my fingers along his jaw, feeling the warmth beneath my fingertips.

"Okay," I whisper. "I'll go."

A slow, wicked smile curves his mouth—one that still somehow manages to be gentle. He lowers his head and kisses me softly, tender where the rest of the night was anything but.

"Good," he murmurs against my lips. "Then tomorrow, we begin something new."

I melt into him, letting his warmth sink deep beneath my skin. Newt hops onto the back of the couch, gives us a look so judgmental I swear Slade nearly laughs again, and flops down in dramatic resignation.

"He hates sharing me," I mutter.

"He hates sharing everything," Slade replies, running his thumb slowly down my arm. "Including the *air* we breathe."

I snort softly into his chest, and he presses another kiss into the top of my head. "Rest now," he murmurs, voice dipping back into that low, intimate timbre that always undoes me. "Tomorrow will be a long day."

I curl closer, my body fitting against his like it's the place I've always belonged. The room fades to a warm haze—the lights, the heat, the lingering scent of him on my skin—and my eyes drift shut.

Tomorrow, I'll step into his estate. His world. His life.

But tonight, wrapped in his arms on this sofa, with my curls tangled against his chest and his breath steady on my skin—I fall asleep knowing everything in front of us is ours now.

And for the first time in my life... I'm ready for whatever comes next.

# CHAPTER 35

*Slade*

Piper is a vision of soft winter warmth and quiet anticipation as she stands in the center of the apartment, fastening a gold crescent-moon comb into her curls. Her hair falls in dark, untamed spirals down her back, catching the light with every movement. She wears a deep forest-green dress, fuzzy socks, boots, a cozy cream sweater, and my coat draped over her shoulders because she insists it's warmer than hers.

She's wrong.

It's warm only because it's mine, and everything that touches her reacts.

Newt perches on the counter like a small, judgmental emperor. He knows something is happening, tail swishing in irritation. He's been fed. He's been brushed. He has no reason to complain.

He complains anyway.

Piper adjusts her bag, tucks a strand of curls behind her ear, then looks up at me with that blend of curiosity and nerves she tries so hard to hide. "So, this is it? I'm meeting... your world."

I cross to her slowly, savoring the sight of her effortlessly taking up space in what used to be my life's quiet corners. "You've already met most of it. Hell. My people. My brother. Lucifer." I pause, letting my thumb brush the side of her jaw. "Now you meet my home."

Her breath shivers across my finger.

"You don't have to be nervous," I murmur.

"Oh, I'm not nervous," she says. Then after a beat—"I'm nervous-adjacent."

A laugh escapes me before I can stop it. She beams at the sound, delighted and a little smug that she's the one who pulled it from me. Newt yowls like he's not the least little bit impressed by the joke.

Piper points at him. "He knows. He can sense a portal coming."

"He suspects he'll hate it," I confirm.

She snorts. "He hasn't even been through one yet."

Newt yowls—long, offended, absolutely certain of his impending doom. I scoop him up. He goes boneless in my arms like he's bracing for cosmic betrayal. Piper snorts behind her hand.

She steps closer and her hand slides into mine like it belongs there. "Okay. Let's go before he stages a coup."

Her trust hits me like a brand—hot, anchoring, absolute.

I raise my free hand and tear reality open.

The portal unfolds in shimmering layers of obsidian and pale gold, curling outward like a living thing. The air hums with familiar power, and she stiffens only for a moment before leaning subtly into my side.

"Stay close," I murmur.

"As if I'd ever let go."

I chuckle and guide her through. The realm shifts the second we cross. Gone is the apartment's cramped warmth and twinkling Christmas clutter. Here, winter is a different creature—vast, humming with old magic. Snow falls in lazy spirals, glittering like powdered starlight over the obsidian path that stretches toward the mansion.

Piper stops walking, breath catching.

The Athalar Estate rises ahead of us—massive towers of dark stone veined with glowing sigils, pulsing like the heartbeat of an ancient beast.

Lanterns carved into the shapes of serpents line the path, their flames bending toward her as if bowing.

Newt clings to my coat with his claws as if hanging on during the apocalypse.

Piper whispers, "Slade... this place looks like it stepped out of a myth."

"It did," I answer simply. "You're part of that myth now."

Her cheeks flush, and she squeezes my hand. The wards surge at her arrival—recognizing her bond to me, recognizing her as Lady Athalar, claiming her in ways she hasn't yet grasped.

The doors open before us, tall enough to dwarf giants, carved with constellations and ancient runes. Warm air spills out—sweet with incense, firewood, and the faint metallic scent of old magic.

Newt lifts his head, and sees the interior. Then, the *literal* throne I commissioned and picked up yesterday, placing it near the hearth—a velvet monstrosity in midnight-blue, adorned with tiny sigils for protection and comfort.

The cat howls in awe, then leaps out of my arms and sprints inside like he's been reincarnated as royalty.

Piper blinks. "Did you... make my cat a throne?"

"He is a prince of the Ninth by association," I say dryly. "It was overdue."

The joy that bursts across her face nearly brings me to my knees. Piper walks forward slowly, taking in everything—the vaulted ceilings painted with constellations that shift with real celestial movements, the sweeping golden staircases, the enormous windows overlooking forests lit with glowing flowers, the soft hum of magic that drifts like invisible snowfall.

"Slade... this is..." Her voice cracks softly. "It's beautiful."

"It's yours," I say. "All of it."

Her hand finds mine again, fingers intertwining on instinct.

"What do you want to see first?" I ask. "The library? The gardens? The upper levels? The forge?"

She grins. "Show me everything."

My chest tightens. My magic rises. The estate hums in recognition.

"Then we'll start with the heart," I tell her, guiding her deeper into the house. "And show you what it means to be Athalar."

Newt appears beside us with a regal strut, his tail arched like he owns the estate. Piper laughs—soft, delighted—and the estate brightens, every lantern rising half an inch. It's as if the realm itself is pleased by her joy.

And I realize this is the beginning—her first true step into my world, and my world is already reshaping itself around her.

I take her hand gently, threading our fingers together as I lead her from the library into the long, glass passage I only ever walk alone. Tonight, the torches burn warmer, casting molten ribbons along the stone and glass. Her reflection keeps pace beside mine—wild curls, flushed cheeks, lips parted in wonder.

"Where are we going?" she asks, her thumb brushing the back of my hand in gentle swirls.

"You've seen the halls. The library. Newt's throne. Now I want to show you something that's always been mine."

She lifts a brow. "Slade Athalar, if this is some weird demon lord metaphor—"

I smirk. "If I planned to seduce you with a metaphor, Piper, you wouldn't be standing up-right."

Her cheeks flush brighter, magic coiling lightly in the air. And the realm reacts—to *her*. My mate.

We step onto the balcony, the world opening before us.

The terrace stretches wide, its marble floor lit with silver-fire braziers. Far below, the Ninth Realm glows like an endless constellation—terraces carved from dark stone, ribbons of blue fire, swaying silver-leafed trees whispering in the night breeze. Above us, the twilight sky deepens, a wash of blue-black velvet punctured by pulsing, music-making stars.

Piper walks forward slowly, bracing her hands on the carved railing, her breath visible in the cool air. Her hair lifts in a soft breeze, curls haloing her like a celestial crown. "Slade," she breathes. "This doesn't look like Hell."

"This is the east side of the Ninth," I murmur. "The quarter of the old nobility, order, history, and... things we don't speak of lightly."

"And you rule this." She turns to me, eyes wide. "All of this? This is your home."

"Now ours," I say, my voice low. "Everything I have belongs to you."

Her breath stutters. The bond warms between us, steady and sure.

She looks back out at the view. "It feels alive."

"It is," I answer softly. "The stars especially."

She studies them—each pulsing, chiming sphere shifting like distant, blinking eyes.

"They respond to emotion," I explain. "To magic. To intention."

"And what do they hear from you now?" she asks quietly.

"Desire," I say.

The word tangles in the space between us. She doesn't withdraw, or tense. She steps closer.

Slowly, deliberately, she moves into my space until her back brushes my chest. I place a hand on her waist, fingers curving over the velvet-soft warmth of her body, guiding her gently against me. Her exhale shivers through the cold, and the air thickens around us. I bend my head, letting my lips graze the place where her neck meets her shoulder—a soft, reverent stroke of my mouth over her beating pulse. Her hands rise to the railing, tightening around the carved stone as if she needs grounding.

"That spot," I murmur against her skin, "is mine."

Her body arches imperceptibly, offering more. She tastes like winter and warmth. Like *home*. My other hand slips from her waist to her hip, curving around it, guiding her back into me with slow, sinfully deliberate pressure. Her breath catches, the sound small and breakable and perfect.

"Slade..." she whispers.

"Look up," I tell her softly.

She lifts her chin, looking up at the glittering mass above us. The stars swell brighter—responding not to me, not to my realm, but to *her*. To the emotion blooming in her chest that she doesn't hide, or mask.

They pulse in rhythm with the bond.

I slide my hand up her arm—slow, deliberate—until my palm covers her heart. Her pulse leaps against my touch. She lets her head fall back against my shoulder, exposing her throat in a gesture that is instinct, trust, surrender. "You belong here," I murmur, letting my lips brush her ear. "In my world... In my life. With *me*."

Her fingers slide along my arm, knuckles brushing mine, her breath warm and uneven.

And slowly, she turns in my arms—facing me, framed by the soft chiming twilight. Her eyes shine with an emotion that vibrates through the bond like a deep, resonant chord.

"Then show me," she says, her voice low and sure.

The stars flare like a breath caught in the throat of the realm. The night bends toward us.

And I step into her fully—letting the seduction deepen, letting the magic thrum, letting the world around us fade into a warm, pulsing hush.

My hands slide under her dress, finding the lace of her underwear and tearing it aside without ceremony, circling her clit with fast strokes. I claim her mouth with a deep, consuming kiss, silencing the breath that was about to escape her. This is beyond slow seduction now. This is famine, and the Ninth Realm is our witness.

I lift her, turning her so her back presses against the cold marble railing. The contrast makes her gasp into my mouth. I hike her legs, pulling them around my waist, making her entirely dependent on my grip. Then, I peel back the barrier of my clothing, quickly freeing myself, and press my throbbing length against her slick heat.

"Look at the stars, little witch," I demand, my breath heavy against her ear. "See how bright they burn for you."

I drive into her, a single, deep plunge that takes her breath and makes the silver-fire braziers around the terrace flare. She cries out, a sharp, feral sound that is immediately muffled by my mouth clamping down on hers.

I pull back, needing to see her face, to see the pleasure I'm inflicting. Her blue eyes are wide, glazed over with need, framed by her wild curly, dark black hair.

I begin a slow, brutal rhythm, one hand gripping the railing behind her for leverage, the other fiercely kneading the curvy flesh of her hip. I don't move for control. I move for the painful depth of her pleasure.

"Scream for me, Piper," I growl against her throat. "Let the whole damn realm hear what you feel."

She doesn't disappoint. The sound is a ragged, breathless plea that the stars absorb instantly, making them shimmer faster.

I shift her slightly, hooking my forearm under her thighs, lifting her so she is impaled at a dizzying, perfect angle over the railing. She grips the cold marble, her knuckles white, her body stretched and vulnerable.

I slow the pace, needing to savor the intensity. I pull back almost entirely, letting the friction drive her mad, and then sink back in, deep and possessive, making her moan.

"Tell me what you need, my witch," I whisper, my lips trailing down her throat.

"Everything," she begs, her voice dissolving into a choked cry. "Harder. Faster."

I answer by accelerating the pace, driving us both toward the edge. I'm moving with a feverish intensity, pushing deeper, faster, until she's lost to the feeling.

Her climax hits her like a lightning strike—a long, drawn-out scream that vibrates through the entire terrace. Her body tenses fiercely around mine, and the stars explode in response, creating a sudden, beautiful wash of golden, chiming light. I hold her there, trembling and spent, sinking one last, desperate time before pulling free.

I kiss her forehead, setting her gently back down on her feet. She's weak, supported entirely by the railing and my arms.

"That wasn't the payment," I murmur, my voice heavy. "That was just the first offering."

I move her away from the railing, pushing her dress higher, kneeling before her. I look up, taking in the full, powerful view of her body—the flushed skin, the shaking thighs, the heavy, quick breaths.

I hook my fingers under her hips and pull her forward, spreading her thighs slightly. My eyes stay locked on her face for a moment, a silent question and promise. She nods once, a small, trusting gesture.

I lower my head, taking in her beautiful glistening pussy. The shock of my mouth on her is immediate. I use my tongue, my teeth, my lips—licking, sucking, devouring the slick, sensitive skin I just ravaged. I'm relentless, tasting her heat, her desire, driving out the last tremors of her first climax and pushing her straight toward a second.

She cries out, the sound high and uncontrolled. Piper grips my shoulders, fingers digging in, as she whispers my name over and over again. The world vanishes into the hot, humid focus of my mouth.

I don't stop until her second climax hits her—a violent, shattering rush that makes her knees buckle. She collapses forward, gripping my shoulders, whimpering into my black hair.

I stand, pulling her to her feet, holding her against my chest until her breathing evens out.

"Now," I whisper, my voice thick with raw possessiveness. "Let's finish this properly."

I lift her again, guiding her so that she is perched on the marble railing, facing out over the vast, shimmering darkness of the Ninth Realm. Her knees set on the bannister, leaving her pussy exposed and wonderfully vulnerable.

I step between her thighs, and I slide into her with a low growl, gripping her hips, setting a deep, primal rhythm. This is slower, more intense, meant to be felt and absorbed.

Gripping her hair, I pull her head back, her curly black hair fanning across her back like a shadow. She's silent now, lost to the feeling, her face tilted up to the pulsing, chiming stars. I drive my hips forward one last time, deep and heavy, feeling the world tilt on its axis as our release comes. I watch the stars flare into a dizzying white light, celebrating our completion.

I rest my forehead against hers, breathing her in. The cool air, the silver fire, the chaos of the deep realm—it all feels perfect. Pulling back, still deep inside her, I let my hand sweep the curls from her face. "You have my heart, Piper," I murmur, my voice rough with fulfilled promise.

She smiles, her lips swollen and damp, her blue eyes shining with absolute certainty. "I know I do," she whispers back.

# CHAPTER 36

Piper's breath is still unsteady when I finally ease back from her, letting the night air cool the flushed heat between us. The stars above us dim gently, as though politely averting their gaze now that the crescendo has passed.

I brush another stray curl from her cheek, my thumb lingering along the soft curve of her jaw. "Come," I murmur. "There's something else I want to show you."

Her fingers tighten briefly around mine, reluctant to break the spell of the balcony, but she nods. I guide her toward the interior hall, my hand warm against the small of her back, her steps soft and trusting beside mine.

We move through one of the glass corridors, the soft hum of the Ninth Realm's magic shimmering around us. Piper's curls sway with each step, her dark silhouette sharp against the glowing torches. She glances around with that same mix of awe and curiosity she had the first day—yet now it's softened by something else.

*Belonging.*

"Where are we going?" she asks quietly.

"To the dining hall," I answer. "I asked my staff to prepare something special."

The double doors ahead gleam with silver sigils that respond to my approach, parting on a soft exhale of air. Piper steps inside and gasps softly.

The hall is aglow. Hundreds of floating candles drift overhead in gentle spirals, their flames a warm gold that casts the long table in shimmering light. A feast spreads across polished obsidian—fresh bread still steaming from the oven, roasted meats lacquered with honey glaze, fruits glistening like jewels, goblets filled with deep red wine that catches the candlelight.

Piper moves forward slowly, drawn to the spectacle. "Slade... this is beautiful."

"It's for you," I tell her, pulling out her chair. "A welcome, as much as a promise."

She sits, her eyes bright, her curls spilling across her shoulders. I settle beside her instead of across, wanting her within reach. The bond hums warm and steady between us as the meal begins.

She tastes everything with a kind of wonder—herbal soups brewed with soul-warming spices, pastries stuffed with spiced fruit, wine infused with golden magic that warms her from the inside out. We eat, we talk, we laugh, and for a moment the weight of the world feels distant.

Her knee brushes mine under the table. She doesn't move it, not that I want her to. I take her hand gently and brush my thumb across her knuckles. "I wanted your first night here to feel like a beginning."

"It does," she agrees with a small smile. It settles in my chest like the warmth of a fire.

When we rise from the table, she curls her fingers into my palm without needing invitation. I lead her through a side corridor lit by soft moonstone sconces, each step quiet and intimate.

Newt appears in a blur of fur at our ankles, trotting with the smug swagger of someone whose new throne room is merely the opening act.

Piper laughs lightly. "He likes it here more than he likes my apartment."

"I built him a monarchy," I say dryly. "It was inevitable."

She snickers, leaning into me as we walk. My hand drifts to her waist, savoring the feel of her warmth through the soft fabric of her dress.

We stop before a tall set of blackwood doors etched with silver constellations—my chambers. The sigils flare softly at my touch, welcoming her for the first time, recognizing her as mine.

I glance at her, gauging her reaction. Piper's breath catches, her blue eyes going wide as the doors open fully.

Inside, the room glows with a gentle, enchanted light. A massive four-poster bed draped in deep emerald fabrics dominates the space, soft fur throws layered across the foot of it. A hearth crackles quietly, casting golden warmth across the rug. The air smells faintly of cedar, smoke, and the magic that clings to her skin.

Piper steps in slowly, her voice soft as she whispers, "Slade... it's *beautiful*."

"It's yours," I say quietly. "For as long as you'll have it."

The words settle between us—heavy, intimate, true. She turns to me, eyes bright, lips parted in something between awe and affection, and my pulse kicks hard in my chest. Tonight was meant to show her my world. But as she moves closer, her fingers brushing my jaw, her heartbeat steady and certain against the bond—I realize she's becoming my world.

*Completely.*

And when her hand slides down my chest, her body swaying into mine with a slow, deliberate invitation under the soft glow of bedside candle-light... I know the night is far from over.

I'm ready for her. My world narrows to the heat of her touch, the sudden, sharp spike of need that slams into me like a physical blow. The air in the vast chamber grows thick, charged with the magic we're both letting loose.

"*Mine*," I growl, the word tearing from my throat, a deep possessive claim.

I seize her face, cupping her perfect jaw, and my mouth crashes down on hers. It's a kiss that's a promise, a demand, a surrender. I pour every ounce of my hunger, my devotion, my deep love into the fierce contact. Her lips part instantly under the pressure, giving me access, and I ravage the sweetness within, pulling a low, desperate sound from her chest.

My hands don't linger on soft fabric. They plunge beneath the hem of her dress, sweeping up the silk until my fingers find the bare, warm skin of her thighs. Her muscles clench reflexively, and I push harder, lifting her, backing her up without breaking the kiss.

The walls in my bedroom are cold stone, but the contrast only seems to sharpen the molten heat building between us. I slam her back against the rough surface, the impact stolen by her gasp. She wraps her legs instantly around my hips, locking me in place, an exquisite, aching weight. I pin her there, pressing my erection hard against the junction of her thighs, grinding until she arches her neck, her head resting against the stone, a soundless scream pulling at the taut muscles of her throat.

I break the kiss only to feast on the delicate skin of her neck, sucking hard enough to leave a bruise, a dark, tangible mark of my possession. I want her marked. I want the world to know she is mine.

"Slade," she manages, her voice broken, a breathless plea.

I lift her again, my hand dropping to cup her perfect, slick heat right through her panties. I feel the damp fabric, the involuntary spasm of her core.

"Not yet," I bite out, the raw edge of my voice surprising even me. "I take what I want first."

I move toward a small, carved blackwood side table near the window. I set her down, roughly, my hips pushing her dress up completely, exposing her bare, trembling legs and the dark triangle of her underwear. I don't give her time to protest or adjust. I take hold of her hair—the thick, dark, magnificent cascade—and pull. Not gently. I yank, tilting her head back, exposing her throat, and her stunned, needy face.

"On your knees," I command, releasing her hair and grabbing her waist instead, pushing her down, spinning her slightly so her hands brace on the table. I position myself behind her, my belt buckle biting into her backside through the thin fabric of her dress.

Her breathing is ragged, fast, scared and excited all at once. The position makes her submission explicit, and her vulnerability erotic. I shove my hand between her thighs, ripping the scrap of fabric aside, and three hard, demanding fingers find her entrance. She's soaking wet, ready and waiting, slick against my intrusion.

I watch her reflection in the dark window as I slide my thumb over her clit, feeling the immediate, deep tremor run through her body.

"Look at yourself," I instruct, my voice a low, gravelly rasp right at her ear. "See how you take me, how you crave this."

I start to thrust my fingers in and out, the angle deep and deliberate, using the friction of my palm on her wet folds to drive her wild. Each stroke draws a sharp, involuntary cry from her. She tries to brace herself, her hips attempting to escape my control, but I lean down, biting the curve of her shoulder, holding her in place.

"Don't move," I snarl against her shoulder, withdrawing my fingers abruptly.

She whimpers at the sudden loss. I shift, pulling her away from the table, toward the plush rug in front of the crackling hearth, guiding her to the edge of the low coffee table. I make her sit there, eyes wide and utterly confused.

Unbuckling my belt, the leather snaps. It's a sharp, commanding sound in the quiet room. I let my trousers fall to the floor. My erection springs free, hard and demanding. I stand between her legs, spreading them wide, forcing her gaze to my rigid length. The soft light from the fire makes the sweat gleam on my skin. "You take this, Piper," I say, the instruction a low, harsh breath. "You earn what comes next."

Her hesitation lasts only a fraction of a second. The look in her eyes is hungry, desperate. She reaches out, her hand wrapping around me, her fingers surprisingly soft yet firm. She brings my length to her mouth, her eyes never leaving mine.

The immediate, scorching heat of her mouth is an electric shock. Her technique is practiced, greedy, and devastatingly perfect. She sucks me deeply, relentlessly, her throat working, her eyes glistening with tears of need and arousal. I clench my fists, digging my nails into my palms to keep from coming instantly. The sounds she makes—soft mumbles, little gasps—reverberate through my core.

I lean down, my hands gripping the back of her head, guiding her pace, the rhythm of my control absolute. "Good girl. Take it all."

I endure the exquisite torment for what feels like an eternity, every nerve ending screaming. When I know I'm on the brink, when the deep, shuddering climax is clawing at my control, I break away, pulling myself free with a wet smack of skin.

I lift her off the table, moving her swiftly to the floor, where I lay her back against the soft, fur-draped rug. Grabbing her ankles, I pull her legs up and open, draping them over my shoulders in a wide, utterly exposed angle.

I stare down at her, at the dark triangle I just uncovered, slick and throbbing, demanding my attention. My need to control, to claim, to worship is overwhelming.

I drop my head, burying my face in her.

The taste is intoxicating, musky, sweet, and wholly mine. I use my tongue like a weapon, tracing the delicate seams of her folds, then driving straight for the hot, swollen center of her desire. I lap, I flick, I suck, giving her absolutely no respite. I watch her face as I do it, making sure she knows she has nowhere to hide. That she is entirely at my mercy.

She begins to writhe, her fingers knotting into the deep fur of the rug, her breaths becoming ragged, panicked attempts to draw air. The sounds she makes are primal—unintelligible murmurs that turn into sharp, desperate cries.

I focus all my intent on the tiny, exquisite nub beneath my tongue, sucking her deep into my mouth with a demanding pressure.

Her body seizes. Her hips buck violently against my mouth, her back arching, Piper's entire body rigid with pleasure. A long, shuddering cry tears from her, a sound of absolute, shattering release.

"SLADE!" she screams my name, the sound echoing off the high ceilings, a pure, unadulterated declaration of ownership and climax.

I don't stop until the spasms fade into soft tremors. I lift my head, my face wet, my eyes locked on her dazed, sated expression.

I rise above her, grasping her knees, forcing her legs wide, and I position the tip of my erection at her entrance, slick and hot.

I don't wait. I plunge into her, one deep, violent thrust that buries me to the hilt.

She gasps, a strangled sound of overwhelming pleasure. I lean down, covering her mouth with mine, absorbing her sharp cry as I begin to pound into her, deep and relentless. I roll us, flipping onto my back, still buried within her, but now she's on top. I lift my head, admiring the view. I let my hand trace the curve of her waist.

"Ride me," I command, moving her hips with my hands. "Show me what you want."

With a moan of raw delight, she grinds against me, taking the dominance. She takes full control, swiveling her hips slowly, agonizingly so, until I'm buried deep again. She rises, dragging fire along my length, then descends, slamming down hard enough to make my teeth clench. Her eyes are half-lidded, glazed with power and lust.

She controls the flow—slow, languid circles that drive me insane with anticipation, then sudden, violent drops that steal my breath. I watch the rise and fall of her breasts, the sweat on her skin, the determination on her face. Her power, her willingness to take what she wants, is the most exquisite thing I have ever witnessed.

I lift my hands, cupping her hips and matching her rhythm. My throbbing pulse drives her harder, faster. The magic around us flares, a tangible rush of heat and energy, locking our bodies and souls together in one, final, ecstatic explosion.

I feel her collapse onto my chest, the warm weight of her body against mine. I'm breathing hard, the scent of her arousal and my own satisfaction filling my lungs, taking root deep within. I'm still buried deep inside her, the heat of our connection solid and undeniable. I have claimed her completely. She kisses my cheek, and nips at my ear, nuzzling the sensitive skin with her nose. My arm tightens around her as the realization settles deep within my bones...

I'm *home*.

# CHAPTER 37

*Piper*

I wake to heat.

Not the wild, molten kind from last night—though my thighs tremble at the memory—but a softer, steadier warmth that sinks into my skin like I'm lying on the sun itself.

Slade is behind me, one muscular arm slung heavy over my waist, his breath a slow, controlled rise and fall against the back of my neck. The massive emerald duvet is tangled around our hips, half-dragged to the floor during what I can only describe as a marathon of worship and destruction. My body feels tender, used, adored. My every nerve is a hum of lingering magic.

I shift, just barely, and a low sound rumbles in his chest—an approving purr that vibrates straight through me.

Oh gods.

Everything inside me clenches with immediate, aching need.

"Don't start," he murmurs against my hair, voice still rough with sleep. "You're not fed yet."

I almost laugh. Almost.

"Slade... I'm starving for something else entirely."

His hand tightens on my hip in warning—a warning that sends another little shockwave through my core.

He presses his lips to the back of my shoulder, slow and deliberate. "I know, little witch." His voice is velvet dipped in sin. "But if I touch you again right now, you won't leave this bed for hours, and I need you walking for the tour."

A whimper slips out before I can stop it.

A pleased, sinful sound vibrates in his throat. "Exactly."

I turn slightly so I can see him. His hair is a wild, glorious mess across the pillow. His eyes are half-lidded, dark green and molten, the kind of look that promises everything and threatens my sanity.

"Come here," he murmurs.

I shift onto my back, and he immediately rolls over me—not heavy, not demanding, just covering me like he's making sure I'm still real. His thigh slides between mine, and I swear my soul tries to leave my body.

He feels it, and grins like a demon who knows he owns me. "Later."

"Cruel," I whisper.

His mouth brushes my cheek, my jaw, the place just beneath my ear that makes my spine arch without permission. "Efficient," he corrects. "And you need food. Water. Maybe a healing potion."

I shove him lightly. "I'm not that wrecked."

"You are *absolutely* that wrecked," he says, leaning back enough to rake his eyes slowly down my naked body. "And you look *perfect*."

Heat floods my face, down my throat, between my legs. Slade groans under his breath like the sight alone is enough to undo him. He kisses me—slow, deep, maddeningly restrained—before finally pulling himself away and rising from the bed in one lazy, predatory stretch.

I watch shamelessly.

He notices within seconds. Slade smirks and offers me his hand. "Come. Bath. Food. Then I show you the realm."

Our realm.

The realization flutters in my chest as he helps me stand, steadying me when my knees wobble.

"See?" he murmurs, amused. "You absolutely need the potion."

I glare. He kisses my forehead in apology. Or condescension. Or both. Hard to tell.

He guides me through the screened archway into a bathing chamber carved from black stone veined with glowing gold. Steam curls lazily from the wide pool sunk into the floor, the water sparkling with suspended motes of magic. He lowers me in first, then sinks behind me, drawing me between his legs.

The warm water immediately soothes the delicious ache radiating through me. I melt against him with a soft sigh.

"That's better," he breathes into my ear.

"Mm. You just like having me trapped."

"That too."

We stay in the bath until my muscles stop trembling and he decides I can be trusted to walk without falling apart. He wraps me in a thick, emerald towel, drying every inch of me with slow, reverent hands that make my pulse skip.

Breakfast waits on a nearby table—fresh fruits, warm bread, spiced meats, and something that looks suspiciously like a dish Slade made specifically because he knows I love it.

We eat together, knees touching, his hand resting on my thigh every time he reaches for his cup. I steal bits of fruit off his plate. He lets me—*barely*.

By the time I finish my meal, I'm warm, full, and steady again.

Which only makes the hunger for him sharper.

I lean closer, brushing my lips against the edge of his jaw. "So... what does this tour include?"

He stands, pulling me gently to my feet. His eyes darken with slow, promised heat.

"Everything," he says. "The gardens. The living flame springs. The old throne hall."

"And then?"

He sweeps his thumb across my lower lip.

"And then," he murmurs, "I bring you back here... and ruin you properly."

Heat pools low and sweet inside me. I lace my fingers with his, letting him lead me toward the wardrobe where clothes for both of us wait. He pauses in the doorway, looking down at me with something warm and fierce and newly settled. "Ready to see your realm, Piper Athalar?"

My breath catches. Not Piper the cursed witch, or the outsider. Piper *Athalar*.

I nod, heart tripping hard in my chest. "Show me everything."

He smiles—a slow, wicked, devastating thing—and opens the door. "Good," he says. "Hold on to me."

And gods help me, I always will.

***

Slade leads me through the archway, and the moment we step into the corridor, the entire estate seems to inhale—recognizing him, recognizing me.

Torches flare brighter. Shadows shift like bowing attendants. Magic hums down the marble floors like welcome home.

His hand stays wrapped around mine, thumb brushing my knuckles in lazy, possessive circles.

"Where first?" I ask, trying not to gape like a tourist.

"The gardens," he says, voice low with something close to pride. "You'll like them."

We move through the palace until a set of carved obsidian doors swing open at his mere approach. Beyond them, the world expands into a breathtaking, impossible landscape—an underworld Eden.

The air is warm, threaded with faint jasmine and something spicy and wild, like cinnamon bark burning in the distance. Blackstone paths curve around bioluminescent blooms, each flower casting its own soft glow—violet, ember-red, ghost-white, deep gold. Some float, some pulse with an internal heartbeat, others shift shape as if dreaming.

Slade watches my reaction like he's memorizing it.

"It's beautiful," I breathe.

"It's ours," he corrects.

We walk slowly, our fingers still laced. Trees rise tall around us, their leaves shimmering like brushed metal. Strange birds—inky creatures with ember eyes—flit overhead, leaving brief spirals of glowing dust behind them.

I pause beside a massive blossom shaped like a flame. When I reach out, it curves toward my palm, warm as breath.

"It recognizes you," Slade murmurs.

"Because I'm your...?"

He steps close behind me, his chest brushing my back. "Because this realm bends to power. And you have more than you realize."

Heat blooms low in my belly. Not lust—well, okay, also lust—but something deeper. Something that feels like belonging.

We continue on, and the garden gives way to a series of stone steps leading to a cliffside balcony.

Below us, the Ninth Realm sprawls in a breathtaking tapestry of glowing rivers, jagged obsidian spires, shimmering plains, and distant cities lit from within by magic. The sky above is a deep, rich violet—almost black—with drifting constellations that shift and reform like living stories.

"What... are those?" I whisper, pointing to the slowly changing star patterns.

"Fragments of lost souls," he says softly. "Ancestors. Old gods. The realm keeps their memories as light."

I press a hand to my heart. "They're beautiful."

"So are you," he murmurs, brushing a kiss to my temple.

We linger there, the wind warm and strange against my face, carrying the scent of smoldering stone and rare flowers.

Then he leads me down a winding path to a glimmering pool carved into the earth. The water glows from within—liquid flame, dancing gold and soft white. "The Living Flame Springs," he says quietly.

The air vibrates with ancient magic.

Slade stops at the edge. "The springs amplify whatever burns in your heart. Passion. Power. Grief. Hope."

I dip my fingers in, and warmth spreads through me, curling along every vein like it wants to unlock something inside me. Slade takes my hand again, steadying me. Protective. Present. "It likes you," he says quietly.

"Everything in your world seems *weirdly* friendly to me."

Slade chuckles softly, shaking his head at me.

We leave the springs behind and continue toward the oldest part of the estate—a towering structure carved directly into the rock face.

The doors open with a moaning groan, ancient magic stirring. The hall is magnificent—vaulted ceilings painted with old wars, old kings, old sacrifices. Massive braziers line the walls, flames shifting colors that don't exist in the mortal world.

At the center sits a throne of blackstone and gold veins, carved so intricately it almost appears woven. Behind it is a smaller chair—elegant, curved, with a cushioned seat of deep green velvet.

My heart stutters, flip-flopping in my chest like a fish on land. I don't bother hiding the grin as it spills across my face. "You have a throne," I tease.

He gestures toward the smaller one. "You have a throne, too."

I freeze. "Slade..."

"You *are* Lady Athalar." His voice holds no hesitation. "The realm knows it. I know it. That throne will accept no one else." Emotion rises unexpectedly in my throat. He notices instantly, pulling me gently into his arms. "You don't have to rule anything," he says, low and warm. "You don't have to claim anything. This just means... you have a place here. A home. With me."

I breathe him in, and the ancient hall seems to breathe with me.

"I love it," I whisper.

He exhales slowly, as if I've told him something important. Then he pulls back and lifts my chin with two fingers. "One more stop."

He leads me back outside, up a long spiral ramp that winds along a natural spire of stone until we reach a private balcony overlooking the entire realm. The sky above shifts—constellations flickering, swirling, reshaping. Stars pulse brighter as if greeting us. "It's... stunning," I breathe.

Slade steps behind me, wrapping his arms around my waist, his chest pressed warm and solid against my back.

"Every night is like this," he murmurs. "Every night since the old war ended."

"And you sometimes... watch this alone?"

"I did." His hold on me tightens. "But, not anymore."

I turn in his arms, tilting my face up to his. And gods—his eyes under this strange starlight are something out of myth. Dark green, glowing at the edges, fierce and tender all at once. The wind carries the scent of warm stone and distant fire. His thumb slides along my lower lip, and my pulse jumps.

"Piper," he whispers, voice dipping into something molten, "come here."

I step into him without hesitation.

His mouth meets mine—slow, reverent, a kiss that tastes like a vow whispered straight into my soul. His fingers stroke the sides of my waist, his touch gentle but full of promise. He kisses me again. And *again*. Drawing me flush against him.

Tension coils low and hot in my belly. My hands slide into his hair. He groans softly—one of those rare, quiet sounds he only makes when he's losing control. The stars swirl above us, echoing the dizzying heat climbing through me.

He presses his forehead to mine, breath mingling with mine. "Tonight," he murmurs, his voice rough enough to scrape pleasure down my spine, "I show you the rest of my realm."

His thumb traces my jaw, slow and possessive, then drifts down the column of my throat, lingering where my pulse jumps beneath his touch.

"Not the halls," he continues, "not the quiet parts you've already seen... but the living heart of it. The streets. The pulse. The creatures that come alive after sundown."

My breath catches. He leans in, his lips a brush against mine—barely there, a spark suspended between us. "You'll see the Ninth Realm as it truly is," he whispers, "colorful and wild and loud... the demons who don't look human, the ones who shimmer and crackle and glow. The ones who shape the night like music."

His mouth grazes my lower lip, sending heat spiraling through me. "And you," he adds, eyes burning gold at the edges, "will walk beside me like the Lady you are."

The words settle between us—heavy, electric, full of heat and promise—not the end of a moment, but the doorway into the next one.

And when he finally takes my hand and leads me toward the glowing city below, the air itself seems to shift... as if the Ninth is holding its breath for us to arrive.

***

The promise from earlier is thick and intoxicating, settling into my skin deeper than the chill of the high spire. I turn fully in his arms, and the sight of his fierce, glowing eyes in the shifting starlight makes my heart race.

"I'm ready for the wild and loud," I tell him, my voice barely a whisper, yet firm with conviction.

He's smiling, a slow, predatory curve of his mouth that only makes him more beautiful. Slade releases me, pulling a dark, shimmering cloak from the air—spun from shadow and midnight, it settles over my shoulders, heavy with protective power.

"But not like that," he murmurs, his gaze sweeping over my dress. "The streets require armor."

I watch as he lifts his hand, the air around me crackling with raw magic. The fabric of my dress shifts, reforming. My casual dress morphs instantly into something tighter, darker, and cut with wicked defiance. It is obsidian black, clinging to my curves, plunging low in the front and hiking high up my thighs, shimmering like liquid shadow. On my feet, flat sandals are replaced by high, aggressive heels of polished, dark crystal that feel lethal and empowering.

I'm the Lady of the Ninth, and *this* is my armor.

He's dressed the same—sleek, tailored black that makes him look like a creature carved from the darkest night. He takes my hand, and the world spins in a blur of purple light and searing heat.

We land hard, the impact jarring but exhilarating.

The air hits me—a wall of heat, sound, and a thousand overlapping, primal scents—burnt sugar, blood wine, and musk. The noise is a physical force, a deep, aggressive music that vibrates in my chest and skull, distorting everything.

We're in the Lower Levels, the heart of the Ninth Realm's nightlife. The street is a winding canyon of basalt and glowing plasma, lined with open-fronted clubs and bars that spill light and chaos onto the pavement. The creatures here are magnificent and terrifying. Hulking, shadow-skinned demons with blazing eyes, serpentine forms that glide through the crowds, and towering beings covered in crystalline scales that crackle when they laugh.

My breath catches, but I force myself not to gape.

Slade grips my hand, his thumb stroking my knuckles in a slow, possessive warning to the crowd. "Welcome to the Harrow district," he shouts over the thundering bass, his voice rough but clear. "The pulse of the realm."

He guides me toward a doorway, a gaping maw of black stone that pulses with deep red light. I walk with a new, deliberate power, matching his stride in my vicious heels.

The moment we step inside the club, the noise is deafening, the air thick with sweat and pheromones. We're in the Harrow, apparently notorious... and I have to admit... rather magnificent.

Slade pulls me instantly into the crush of bodies on the main floor. The music is a deep, pounding rhythm that demands movement. I let it take me, allowing the chaotic energy of the crowd to fuel the heat already simmering in my core.

He locks his gaze on mine, his dark green eyes glowing gold at the edges. Slade presses his hips against mine, making every accidental brush of our bodies an explicit act. "Drink this," he commands, seizing a glass of glowing liquor from a passing waiter—a fiery, spiced liquid that smells of temptation. "You'll love it."

I take a deep, daring gulp. The liquor is scorching, but it instantly sends a delicious warmth through my veins, sharpening my focus, stripping away my last inhibitions. I smile back at him, sharp and wild.

I'm dancing, my body moving with a raw, feral abandon I didn't know I possessed. My hips roll, deliberately brushing the erection straining beneath his pants. I let the other demons look, letting them crave what they cannot have.

He leans close, his breath hot against my ear, the bass vibrating his words into my core. "That dress is driving them *mad*. Show me more, little witch."

My hips answer him, pushing my pussy hard against his length, a silent, demanding promise. "I *am* showing you," I breathe back, a thrilling arrogance flooding me.

I feel his grip tighten on my wrist. He pulls me sharply through the crowd, past twisting, writhing bodies, toward a dark corner near the back. Slade shoves an unmarked iron door open, dragging me inside.

The room is tiny, black, and silent compared to the club, lined with rough, padded leather. The only light is the crimson glow seeping from beneath the door. He slams the door shut, spinning me around, throwing me back against the cool, dark leather. His mouth crashes onto mine, a violent, desperate claim that steals my breath and my thoughts. He spins me around, slamming my chest against the wall.

His hands are on the back of my dress, instantly finding the zipper. He rips it down with a vicious snap, shoving the silk aside. My panties are already wet, hot, and soaked.

He growls, pulling me tight against him so I feel the solid, desperate heat of his erection. "You are going to take every inch of me, right here, right now."

I lift my hips, desperate, shoving my knees apart for him. I feel his hands grip my waist, pushing me forward against the leather.

He is kneeling on the floor, pushing the dress up, finding my burning, dripping core.

I scratch at the leather as his mouth closes over my pussy. The noise outside is a muffled rhythm, but the sound of his hungry sucking is deafening in the tiny space. His tongue is a weapon, driving deep into my wet folds, consuming me, giving me absolutely no quarter.

I cry out, a silent, desperate scream caught in my throat, my head thrown back as I push my pussy against his mouth. My body is writhing, my hips bucking wildly against his face.

"Tell me how much you need it, little witch," he demands, his voice a dark rasp against my skin. "Tell me I am the only one who tastes you."

"Yours!" I gasp, the word tearing from me. "I'm yours! Don't stop!"

I'm shattering, my body seizing. The climax is a deep, shaking explosion that leaves me trembling and slick against the cold leather. I scream his name into the silent room. He pulls back, rising above me, his length sprung free, hard and demanding. He pulls me up, spinning me to face him, and I guide him, my hands gripping his erection. Slade wraps my legs around him, and plunges into me, one deep, violent thrust that buries him completely.

I meet his aggression, my hands locking around his neck. He pins me to the wall, and the fierce rhythm begins—fast, hard, primal, powered by the feral energy of the club outside.

I ride the edge of control, my eyes locked on his, my own voice lost in the rhythmic, guttural sounds he tears from his chest. This is pure, unadulterated pleasure and power.

He leans into my ear for one final declaration. "This is *your* realm, you hear me? And *you* are... *mine.*"

The climax is sharp, violent, and complete, locking our bodies together in a shaking, gasping union. I cling to him, my body heavy and satiated. He pulls us back together, slowly zipping the dress, fixing the chaos we unleashed. He kisses my forehead, his touch reverent, protective.

"Now," he whispers, steadying me. "The night is young. Let's show them the Lady Athalar is still hungry."

I nod, the raw power still burning in my eyes. I take his hand, and we step back out into the light of the Ninth Realm, ready to conquer the rest of the night.

I'm standing beside him, the loud, aggressive music of the Harrow washing over my senses. The fresh, delicious throb of being completely sated is a steady pulse that has me clenching my thighs tighter while we walk. I'm still riding the high of the tight, dark space, knowing exactly what we just did and *where* we did it.

"Night life, you say?" I whisper, my voice rough with residual need, my gaze challenging him. "You haven't shown me the real secrets yet, Slade."

He's looking down at me, his eyes gleaming with dark amusement, acknowledging my desire for more chaos. "My Lady is *insatiable*," he murmurs, his hand tightening on mine. "Very well. There are places even the Harrow avoids. They're not pretty, but they're honest."

He's leading me out of the crushing throng of the main street, pulling me toward a narrow alleyway choked with steam and shadows. The air here is cooler, thicker, and carries a distinct smell of burnt metal and ancient incense.

We're moving deeper into the basalt canyon. The clubs are giving way to cramped, unmarked doors and windows covered with thick, oily grime. The creatures here are different—more angular, their glowing eyes fixed, their movements slow and heavy with something ancient.

I'm feeling the power emanating from Slade intensify. Here, in the true underbelly, he's not just the Lord of the Ninth. He's the Apex Predator.

We stop before a door that is nothing more than a sheet of rust-pocked metal. It bears no sign, only a single, slow-flashing blue light above it.

"The Velvet Pit," he announces, his voice low and devoid of warmth. "It's where deals are made, secrets are traded, and the rules of the surface realm don't apply."

I feel a dangerous thrill shiver down my spine. "It's perfect."

Slade pushes the door open with a single, sharp shove.

The noise isn't music here. It's a low, constant roar—a thousand voices speaking in sharp, aggressive clicks and guttural tongues. The light is dim, supplied by sickly green lamps that cast long, unsettling shadows. The air is thick with smoke and a heavy, sweet narcotic vapor.

The room is enormous, a sprawling labyrinth of partitioned booths, low tables, and velvet-draped alcoves. Every surface is worn, stained, and richly decadent in its decay.

Slade guides me through the crowd. I see demons with extra limbs, creatures whose skin shimmers like oil, and ancient beings who look like they're slowly turning to dust. They're talking, gambling with glowing fragments of bone, and drinking thick, black substances from ornate goblets.

Every eye follows us. The silence that descends around our path is more deafening than the club's bass. They're recognizing Slade. They're recognizing me.

He leads me to a booth tucked away in the deepest corner—a crimson velvet horseshoe with heavy black curtains. He sweeps the curtains aside, and we slip inside, claiming the space. The velvet is worn smooth, and the air is heavy with the cloying scent of cheap perfume and old power.

I'm sliding into the booth. Slade is sitting opposite me, leaning forward, resting his elbows on the chipped table, his eyes never leaving mine.

"This is where the realm unmasks itself," he tells me, his voice barely audible. "Look around, Piper. Absorb their power."

I'm doing as he asks. I'm peering through a slight gap in the curtain. I see a creature with eyes like liquid mercury staring directly at our curtain, its posture aggressive and territorial.

Slade catches my gaze. "He's curious. He's hungry. He's wondering why I'm bringing mortal sweetness into his den."

I reach across the table, my fingers tangling with his. "Then remind him why," I challenge, a fierce, wild energy rising in me. The liquor and the recent climax are still burning hot. I want to claim this space.

He smiles, a slow, deliberate unveiling of his full power. He's pulling our hands away from the table, lifting them into the shadow of the curtain. His thumb is moving to trace the curve of my palm, then gliding up my wrist, finding the smooth skin beneath the lace cuff of my dress.

"You truly are insatiable," he repeats, his voice a dark, rough velvet. "And I'm prepared to worship you again."

He's slipping his hand under the table, his eyes locked on mine. I'm bracing myself, my breath catching as I feel the heat of his touch on my thigh, sliding high beneath the skirt of the armor dress.

I'm leaning forward, my body trembling slightly. The tension is exquisite—the filth of the environment, the hidden intimacy, the sheer audacity of what we're about to do with a room full of dangerous predators just inches away.

His fingers are stroking my soaked pussy, the dark cloth of my underwear already useless against the torrent of my need. He easily pushes the fabric aside, his fingers finding the slick heat of me. I gasp, forcing a nonchalant cough to cover the sound.

"You're already dripping for me," he murmurs, his voice dangerously low, eyes bright with dark triumph. "Look at me, Piper. Let them think we're only talking."

I'm looking at him, eyes wide, my lips parted. I'm forcing myself to maintain an appearance of calm dialogue while his fingers are driving me wild beneath the table.

He's finding my clit, circling it with a relentless, demanding pressure. I'm biting the inside of my cheek, suppressing a moan as the waves of pleasure begin to crest.

"I'm going to drive you mad here," he promises, his voice a sharp, seductive rasp. "I'm going to make you scream in the middle of this den of thieves. And they'll hear you, Lady Athalar, but they won't know what you're screaming for."

His fingers are quickening their pace, relentless and perfect. I'm arching my back, pressing myself hard onto his hand, begging for more pressure. My vision is blurring. I can't fucking breathe, but gods, it's delicious.

"Give it to me," I whisper, the words strangled, focusing all my energy on keeping my voice steady.

He's plunging a finger deep inside my cunt, stretching me, dominating me—hitting the right spot, the pleasure so sharp it's bordering on pain. Slade's withdrawing and plunging again, a rhythm born of desperation and control.

I'm seizing, my legs trembling violently under the table. The climax is a silent, internal explosion, shaking my core, pulling a choked sob from my throat. I'm grabbing the edge of the table, my knuckles white, my eyes squeezed shut.

He waits until the tremors subside, withdrawing his hand slowly, lingering just long enough to draw out the last wave of bliss. He's wiping his wet fingers on the expensive velvet of the booth, a dark smile on his face.

I open my eyes, utterly spent, panting softly.

Slade leans in, claiming a soft, sweet kiss from my swollen lips. "Now," he whispers, the dark energy around him palpable. "We're going to drink. And then, we're going to leave. I'm going to take you back to my throne room, and I'm going to keep you beneath me until morning."

I nod, unable to speak. The heat of the experience settles into a fierce, deep determination. I'm ready to go back, and so fucking ready for the throne room.

# CHAPTER 38

*Slade*

I'm the Lord of the Ninth, but right now, I'm nothing but pure appetite. I always seem to instantly crave her again. *Only* her. I'm going to devour every inch of Piper Athalar until the sun rips its way across the sky.

The moment we're through the massive obsidian doors of the throne room, the restraint I'd maintained in the Pit snaps. I've waited too long. I don't even bother to set her down. We barely make it through the throne room, and I'm shoving her against the nearest wall, crushing her dress between us.

"You think you know chaos, Lady?" My voice is a low growl, the sound of a beast finally closing its jaws. I'm ripping at the fabric, tearing the useless lace of her sleeve, desperate to see skin, to see the marks I'm about to leave. "You haven't seen anything yet."

She isn't meek. No, she never is. Her legs wrap tight around my waist, urging me closer, her mouth locking onto mine in a savage, breath-stealing kiss. She's already wet, the scent of her arousal—musk, sweetness, and the lingering filth of the Velvet Pit—driving me insane.

I slam my cock into her pussy against the cold stone of the wall, letting her feel the full weight of my need. She shrieks, muffled against my shoulder, a sound of pure, helpless pleasure that I'm meant to possess.

The marble of the long audience table is next, its surface cool and slick beneath her heated skin. I've got her bent over the edge, her ass lifted high, as I'm driving into her pussy from behind. I grip her hips like handles, the heavy, rhythmic force of my body meeting the frantic, shaking tremors of hers. I'm whispering obscenities into her ear, telling her exactly how deep I'm going, how much I'm enjoying watching her ass quiver.

Gods, she's breathtaking.

Then the plush, heavy carpet near the fire pit. I place her on her back, my tongue trailing licks of fire down her body, over the sharp jut of her hips, across the plane of her belly. I lower myself, making a slow, decadent meal of her. Savoring the salty, sweet flavor of her cunt until she's weeping my name.

"Look at this," I demand, lifting her hips so I've got the perfect view. "It's *all* mine."

I lower her gently, and she slides down, reversing us expertly until we're in sixty-nine, her perfect ass sitting directly on my face. She's relentless, focused, using her hands to grip me, her mouth working me with skilled, intoxicating suction. I'm lost entirely in the sensation, groaning, my own hands braced on the back of her thighs as I return the favor. Licking, sucking, and teasing the velvety heat of her pussy.

When she's close to the edge again, I pull her up, lifting her high onto the actual throne—*my* throne—the velvet dark against her pale skin. I'm kneeling behind her, plunging my cock into her cunt in a deep, agonizing slow motion that has her arching her breasts against the chair.

"I'm gonna show you where true power lies, Piper," I pant, leaning down to nip her shoulder.

As I ride her, pounding into her deeply on the hard stone and velvet of the throne, my hands find her waist. My lips ghost across the delicate skin behind her ear before my tongue slides lower, down her body. I exit the sweet heat of pussy, sliding lower until finding the tight, sensitive ring of her asshole. I lick the entrance in a slow, hot, possessive caress. She cries out, a raw, shocked sound that spurs me on.

I slide back up, thrusting into her quickly, using my thumb to rub the sensitive ring of her ass. While I'm driving my cock into her pussy, my fingers sink to the hidden crevice. One finger, then two, pushing gently, steadily, into her asshole. Spreading her, and preparing her for the next wave of pleasure. The dual invasion—my cock dominating her cunt, my fingers ravishing her ass—has her seizing, completely undone.

Finally, I'm collapsing onto the steps of the throne, pulling her down with me, slick skin against skin, our hearts hammering in unison. She is boneless beneath me, utterly annihilated.

"I'm *so* glad I've got that Witch's Brew," she says, her voice a rough whisper against my collarbone. She's running a tired, satisfied hand over my chest. "I'd be pregnant on every surface of this room right now."

I laugh, the sound dark and low. I roll us onto our sides, tucking her head under my chin. "We're more than ready for kids, little witch. Look at our perfect son, Newt. We just aren't ready for a second one yet."

"You're incorrigible, Slade," she murmurs, tracing the line of my jaw with a thumb.

"I'm only getting started," I promise, my gaze locking on hers. That familiar, dark hunger already coiling in my gut. I'm shifting my weight, reaching between her legs, finding she isn't quite as spent as she thinks. "Come here, *wife*. I'm going to fuck you senseless all over again."

She blushes prettily from head to toe, "I'm not your wife, yet, Slade Athalar."

"Not yet," I agree. "But you will be."

I pull her onto my lap, my length already hard and ready for her. She straddles me, facing away, settling the weight of her ass onto my cock. The friction is immediate, sharp, and brutal.

"Ride me, little savage," I demand, my hands shooting out to grip her throat, exerting just enough pressure to make her gasp and arch her back onto my chest. I'm watching her reflection in the dark mirror above the fireplace—her eyes wide, the pleasure and fear a perfect, combustible mix. She's bouncing hard on me, controlling the pace, grinding my balls with her ass.

My other hand finds her breasts, the dark nipples taut and begging for abuse. I'm pinching them, twisting the sensitive peaks between my thumb and forefinger, eliciting another sharp, choked cry from her. I drive my hips up, meeting her brutal descent, slamming deep into her throbbing pussy.

"You're *insatiable*," she whispers, twisting her head to look back at me, the words breathless.

"It's the bond, Piper," I rasp, my breath hot on her neck. I'm tightening my grip on her throat, my control absolute. "It's solidifying, and doesn't want us apart. And I'm going to teach you to crave every moment of it."

I roll her onto her back on the cold marble floor, gripping her calves and lifting them over my shoulders. This position is brutal, exposing her completely, allowing me to bury myself up to the hilt with every stroke. I'm relentless now, letting go of any semblance of control, letting the raw energy of the Ninth consume me.

"Say it!" I growl. I slam into her, faster, harder, until the air is punched from her lungs. "Scream it! Tell me who owns this sweet pussy!"

"Slade! Oh, God—*Slade!*"

The sound is deafening, a raw, ragged shriek of release that cracks the air. I bury myself deep one last time as she goes rigid beneath me, her ass lifted, her calves convulsing violently around my neck. Her internal muscles clench around me, and

I'm roaring too, collapsing beside her, feeling the dark, beautiful completion settle over us like dust.

We lay there for a long time, the only sound the crackle of the fire and our ragged breathing. Finally, I move, sliding out of her slick, spent body. I'm still hard, still possessive, but the immediate, sharp hunger is replaced by a deep, protective satisfaction.

"Come here, little witch."

I lift her, carrying her toward the washroom. The water for the enormous stone tub is already running, hot and infused with salts and oils that smell of earth and calm. I'm not letting her do a single thing for herself, not when I can take care of her. I settle her into the bath, washing the sticky evidence of our chaos from her body. Her eyes are half-closed, heavy with exhaustion. She's completely trusting me, and my heart twists painfully at the realization.

When she's clean and wrapped in a thick, sable-lined robe, I carry her to the massive bed. I pull back the heavy furs, tucking her against the linen sheets, and kiss her forehead with a soft reverent press of my lips. "Sleep, Piper. I'll be right here."

I sit in the chair next to the bed, watching her face soften into deep sleep. I've broken her wide open, filled her with my power, and then put her back together again.

It's the most satisfying work I've ever done.

She is *mine*. And tonight, the bond sealed it... *forever*.

# CHAPTER 39

*Piper*

Breakfast in Slade's estate feels like something stolen out of a myth—warm, indulgent, and too intimate to catalog. Steam curls from the plates he's prepared, the air sweet with ember-honey and cinnamon, the hearth casting a soft glow across the obsidian floors. I'm wrapped in one of his robes, my legs tucked beneath me, deliciously sore in ways that make heat crawl up my throat whenever Slade looks at me for too long.

He watches me eat like it's a private pleasure, one he savors slowly.

"More?" he asks, offering another slice of fire-glazed fruit with his fingers.

"I swear you're trying to keep me from leaving this bed ever again," I murmur, taking the bite.

Slade's smile is all wicked promise. "I don't need to try."

Before I can respond, Newt hops onto my lap with the dramatics of a dying opera singer. He plants his fluffy butt firmly on me, tail flicking, ears flattened in full betrayal.

Slade lifts a brow. "He knows we're getting ready to leave."

"He's pouting," I say, scratching under his chin.

Newt emits a tragic groan, the sound vibrating through his entire body. It's the same noise he made the last time he was forced through a portal—right before he tried to climb Slade's leg like a tree and failed spectacularly.

Slade shakes his head. "He *hates* portal travel."

"Hates is generous," I sigh. "I'm pretty sure he believed he saw the afterlife."

At the mention of another portal, Newt crawls up my chest, shoving his face under my jaw as if attempting to physically anchor me to the realm. Slade watches the scene unfold, something amused but undeniably soft warming his expression. "He's made his preferences clear."

"Yeah," I breathe, holding Newt close, "he really has."

Slade steps behind me, placing one hand on my shoulder, his thumb brushing lightly over my skin. No pressure. No persuasion. Just presence.

"You could stay here," he says quietly—not as a command, not even as an invitation. More like a truth he's finally speaking aloud. "Portal to work. Come and go when you want. This place... it's yours as much as mine."

I freeze—not in fear, but in the kind of stillness that arrives when something clicks perfectly into place.

Newt wriggles off my lap then, trotting proudly across the room toward the ridiculous miniature throne Slade had crafted for him. All polished blackwood, crimson cushioning, and carved paw motifs that make Slade look embarrassingly proud of himself. Newt hops up and settles into it with a satisfied chirp.

Slade glances between us, smirking faintly. "I believe the cat has spoken."

I exhale, my heart expanding in my chest until it feels too full, too bright. The realization washes over me—not a lightning strike, but a sunrise. I already chose. Somewhere between the bond, the laughter, the last couple of nights spent tangled in his sheets, the Ninth, and the way Newt struts through these halls like a tiny tyrant, this place became home.

"I think..." I run my fingers along Slade's jaw, pulling him closer until our foreheads touch. "...I'd like that."

His breath stills. "You would stay," he says, voice dropping into something raw and reverent, "by choice?"

"Yes." The answer slips out easily, naturally. "By choice."

His hand tightens faintly at my waist, the only sign that the admission hits him with more force than he lets on. Heat flares between us—deep. Anchoring.

Newt chirps impatiently from his throne as if commanding us to finish the moment so he can resume being worshipped.

Slade lets out a low laugh, rarely this soft, or this unguarded. "We should go. Your friends will be expecting you."

I lace my fingers with his. "New Year's Eve waits for no witch."

"And no demon," he murmurs.

When the portal opens—gold-edged, humming gently—Newt begins yowling with operatic despair. I scoop him into my arms, pressing kisses to his head as he trembles in outrage.

Slade stands beside me, one hand on my lower back, steady and warm.

"You know," I say, rubbing Newt's ears, "he might never forgive us for taking him away from his kingdom."

Slade's eyes gleam with quiet pride. "Good. It means he's settled. It means you are too."

And as we step through the shimmering light—Newt howling, Slade smiling like sin, my heart steady and certain—I know he's right.

I'm not just visiting his world anymore.

I belong to it, and belongs to me.

***

The moment we step into the mortal realm, Newt launches himself out of my arms and sprints up the hallway of my apartment building like he's reenacting a prison break.

Slade watches him go, hands in his pockets, thoroughly amused. "He runs quickly for someone who believes he's perpetually dying."

"He has dramatics in his blood," I say, unlocking my apartment door.

"Wonder where he gets that from," Slade murmurs—right into my ear.

I elbow him. He smirks, entirely unrepentant.

The door clicks open. Newt darts inside, then stops dead in the middle of the living room, tail puffed, glaring at everything in total disgust. He swivels slowly to face us, pupils blown wide and voice trembling with betrayal.

"Mrrroooow."

"Oh my gods," I exhale, dropping my coat. "He's *scolding* us."

Slade enters behind me with the unbothered confidence of a man who has ruled Hell for centuries. "I wasn't aware cats had the capacity for moral indignation."

"He's not a cat," I mutter. "He's a tiny, fluffy *menace* with a superiority complex."

Newt hops onto the coffee table, deliberately knocking a coaster to the floor while maintaining direct eye contact.

Slade folds his arms. "Is he... threatening us?"

"He's expressing his feelings," I say sarcastically.

"Those are threats," Slade counters. Newt opens his mouth, unleashing a long, quivering yowl of pure, operatic heartbreak. Slade blinks. "This is emotional blackmail."

I sigh dramatically and scoop up the furry tyrant. "Okay, fine, you can be mad at us. We know you love Hell. You literally have a throne."

Newt bats my chin in protest.

"A throne," Slade reminds him solemnly. "Hand-carved. Crimson upholstery. A name-plate."

Newt hisses softly, offended that the throne is being used as leverage.

Slade gestures. "Ungrateful."

"He's sensitive," I whisper, kissing Newt's head.

"He's *spoiled*," Slade corrects—but he's hideously proud about it.

I set Newt down before he stages a coup. "We're packing," I announce. "You can stay mad about it."

Newt relocates to the top of the sofa and glares down at us with the intensity of a disappointed monarch.

Slade points up at him. "That's not resentment. That's judgment."

"It's both," I say. "He's multifaceted."

Slade watches me walk into the bedroom, his eyes darkening with an appreciation I feel all the way down my spine. "You're enjoying this."

"Maybe," I call over my shoulder. "Maybe I like seeing you negotiate with someone smaller than your boot."

"I negotiated," Slade says, following me inside, leaning in the doorway. "He refused diplomacy."

Inside my bedroom, I pull out three suitcases and flop them open on the rug, chuckling softly to myself. Slade takes stock of the room with fond curiosity—as if wanting to memorize the space I lived in before him. Before us.

"Pack whatever you want," he says, voice low and warm. "You won't need much, but I want you comfortable."

"Oh, trust me," I murmur, tossing in clothes, lingerie, candles, three sweaters, and a stack of books, "comfort is the goal."

Slade arches a brow at the mountain I'm making. "You're packing enough for eight women."

"I need options."

He steps behind me, hands landing lightly on my hips. "You always have options, Piper."

The words settle deep in my chest—comfortable, certain, full of promise. I slip into the closet, choosing an outfit for the rest of the day. A soft, midnight blue velvet gown edged in gold, and a delicate gold necklace that settles right above the mark Slade left on my collarbone.

When I step out, Slade goes still.

"You're staring," I tease, smoothing the sweater over my hips.

"I'm admiring," he corrects. "There's a difference."

"Is the difference... you're *horny*?"

"Yes."

Before he can close the distance between us, Newt stomps into the bedroom, plops beside the suitcases, and lets out a low, pitiful moan.

Slade gestures at him, dead serious. "He's doing this on purpose."

"He's dramatic," I say, hoisting the last suitcase shut. "He'll get over it."

Newt hides his face under his paw.

Slade sighs. "Or not."

I lift Newt into my arms, burying my face in his fur. "You *love* your new home," I murmur. "You literally refused to leave your throne. Don't pretend you're in pitiful shape, you're not."

Newt blinks at me with offended resignation.

Slade grabs the suitcases with ease, all three in one hand like they weigh nothing. "We'll leave these here for when we return."

"Tomorrow?" I ask softly, stepping beside him.

"Tomorrow," he promises. "Tonight we celebrate. The mortal realm gets you for one more holiday."

Newt meows dramatically.

Slade deadpans, "And then we go home."

The word home settles around us—warm, certain, inevitable.

I thread my fingers through Slade's, Newt tucked between us like a furry little prince.

"Ready?" Slade asks.

I smile. "Always."

# Chapter 40

*Slade*

The Bellamy manor rises before us like a living constellation—balconies lined with gold-twinkling lights, frost glittering across carved stone, warmth spilling from the windows in soft amber ribbons. The last time we were here, the halls held the magic of Yule.

Tonight, the air feels different. Charged, expectant, heavy with everything I've planned—and everything I'm terrified she'll see before I'm ready.

Or maybe that weight is simply my heart trying to beat its way free.

Beside me, Piper adjusts the midnight-blue velvet of her gown, the gold thread catching in the lantern light as she turns. Her eyes flick down to my hands just as I adjust my collar for the fourth time.

"Nervous?" she asks, smirking.

If she knew why, she'd be the one nervous.

"Bellamy gatherings are... unpredictable," I say smoothly.

She laughs softly. "You love unpredictable."

I love her. The rest is insignificant.

Her fingers slip around my arm, warm and sure. Newt perches on my shoulder wearing his gold bow tie as though he's descended from royalty. His tail flicks—imperious, dramatic—as if he personally approves tonight's aesthetic.

The great doors open before our hands touch them.

Warmth crashes out—music, laughter, clinking glasses, and the layered chorus of too many conversations happening at once. A celebration of endings and beginnings, drenched in magic.

We step inside—and Piper stops.

"What the hell?" she whispers. "Slade... this was supposed to be immediate family."

I scan the crowd, realizing she's right.

Aunt Petunia's "little gathering" looks more like a magical summit. Cousins. Great-aunts. Matriarchs. Families I've never seen. People I would swear aren't even fully human. Bellamy's have multiplied like enchanted rabbits.

Piper's brows shoot up. "Petunia said small. This is not small."

I lean closer. "Your family must have a different definition."

"Yeah," she deadpans. "Apparently 'immediate' means the entire fucking bloodline plus half of Europe."

Her irritation is adorable. I hide my smile behind my hand.

"Slade," she whispers, "why are there so many people here?"

Because your aunt is a menace who somehow sensed I'm proposing tonight. Because this family treats events like omens and wants witnesses. Because the Bellamys never do anything quietly. *Ever.*

But I *cannot* tell her that.

"I'm sure there's a reasonable explanation," I say solemnly.

She gives me a suspicious squint, but before she can interrogate me further, Rhea spots us practically breaking her neck to change directions. "PIPER! SLADE!" she shrieks, barreling through the crowd like a glamoured hurricane. She slams

Piper into a hug, then jabs a finger at me. "*Be-have.*"

"I always behave."

She snorts so loudly a passing witch chokes on her champagne.

Elle glides up behind her—gold gown, amber eyes bright. She kisses Piper's cheeks, then gives me a look that promises polite, glitter-covered as-sassination if I break her cousin's heart.

Then—unexpectedly—Draven and Caelan ap-pear.

"Pipes!" Caelan grins, scooping Piper into a de-lighted spin that sends her laughing.

Draven stands beside Rhea as though he's been summoned by destiny or sheer mischief. His smirk is all knowing villainy. "Slade," Draven drawls.

"Draven."

Rhea elbows him so hard he doubles over. Draven wheezes. "I was being friendly!"

"It was suspicious," she snaps.

They bicker their way into the crowd, and I lean down, murmuring into Piper's ear, "They'll be mated within three months."

"Three weeks," she whispers, eyes sparkling.

Her laughter warms through the bond, curling under my ribcage like a private sunrise.

I rest my hand on her waist—because I can, because she's mine, because tonight I intend to make that forever. The ring burns in the inner pocket of my coat. Dark green stone. Black diamonds. Forged with ancient Ninth Realm magic. A promise waiting for her hand.

At the stroke of midnight, I'll ask Piper Bellamy to marry me.

The thought tears through my composure like a blade.

Aunt Petunia materializes out of nowhere—glittering, regal, chaos incarnate. "Children! There you are!" She hugs Piper fiercely, then pats my cheek like I'm her favorite cursed nephew, and Newt practically dives off my shoulder for Piper's arms. "Take care of her tonight. And bring her around after midnight so I can brag to the ancestors."

I choke.

Piper blinks. "Brag about what?"

"Your future!" Petunia chirps, floating off before I can collapse on the spot.

Piper turns, brows arched. "Any idea what she means?"

I lift her hand and kiss it. "Not a clue."

Lie. I'm sweating under immortal composure. She watches me for a long moment—as though she feels the truth thrumming beneath my skin—and smiles softly.

The night unfolds like a tapestry. Champagne. A dozen dances. Elle's laughter ringing like bells. Rhea out-drinking Draven. Caelan conjuring indoor snowflakes to impress Elle. Newt staring judgmentally from Piper's arms like the world's fluffiest chaperone.

The lights dim, and the orchestra swells. The countdown magic begins shimmering in the air—the veil between this year and the next stretching thin.

I tighten my arm around Piper's waist. The ring feels heavier in my pocket, as the moment draws closer. Every heartbeat thrums like fate knocking on my ribs.

Piper turns toward me, eyes gilded by candlelight. "Slade? You okay?"

I cup her cheek gently. "More than okay."

She must feel it—my magic trembling, anticipation rising like a tide. She leans into my touch, trusting, open, perfect.

One more hour. One more dance. One more breath before I kneel before her.

Tonight, I offer her my future. I ask her to be mine past death, past realms, past eternity. New Year's Eve is endings and beginnings.

But with her? It feels like destiny.

And nothing—not hell, not fate, not prophecy—will stop me from claiming forever with Piper
Bellamy.

# CHAPTER 41

*Piper*

The last hour of the year winds itself around the Bellamy manor like a spell, slow and glittering and full of suspended breath. The ballroom hums with music and laughter and the soft clink of crystal, but all I really feel is the weight of Slade's hand at my waist and the way my heart keeps stuttering like it is trying to keep time with some secret rhythm only he knows.

Gold and silver lights drape from the vaulted ceiling like captured stars, flickering in the polished marble and scattering over swirling gowns and dark suits, and every so often, when I catch my reflection in one of the tall windows, I almost do not recognize myself. Deep midnight-blue velvet hugging every curve, the sweetheart bodice holding my breasts in a way that makes Slade's eyes darken every time he looks at me, the gold snowflake belt at my waist blazing with diamond fire—a Bellamy heirloom that feels like it has chosen me as much as I chose it. My curls are piled up and pinned with delicate gold leaves, my neck bare except for a simple chain that catches the light when I move.

Newt is draped across my arms like a spoiled, purring brat in his tiny gold bow tie, smug, regal, and perfectly aware that everyone in this house worships him. The orchestra shifts into something slower, richer, notes spilling like warm wine, and Slade turns toward me with that look—the one that burns and softens at the same time, the one that says I am his whole world and he cannot quite believe it is allowed.

"Dance with me," he murmurs, like he is asking for a lifetime and not a song, and when he takes Newt carefully from my arms and deposits him with dignified ceremony into Elle's waiting hands—"Guard her, Your Furry Highness"—my heart does a foolish little flip because he treats my cat like a king and me like something even more sacred.

He leads me out into the center of the ballroom and the crowd eases back as if some unseen hand smooths them away, leaving us a circle of polished marble and candlelight. His hand slides to my waist, warm and sure, his other taking my fingers, and when he pulls me in, our bodies fit together as though every dance for the last five hundred years has been rehearsing for this one.

The music threads around us, low strings and a lilting piano that tastes like nostalgia in the air. I let my head tip toward his chest, close enough to smell cedar smoke and winter air and that faint thread of lightning ozone that clings to his skin no matter which realm we are in. "You're quiet," he says softly, guiding me through a slow turn, the skirt of my dress whispering around my legs. "Unusual for you, little witch."

I smile up at him because he is right. My words feel lodged somewhere behind my ribs tonight, caught between the joy of the bond thrumming steady and warm in my chest and the awareness that something is gathering in him, something heavy and bright and edged with nerves he is trying very hard to hide. "I'm thinking," I say, my voice barely above the music. "About how two months ago my biggest problem was cursed mistletoe and now I'm dancing with a demon lord at a New Year's Eve ball wondering if I own enough sensible shoes for my new part-time life in hell."

His mouth curves, slow and reverent, and his thumb brushes an absent pattern against my waist. "You don't need sensible shoes," he replies. "You have me."

"You're the opposite of sensible," I whisper, but it comes out soft and fond and so full that my chest aches.

He leans down, his forehead almost touching mine, and the lights catch in his eyes, turning the deep green into something brighter, almost golden. "And yet you chose me," he says, and there is wonder in it still, like he keeps expecting to wake up and find himself alone again.

I think of the curse breaking under Yule's light, the way the bond snapped fully into place with that last, breathless yes, the way my magic has settled since, no longer flaring in panic but flooding me with something steady, rooted, whole. I think of Newt's throne in the Ninth Realm, of waking up tangled in emerald sheets and demon arms, of the smell of coffee and warding smoke and faint brimstone in our kitchen.

"I did," I answer, and I press closer, because it feels important that he feel this truth against his skin. "And I would again. Every time."

The song swells and our bodies move together as if the music is inside our bones, as if every step is a promise. Somewhere to the left, I hear Rhea's delighted shriek of laughter as Draven pretends to be scandalized by something she has said, and Elle's softer giggle as Caelan whispers in her ear.

Aunt Petunia glides past, arms full of what looks like an entire armory of enchanted party poppers and confetti charms, her silver hair piled high and skewered with a wand that glows faintly red at the tip. She gives me a look so full of mischief my stomach flips and mouths something that looks suspiciously like "Get ready," before winking and disappearing back into the throng.

The giant clock at the far end of the ball-room begins to glow faintly, numbers outlined in gold fire above the musicians' platform, reminding everyone that midnight is no longer a distant, glittery idea but a destination. Slade's hand tightens at my back, just a fraction, but I feel it like a storm rolling in. "Piper," he says, and my name on his tongue is a caress, a vow, a slow inhale. "Come with me."

Before I can answer, he guides us smoothly out of the circle and toward one of the tall glass doors that lead to the balcony, his body a shield between me and any curious eyes. Newt, who has apparently decided Elle and Caelan are inadequate staff, leaps gracefully from her arms and trots after us, tail high, bow tie aggressively jaunty.

The cold hits me the moment we step outside, crisp and sharp. Full of the metallic tang of coming snow, but it's chased quickly by the heat radiating from Slade's body as he closes the door behind us and pulls me toward the stone balustrade.

The city below is a sea of flickering lights and distant laughter. The sky overhead is dark velvet pricked with stars, and the faint shimmer of warding spells woven over the manor like fine lace.

Newt hops neatly onto the railing and settles against my side, his purr a low, rumbling counterpoint to the soft music spilling through the glass. Somewhere far off, fireworks are already beginning—small, early bursts of color that bloom and fade against the darkness like scattered, impatient wishes.

For a breath, we simply stand there, the three of us pressed together against the cold stone. The world narrows to the feeling of Slade's hand over mine on the rail, and the way our joined magic hums in quiet contentment under my skin. Then he turns to face me fully and the look on his face steals whatever air the winter breeze left behind.

There is no teasing there, no lazy arrogance, no sharp, dangerous edge. There is only intensity—raw and open and luminous, like someone took every locked-away emotion and pulled it to the surface.

His hand lifts, fingers brushing along my jaw with a tenderness that makes my eyes sting, and when his thumb grazes the corner of my mouth I feel my heart tip forward in my chest like it's about to fall into his palm.

"You changed everything," he says quietly, the words a low vibration between us. "You summoned me into your living room with a miscast spell, a bad idea and somehow, instead of binding me with chains, you gave me a home."

I laugh, a wet, shaky sound. "I also almost set my Christmas tree on fire."

His mouth curves, but his gaze does not soften. "Yes. That too."

His fingers drift down, resting against the gold snowflake at my waist, the diamonds flashing as if they are listening. "I have walked realms that mortals have never heard of," he continues, voice threaded with memory, with old loneliness. "I have held power that made kings tremble. I have commanded legions and walked alone through decades, convinced that was my fate. Necessary. Inevitable."

He inhales, and the cold air clouds between us, briefly visible before vanishing. "And then you looked at me with wild hair, stubborn eyes and told me I was being dramatic. The Ninth Realm has not been the same since."

My throat tightens. Tears slide hot and uninvited to the corners of my eyes, and Newt headbutts my elbow in what I decide is emotional support. "Slade..." I whisper, but he shakes his head slightly, his hand tightening at my waist as if he is anchoring himself with me.

"You broke a curse older than your coven," he says. "You chose to face the truth instead of hiding from it. You chose to trust me when you had every reason not to. You chose a demon lord, Piper Bellamy, and in doing so you gave me something I didn't know I could have. You gave me a life I want to keep waking up in."

My vision blurs.

The bond pulses strong and bright, carrying his sincerity straight through every shield I have ever tried to put up. Behind the glass, I hear the murmur of voices rising, the subtle shift of the crowd as people move toward the center, and the clock inside begins to chime the warning for the final countdown, each tone ringing through the magic-warmed air like a distant bell.

Slade takes a slow breath, and then—without breaking eye contact, without a single ounce of his usual showmanship—he drops to one knee on the cold stone. The sight of him kneeling there, dark suit dusted with snowflakes, verdant eyes lifted to mine with reverence and a hint of very real fear, knocks the wind from my lungs.

Newt lets out an indignant chirp at the movement and climbs higher into my arms, pressing his warm, solid weight against my chest as if he refuses to miss a single second. Slade reaches into the inner pocket of his coat and pulls out a small velvet box, black as a starless sky, and when he opens it the faint light from the manor catches on deep green and dark fire.

The ring is breathtaking. An emerald so dark it's almost black at the edges, cut to catch hidden flashes of forest and storm, encircled by a halo of black diamonds that glitter like captured void. All set into a band of black gold etched with delicate runes that glow faintly in response to our bond. It looks like something that belongs in both worlds—witchcraft and hellfire, winter forest and midnight throne. It looks like it was always meant to find its way to my hand. My breath comes out in a shaking rush. "Slade," I say again, but now it is not a warning or a protest, it is a plea, a prayer, a tremor.

He looks up at me as if I am the only star in a sky he thought was empty. "Piper Bellamy," he says, voice steady even as his magic trembles against mine, "you are my mate, my equal, my favorite catastrophe. You are Lady Athalar in all but name. I love you in this realm and every realm, in every season, in every quiet morning and every reckless night. I love the way you burn and the way you heal. The way you care for a ridiculous cat, a cursed bloodline, and a demon who never thought he deserved any of it. I want every mundane moment and every impossible one. I want to fight with you, laugh with you, cook too much food with you, and spend the next hundred New Year's Eves arguing about which movie we watch after midnight." His eyes shine, wet at the edges, and something in my chest cracks open and floods with light. "Will you marry me?" he asks softly, holding the ring up like an offering. "Will you be my wife, my queen, my partner in all things? Will you stand with me in hell, in your shop, and everywhere in between and let me love you for the rest of this immortal mess I call a life?"

There is a beat where the world seems to hold its breath. Inside, I can hear the muffled chant beginning—Ten... nine... eight....—voices rising with giddy anticipation.

Newt shifts in my arms and plants one soft paw on my collarbone, as if he is physically holding me upright, and something inside me aligns so completely it almost hurts. Every fear, every unanswered question, every shadow of Veda's story, every weight of the curse that used to press on my spine, all of it feels distant now compared to this clear, overwhelming truth.

I love him. I choose him.

Not because the bond demands it, not because fate wrote it, but because somewhere between hexed mistletoe, Lucifer's Christmas Ball and hellfire bubble baths... This impossible, infuriating, devoted demon became the safest place I know.

Tears spill freely down my cheeks, hot on my cold skin, and I laugh through the sob. Because of course I'm crying while holding a fat cat in a bow tie. All on a balcony while my demon lord kneels in the snow with a ring forged of hell. "Yes," I choke out, my voice breaking on the word, and then stronger, fuller, more sure.

"Yes, Slade Athalar. I will marry you. I want all of it. The shop, hell, Newt's ridiculous throne, and every version of us that exists. I love you." The bond surges. A bright, resonant chord that rings through my magic and his. Through the wards around the manor and the very stones under our feet, and for a moment I swear the stars above us flare a little brighter.

He exhales a sound that's half laugh, half ragged relief, and his hands shake just enough that I see it as he slides the ring onto my finger. The metal is cool against my skin, then warms instantly, adjusting, accepting, sealing something that feels both ancient and brand new. Newt leans down and sniffs it, then gives a tiny approving trill like he has just signed off on a sacred contract.

Inside the ballroom, the countdown reaches three... two... one... and the instant the crowd roars "Happy New Year!" the sky above the city explodes into color.

Fireworks bloom in cascading arcs of gold and red and sapphire, reflections dancing in Slade's eyes as he rises to his feet and pulls me into his arms just as the first brilliant flare bursts overhead. Behind us, there is a sudden, deafening pop and the muffled shrieks of delighted shock.

Aunt Petunia's confetti bomb goes off right on cue, magically amplifying it so that shimmering bursts of gold and silver paper shower the ball-room. All of it whirling past the glass like enchanted snow, some of it magically drifting out onto the balcony in lazy spirals.

It clings to Slade's dark hair and catches in my lashes, sparkling in Newt's fur. When Slade cups my face and kisses me—really kisses me, slow, deep, reverent, with his hands cradling my jaw as if I am something priceless and irreplaceable.

The taste of champagne and winter air and his devotion mixes with the faint paper-sweet tang of confetti dust on my lips.

The cheers from inside swell, muffled but joyful, and I hear Rhea's voice rise above the din—"SHE SAID YES, DIDN'T SHE? I KNEW IT!"—followed by Draven's amused drawl, Elle's delighted squeal, and Aunt Petunia's triumphant, "I told the ancestors!" but all of it feels far away, like background music to the only moment that matters.

Slade rests his forehead against mine when the kiss finally breaks, both of us breathing hard, Newt wedged snugly between us like a small, purring barrier of judgment and approval. "Happy New Year, Piper Bellamy," he whispers, his voice rough with emotion.

I smile through my tears and hold up my hand so the ring catches the exploding light. "Happy New Year, Slade Athalar," I whisper back. "Fiancé." The word feels wild and perfect on my tongue.

He smiles, slow and unguarded, undone in the most beautiful way. Above us, fireworks break open the sky. Confetti drifts in shimmering arcs. Newt purrs steadily against my ribs. And standing here—on this balcony, with my engagement ring warm on my finger—I *finally* understand.

There is nowhere in any realm I would rather be. Not in another life. Not under another sky. Only here, with him, at the start of forever.

# CHAPTER 42

*Piper*

Three months later...

Spring doesn't simply arrive at the Bellamy manor—it *erupts*.

At dawn, the estate stirs under a wash of rose-gold sunlight, every window catching the glow like a held breath. Flowers—Bellamy-bound and wild—burst open across the grounds the moment my feet touch the balcony. It's as if the land has been waiting for me to wake, waiting for this day, waiting to bloom.

My wedding dress hangs in the center of the room like a small miracle.

Ivory silk forms the base—smooth as water, soft as moonlight. Woven through the entire bodice and cascading down the skirt are faint blush-toned florals. Magnolia, hellebore, anemone. Not printed, or embroidered—*stitched in with protection sigils,* the Bellamy way. Their runic seams pulse faintly as I approach, shimmering rose-gold at the edges, each one whispering quiet blessings. Protection, longevity, devotion, and fertility.

My veil lies beside it—long, flowing, with delicate floral points embroidered at the hem. Snowdrops, foxglove, and early roses—each enchanted to sway as though caught in the gentlest of breezes, even indoors.

Rhea clasps a hand over her mouth the moment she sees me step into the gown. "Piper Leigh Bellamy, if you don't stop looking like the goddess of spring herself, I'm going to cry directly onto your bodice."

Elle pushes past her, already crying. "You are *so* rude. You promised you wouldn't bawl first."

"I said I wouldn't bawl at the *altar*. This is pre-altar," Rhea sniffs.

They work around me in practiced tandem. Rhea adjusts the sigil placement on the skirt, fingertips glowing faintly. Elle pins my curls back into a soft half-up twist, sliding in the flowered circlet—tiny evergreen tips mixed with blush florals, bridging Yule to Ostara.

"You look like the first breath of spring," Elle whispers.

Rhea nods, awed. "Slade's going to black out."

I breathe, slow and steady. "Is he... ready?"

Elle smirks. "He's been ready since the Yule Ball. Today he's downright feral about it."

They help me into my shoes—ivory satin with tiny gold sigils etched across the straps—and step back, quiet, reverent.

"Let's go get you married," Rhea says softly.

***

The Bellamy gardens have been transformed into something out of myth. A canopy of arching willow branches sweeps over the aisle, their leaves glinting with dew. Blooms spill across every surface—blush, white, pale green—as though the earth has been coaxed into peak spring overnight.

Floating candles circle slowly above us, drifting like tiny suns. Petals fall from nowhere, slow as snow.

And at the end of the aisle—*Slade*.

My breath leaves me in a single rush. He wears charcoal-gray that fits him with sinful precision. A black shirt, and muted sage tie, with an evergreen sprig resting in his lapel, tied in black silk. His hair is swept back. His five-o'clock shadow sharpens every line of his face.

But it's his eyes—dark green, edged in storm—that nearly stop my heart.

In his hand, resting against his chest, is the ring box.

I know what's inside. I still nearly falter at the sight. An emerald so dark it verges on black at the edges—cut in a shape that catches hidden flashes of forest and storm when the light touches it. Encircled by a halo of black diamonds that glitter like captured void. And set into a band of black gold, etched with runes that glow faintly whenever our bond stirs.

A ring forged of witchcraft and hellfire. Of winter forest and midnight throne. A ring that belongs to both of our worlds.

Slade looks at me—and the storm in his eyes softens into wonder.

Petunia officiates, of course. In a gown that looks like she stole it from a solstice queen.

"We gather," she begins, voice soft but carrying, "in the Blooming Hour. At the turning of Ostara. Under the veil of new life and old magic, to unite Piper Bellamy and Slade Athalar."

Magic trembles in the air, as Rhea and Elle step forward first—the Bellamy blessing.

Rhea places her hands over mine. "For protection."

Elle places hers over Slade's. "For devotion."

Their combined magic blooms around us in a shimmering blush-and-emerald haze.

Then the handfasting cord is brought forth—evergreen braided with rose-gold silk and a thread of shadow from Slade's realm. As Petunia winds it around our wrists, the sigils on my gown glow brighter, responding to the bond knitting between us.

"Piper," Petunia asks, "do you welcome Slade as your partner in all cycles, all realms, all magic?"

"I do."

Her voice gentles. "Slade Athalar, do you welcome Piper as your equal, your tether, your chosen match in fate and eternity?"

Slade never looks away from me. "Always."

The cord flashes with light—rose-gold, emerald, black-gold—and our sigils burn into visibility beneath our skin. Matching sigils flare beneath our skin, shimmering just long enough for the gathered magic to recognize them, to seal them, to claim them.

For a heartbeat, the world stills. The garden holds its breath. The candles steady. Every blossom seems to turn toward us, petals trembling with a magic older than the Bellamy line itself. The air warms, infused with the scent of new spring—honeysuckle, rain, earth waking beneath sunlight.

I feel Slade's magic thread around mine, dark heat brushing against my warmth in a slow, reverent spiral. Our bond tightens—not the fierce, desperate snap of survival, but something gentler. A promise.

Petunia's smile brightens, her voice soft as she declares, "You are bound."

The cord unfurls from our wrists in a shimmer of stardust—and Slade doesn't wait for permission.

His hand comes to my cheek, tender and sure, the other sliding to the small of my back as though my body has always belonged beneath his touch. Then his mouth is on mine—soft, reverent, devastating—stealing the breath from my lungs and the rhythm from my heart. The kiss tastes like spring rain, like wildfire, like eternity.

The guests erupt around us.

Flowers release their petals in a sudden swirling cascade, drifting like enchanted snow. Floating candles flare brighter. Magic hums through the Bellamy gardens like a song.

Rhea sobs—loudly, dramatically, while Draven looks positively uncomfortable. Elle fans her with a handkerchief embroidered with tiny foxglove blossoms and Caelan grimaces in her direction. Petunia wipes a delighted tear onto the sleeve of an unfortunate fae lord who looks entirely unprepared for Bellamy affection.

Newt lets out a triumphant, echoing meow, tail flicking with the smugness of a creature who believes this entire wedding was orchestrated for him personally.

Slade pulls back just enough that our lips still brush, breath mingling in the charged air between us. "Mine," he murmurs, low and reverent.

"Yours," I breathe back, dizzy with joy, with magic, with the sheer enormity of this moment.

He presses another kiss to the corner of my mouth, slow and tender, as the applause swells and magic curls around us in warm spirals. Petunia lifts her arms, proclaiming us joined before realms, before spring, before fate itself.

And as Slade threads our fingers together—our rings glinting, our sigils still faintly glowing—I know with absolute certainty.

This is the beginning of our forever...

And the world is blooming with us.

# About The Author

B is a devoted wife and dog mom who has always had a passion for writing. When the opportunity arose, she channeled all her energy into creating an immersive world that captivated readers from the very first page. B loves traveling, reading, photography, and video gaming with her husband. B actively shares her journey on social media, connecting with readers who love paranormal, dark, and fantasy romance.

# ACKNOWLEDGEMENTS

*Hex the Halls* wouldn't exist without the people who held me together, hyped me up, and gently shoved caffeine into my hands when I needed it most.

**To Letta and Yvonne — my Golden Light Publishing sisters:**
Thank you for being the backbone of this whole operation and the reason I didn't lose my mind somewhere around draft three. You listened, encouraged, screamed with me, and reminded me that sleep is, in fact, optional during a deadline. Thank you for being my safe space and my sounding board. Your feedback, your honesty, your hu-

mor, and your unwavering support turned this little chaotic idea into a real book. I'm grateful for you both more than these pages can say.

**To my husband:**

Thank you for putting up with my insomnia-fueled writing sprints, my "wait, let me write this down" moments in the middle of conversations, and the ever-growing collection of notes I scatter like confetti. Your patience and love make every story possible.

**To Jackie:**

Thank you for alpha reading, for catching the things my brain refused to see, and for cheering me on through every twist, hex, and bit of holiday chaos.

**And to my readers:**

Every one of you who picks up my books, shares them, reviews them, recommends them, or simply messages to say a line hit you — you are the magic in all of this. I couldn't do this without you all.

Thank you for continuing to show up, continue to care, and continue to believe in my worlds.

This book is for you.

-B

# ALSO BY B WILLS

The Eternal Darkness Chronicles:

Book 1: Shadows & Starlight

Book 2: Coming Soon...

The Sacred Flames of Ruin:

Book 1: Chasing The Flame

Book 2: Coming Soon...

The Bloodwritten Flames of Ruin:

Book 1: Written In Blood

Book 2: Coming Soon...

9 781970 692006